Acclaim for Robyn Harding's previous novels

"Laugh-out-loud funny."   —*Publishers Weekly*

"An enjoyable read from beginning to end."
                    —Mary Francis Moore, coauthor of *Bittergirl*

"Funny and wholly engrossing . . . you won't be able to put it
down."   —Sarah Mylnowski, author of *Me vs. Me*

"Wonderful . . . I loved it!"
    —Carole Matthews, author of *The Chocolate Lovers' Club*

"Painfully funny . . . Harding is a skilled writer who is able to
transcend and even exploit cliché."   —*The Boston Globe*

LIVINGSTON PUBLIC LIBRARY
10 Robert H. Harp Drive
Livingston, NJ 07039

Chronicles of a Midlife Crisis

Robyn Harding

BERKLEY BOOKS, NEW YORK

FIC
HARDING

9.30

THE BERKLEY PUBLISHING GROUP
Published by the Penguin Group
Penguin Group (USA) Inc.
375 Hudson Street, New York, New York 10014, USA
Penguin Group (Canada), 90 Eglinton Avenue East, Suite 700, Toronto, Ontario M4P 2Y3, Canada
(a division of Pearson Penguin Canada Inc.)
Penguin Books Ltd., 80 Strand, London WC2R 0RL, England
Penguin Group Ireland, 25 St. Stephen's Green, Dublin 2, Ireland (a division of Penguin Books Ltd.)
Penguin Group (Australia), 250 Camberwell Road, Camberwell, Victoria 3124, Australia
(a division of Pearson Australia Group Pty. Ltd.)
Penguin Books India Pvt. Ltd., 11 Community Centre, Panchsheel Park, New Delhi—110 017, India
Penguin Group (NZ), 67 Apollo Drive, Rosedale, North Shore 0632, New Zealand
(a division of Pearson New Zealand Ltd.)
Penguin Books (South Africa) (Pty.) Ltd., 24 Sturdee Avenue, Rosebank, Johannesburg 2196,
South Africa

Penguin Books Ltd., Registered Offices: 80 Strand, London WC2R 0RL, England

This is a work of fiction. Names, characters, places, and incidents either are the product of the author's imagination or are used fictitiously, and any resemblance to actual persons, living or dead, business establishments, events, or locales is entirely coincidental. The publisher does not have any control over and does not assume responsibility for author or third-party websites or their content.

Copyright © 2008 by Robyn Harding.
Cover design by Annette Fiore DeFex.
Cover photo of empty bed by Ryan McVay / Getty; cover photo of bra on lampshade by ImageSource / Getty.
Text design by Laura K. Corless.

All rights reserved.
No part of this book may be reproduced, scanned, or distributed in any printed or electronic form without permission. Please do not participate in or encourage piracy of copyrighted materials in violation of the author's rights. Purchase only authorized editions.
BERKLEY® is a registered trademark of Penguin Group (USA) Inc.
The "B" design is a trademark of Penguin Group (USA) Inc.

PRINTING HISTORY
Penguin Canada trade paperback edition / 2008
Berkley trade paperback edition / September 2010

Library of Congress Cataloging-in-Publication Data

Harding, Robyn.
   Chronicles of a midlife crisis / Robyn Harding.—Berkley trade pbk. ed
      p.   cm.
ISBN 978-0-425-23647-5
   1. Middle-aged persons—Fiction. 2. Separated people—Fiction. I. Title.
PR9199.4.H366C48   2010
813'.6—dc22

                                                                        2010017351

PRINTED IN THE UNITED STATES OF AMERICA

10   9   8   7   6   5   4   3   2   1

For my mom

Lucy

I SHOULD HAVE seen it coming. That night, when I walked into the master bathroom and saw my husband dabbing his ring finger delicately around his left eye, I should have known. "What are you doing?" I asked, trying to keep the smirk out of my voice.

"Moisturizing," came his curt reply.

It was a sign, obviously. But I was so trusting, so naive, that I actually thought it was sort of a good thing. Trent had never cared about his skin before, and I took this late-blooming interest in his epidermis as a sign of long-term maintenance, not vanity. The clothes were another clue.

"What are you wearing?" I asked, trying to keep the smirk out of my voice.

"They're skinny-leg trousers," he'd replied defensively. "They're in fashion."

In hindsight, it seems so obvious. What forty-three-year-old man would wear skinny-leg trousers unless he was in the throes of a severe midlife crisis? But unfortunately, I still didn't clue in. I thought a later-in-life sartorial bent was better than none at all—even if the pants did make him look as though he'd entered a Mick Jagger look-alike contest.

Unfortunately, these clues, so obvious in retrospect, have done nothing to prepare me. As I sit on the living room sofa facing Trent, I am completely blindsided by his words.

"It's not that I don't love you, Lucy. You're a wonderful woman . . . really. It's just that . . . I feel like I've missed out on a lot. We've been together for a long time now, and there's still a lot I need to experience . . . *on my own.*"

I stare at him, speechless. Despite the skin care and new pants, I still can't believe my husband is leaving me.

"We don't need to look at this as an ending," he continues. "Let's look at this as an opportunity to explore who we are as individuals. I want you to take this time to really find out who you are, too."

"I know who I am!" I snap. "I'm your wife! I'm Samantha's mother! I'm forty years old, I'm a Libra, and I'm a props buyer for the film industry!"

He looks at me with pity. "Is that all?"

I shriek, "Is that not enough?"

"I didn't mean the question so literally. I want you to find out who you are on a deeper level, Luce. I just . . . it's hard to explain."

"Who is she?" I growl. All this finding himself shit is so transparent. "Is it someone at work? Some twenty-five-year-old at the gym? Who is it? Tell me!"

"This isn't about anyone else. It's about us. We haven't really been connected for years now, Lucy. We work, we co-parent, we pay the mortgage together, but we're not together, not like we used to be."

"It's called life, Trent," I fire back. "It's called raising a family."

"Well, that's not the way I want to live my life. I want more—for you and for me."

Oh, for fuck's sake! "Fine! Have your midlife crisis. Pack your clothes and get the hell out!"

Slowly, without looking back, he leaves the living room and moves to the staircase. His posture, the slump of his shoulders, says: I tried, but there's no reasoning with her. I hear him ascending the stairs, moving deliberately to our bedroom and retrieving his suitcase from the closet. I hear the dull thud as he places it on the bed, unzips it, and begins filling it with his fashionable pants and skin care products.

I always assumed I'd have a much more dramatic reaction to my husband's desertion. Not that I'd ever given it much thought, but I'd considered myself the type to slap him, throw dishes, or, potentially, light him on fire. Instead I just sit, still and quiet, on the leather sofa as I listen to my husband preparing to leave me. Other than a slight nausea, I am completely numb.

It seems like hours, but eventually he reappears. He has left his suitcase by the front door. Hesitantly, he approaches me, a piece of paper in his hand. "I'll be staying at the Sutton Place Hotel until I get an apartment sorted out. Here's the number."

I look at the piece of paper he's proffering. "Why would I need the number?"

"Just in case Samantha wants to talk to me."

"I hope you plan on explaining to her why you're leaving us."

"Well . . ." He rubs at the stubble on his chin, a sure sign that he's nervous. "I was thinking it might be better coming from you. I mean, you two are so close . . ."

"Ha!" I give a humorless laugh. "Nice try." Since my daughter turned fifteen, *close* is not the word I'd choose to describe our relationship. Something along the lines of *tense*, *strained*, or even *fraught* would be more appropriate. "I'm not doing your dirty work for you. You can tell her how you want to find yourself on your own."

He puffs out his cheeks and lets out a sigh. "Fine. If that's the way you want to be."

This prompts the emergence of the dish-throwing, fire-lighting lunatic I knew lurked inside me. "Get out! Get out, you selfish bastard!" I scream, grabbing the remote control off the coffee table and hurling it at him. "I can't believe I gave you eighteen years of my life just to have you throw them down the goddamn toilet!"

When Trent has scurried out of the house under a hail of remotes, books, and shoes, I collapse on the sofa. Hot tears of anger, disappointment, and loss course down my cheeks. Snot runs unwiped from my nose and a significant amount of saliva coats my face. I sob, I wail, I pound the couch cushions. It is an emotional breakdown entirely befitting the situation. The man I have loved since I was twenty-two years old has just walked out on me. Of course, our marriage hasn't been perfect—or even particularly pleasant for the last three years or so—but still!

I allow myself this unfettered wallowing for forty-five minutes. I could easily have continued for at least another half hour, but my daughter will be home from the mall soon and I don't want her to see me like this. It's not my duty to explain her father's abandonment, and if she sees me covered in all manner of mucus she's going to figure out that something's wrong. Shuffling to the bathroom, I wipe my face with a cloth dampened in cool water. I still look pretty rough, but given that my daughter rarely looks at me anymore, she's unlikely to notice. This thought threatens to set me off again, but I compose myself just in time. I hear Samantha's key in the front door.

"Hi, hon!" I greet her brightly as she enters.

"Oh, hey," she replies, not entirely unfriendly.

I watch my daughter as she slips out of the knee-high suede boots that she simply had to have or she'd be completely ostracized from her peer group. Samantha has her father's sandy blond hair and tall frame, but her heart-shaped face is all me. As much as she wants to look mature and worldly, there's something innocent and childlike in her gray, wide-set eyes that no amount of navy eyeliner can erase. Indicating the small shopping bag in her hand, I ask, "What did you buy?"

"Just some earrings."

"That's nice. Can I see them?"

She looks at me as she hangs up her coat. "They're just plain, fake-gold hoops—nothing fancy."

"They sound beautiful. Let's see."

Despite my only child's self-absorbed and rather surly adolescent phase, she's still tuned into me. "Why do you care about my earrings? Why do you look all puffy? What's going on?"

"Nothing," I reply defensively. "I've got allergies. It's so dusty in here."

"Oh, so now your allergies are my fault? If you want me to dust, why don't you just ask me?"

"I don't want you to dust. I was just saying—"

"Isn't that why you hired a cleaning lady? Maybe you should be getting mad at her instead of me."

"I'm not getting mad at you!" I shriek.

"Whatevs." She dismisses me and marches up to her room.

Well, that went well. At least she didn't ask where her father was. It's tempting to return to the couch and my previous emotional breakdown, but I resist. Now that Samantha is home, I've got to pull myself together. I've got to figure out what I'm going to do next. But the thought of living my life without Trent is overwhelming. The tears threaten to return, and I know I can't get through this on my own. With a shaking hand, I reach for the phone.

The receiver in my grip, I weigh my options. I'm lucky to have two close friends to turn to in my time of crisis: Hope and Camille. Hope and I met at a Mommy and Me playgroup when Samantha was about three and Hope's daughter, Sarah-Louise, was slightly older. It was her companionship that helped me survive those trying and isolating toddler years. Of course, she did sometimes make me feel like a defective model of a mother. While I was frequently overwhelmed by my one tiny daughter, Hope managed her brood of three with frightening aplomb. Seriously, she seemed to find the whole experience of having three children under the age of four rather enjoyable. I didn't get it. But our friendship has endured over the years, and Trent and I spend a lot of time with Hope and Mike. A ragged breath escapes as I correct the tense of my verb: *spent* a lot of time with Hope and Mike.

Camille is a friend from work. We're both props buyers on one of the WB network's hit teen comedies. Our job is to be briefed on the scripts and then provide all the materials the actors will use on set. When I first started in the business, I felt privileged to be spending ten hours a day shopping with someone else's money. But when your list is largely composed of baseball gloves, electric scooters, and algebra textbooks, it loses some of its appeal. In contrast to Hope, Camille is single, childless, and quite happy to remain that way. After ending her "starter marriage" in her mid-twenties, she's been actively involved in the dating scene. Unfortunately, few men are up to her exacting standards and she usually ends up dumping them after a month or two. She used to tell me I was lucky to have married the perfect guy right off the bat. This thought sends a repressed sob shuddering through me.

I start to dial Hope, and then stop. Maybe Camille is a better choice to support me right now? Hope will show up with chamomile tea and a tin of homemade cookies. She'll counsel me to be patient and understanding of Trent's travails. "Give him time," she'll probably tell me. "This is a normal rite of passage for men his age." Camille, on the other hand, will show up with a bottle of wine, if not tequila. She'll call Trent all sorts of nasty names: pig, bastard, selfish prick. In fact, she'll undoubtedly bash his entire gender. "All men are pigs, bastards, selfish pricks! You don't need him," she'll spew. "Get yourself a dildo and you'll actually be ahead of the game."

So who do I turn to for support: Hope with her tea, cookies, and understanding, or Camille with her tequila and righteous anger? I take a deep breath and close my eyes. The sounds of my daughter's CD player drift down the stairs. She's listening to some bouncy pop song, blissfully unaware that her father has deserted her, chosen a life of nightclubs, weekends in Vegas, and one-night stands with cocktail waitresses to being her dad. And as an almost overwhelming surge of anger fills me, my decision is made. I dial the number.

Trent

GOD, THAT WAS ugly. I knew Lucy would be shocked and angry, but it had to be done. And I guess it could have been worse. All I got was some sarcasm and a couple of remotes chucked at me. With a woman like Lucy, you never know how she'll react. I don't think she's really capable of murdering me, per se, but I could see her doing something really crazy, like throwing an iron and killing me accidentally.

I ease the Lexus onto the Burrard Street Bridge and gun the engine. Maneuvering the car through the sparse evening traffic, I feel a newfound sense of freedom. With each mile I put between me and our Point Grey house, I feel more independent . . . more me. It's not that I won't miss my family, Samantha especially, but I need this, I really need this. I've lived half my fucking life and I don't even know who I am anymore. I mean, I know who I'm supposed to be: a father, a husband, and an investment adviser. But I need to get to know myself as a person.

Lucy doesn't understand. She's too wrapped up in presenting a perfect facade to the world: strong, secure marriage; lovingly restored heritage home; artistic, private-schooled daughter; successful careers . . . If she stopped and took a look at our life, she'd see that it's not perfect anymore. In fact, it's not even good anymore. Sure, all the elements are in place, but there's nothing at the core. It's just . . . emptiness. There's got to be more to life than this fucking hamster-wheel existence.

In a few minutes I've reached the circular drive of the Sutton Place, a luxury hotel in the heart of the city. It's where all the stars stay when they come to Vancouver. Not that I'm particularly impressed by this, but someone said Lance Armstrong was here last weekend, and I wouldn't mind meeting him. Now there's a guy who knows what he wants in life and takes it. And he does it all with just one nut. He's an inspiration.

I hand my keys to the valet and grab my suitcase out of the trunk. As I head inside, I wave away the bellboy. It feels good to carry my own luggage, I'm not sure why. It makes me feel in charge. Plus, I don't have any small bills for tipping. Lucy was always on top of that.

The lobby is spacious, austere, and gleaming. The staff members give me respectful nods as I move directly to the bank of elevators. To them I'm just another businessman from Toronto or San Francisco, in town for a meeting or seminar. I'm not some guy from across the bridge who's just left his wife and daughter. I'm thankful for the anonymity.

I ride up to the ninth floor with a good-looking blond guy who might be on that lawyer show I like, but I'm not sure. Samantha would know. She knows way too much about celebrities, if you ask me. But considering that her mother makes a living off the film and television industry, I guess it would be hypocritical to discourage her interest.

Room 906 is a welcome refuge of tranquility and calm. I put my suitcase on the foldout stand and go straight to the minibar. I'm dying for a drink after that scene. Grabbing an eight-dollar bottle of Grolsch, I flop onto the bed and flick on the TV. The Canucks are winning for a change, and I settle back onto the plethora of pillows lining the headboard. Beer, hockey, and solitude: what more could a guy want? But somehow, I can't seem to concentrate on the game. Reaching for my cell phone on the bedside table, I check for missed calls or text messages. There are none. I'm simultaneously relieved and disappointed: relieved that Lucy isn't calling to hurl more abuse at me, and a little disappointed that Annika hasn't contacted me either.

I could always phone Annika, just a friendly call. "Hey, how are you? Whatcha up to? Me? Oh, not much. Watching the game . . . I left my wife tonight." But something about the timing feels wrong. Calling Annika now would be too significant. It would elevate her status from beautiful, sexy coworker to whom I'm most definitely attracted to something more. Because I did not lie to Lucy: Annika is not the reason I left her. My wife and I have been living in separate orbits for years now. Lucy cares about her job, Samantha, the house, and then me— in that order. I'm sure if you asked her she'd say Samantha and I come first, but that's bullshit. You don't spend twelve hours a day running around buying basketballs and zit cream for some teenybopper actor unless you love your job.

If anything, my attraction to Annika has been more like a wake-up call. It's shown me that I'm not completely dead inside, that I'm still capable of intense desire, of passion, of . . . caring about my appearance. I still remember Lucy's smirk when I came home with some stylish pants—as if I'd sidled in like MC Hammer or someone. It pissed me off, it really did. It's emasculating, is what it is. Annika didn't laugh at me. She said, "You look nice today, Trent. New pants?" Even though she's eleven years younger, Annika never makes me feel like an old fool like Lucy does. I mean, Lucy caught me using a little eye cream once and almost pissed her pants laughing.

God, I want to call Annika. I want to call her and ask her to meet me for a drink in the bar downstairs. Then, when she's a little drunk, I'll ask her up to my room where I'll rip her clothes off and ravage her like a sex-starved teenager. A little aroused just by the thought, I reach for the phone. But I can't. I can't invite Annika over mere minutes after I've walked out on my wife and daughter. It would be wrong. It would be sordid somehow. I know . . . I'll watch some porn.

Lucy always said, "It's not that I'm totally against watching porn, but there's a time and a place for it." I'm not sure when that time was or where that place was, but it was most definitely not in our house, not when our daughter, or any other human being for that matter, was within thirty feet of us. Even if we were separated by a solid layer of plywood, Gyprock, and plaster, Lucy could not stomach porn. We had a great sex life once, about a million years ago, but we'd both stopped making the effort.

On the screen, a blond motorcycle cop with enormous fake breasts pulls over a speeding Corvette. "Step out of the car," she instructs the driver, a Tom Selleck look-alike in impossibly tight, faded jeans. "Now," she continues, removing her mirrored sunglasses, "unzip your pants." Of course he complies and the cop proceeds to give him a highly enthusiastic blow job. It's hot, all right; it's porn. But something's wrong. I just can't get turned on by what I'm watching on the screen. It feels sort of . . . dirty and wrong. I flick back to the hockey game, even though I've just wasted eighteen bucks on two minutes of a movie. At least hockey isn't going to make me feel guilty—well, not any guiltier than I already feel.

Lucy

UNFORTUNATELY CAMILLE WASN'T home, so I'm forced to go the tea and sympathy route with Hope. "Have a cookie," she says, offering me the tin of home-baked peanut butter delights.

"I can't eat," I say, sniveling into a tissue. "I'm too upset."

"Oh, honey," Hope says, reaching out to draw me into a tight hug. My friend is the epitome of maternal comfort: warm, soft, and smelling of fabric softener. "I know it's hard right now, but every marriage has its challenges. If you just give Trent a little time and a little space, he'll come back home."

I break free of her embrace. "But what if I don't want to give him time and space? What if I want him to be a man and face up to his responsibilities? Sure, I'd love to run off and stay in a nice hotel and have affairs and get my eyes done. But I'm here, caring for my daughter, trying to give her a stable, loving upbringing so she doesn't turn into an angry sociopath or . . . a serial killer or something."

"Yes, but men are different from us by nature. They don't have the same ingrained sense of family and responsibility. And they have a much harder time coming to terms with their own mortality." Hope takes a deep, cleansing breath before continuing. "Do you remember when Mike was traveling so much last spring?"

I did remember. Why Mike's job as an optometrist required numerous trips to Aspen and the Bahamas was a mystery to me. But Hope, being the patient and loving super-wife that she was, had never questioned him. She just smiled sweetly when he returned home with a tan and a hangover.

"Well, there actually were no optometry conventions in Colorado and the Turks & Caicos."

"Really?" I say, feigning surprise.

"Mike was actually going through an existential crisis. He'd just turned forty-five, his doctor had told him his cholesterol was high, and he was suddenly feeling his age. Those trips were just a last grasp at his misspent youth. He needed to go diving and skiing and drinking with younger women. He needed to get the microdermabrasion and the body sculpting."

"Body sculpting?"

She waves her hand dismissively. "A little minor lipo."

"Mike had lipo?" I can't hide my shock and, well, maybe *disgust* is too strong a word but . . . ewwww!

"No, he had some minor body sculpting on his love handles. It was something he had to get out of his system, and now he's home."

"And you're okay with that?"

"Yes, because it ultimately brought him back to me and the kids, and now I truly feel we're closer than ever."

At this moment, I'm really wishing I could have gotten ahold of Camille and her bottle of tequila. I'm not usually a big drinker, but this is an exception. "I'm happy for you guys, but I just don't know if I could be that forgiving."

"I know." She squeezes my hand. "That's why I brought this." Digging in her large purse, she pulls out a battered paperback book. When she passes it to me, I read the title.

UNTIL HE COMES HOME
How His Midlife Crisis Can Benefit Your Marriage

"Uh . . . thanks, but I don't know if I'm really in the right headspace to read something like this."

"Not yet, but you will be," Hope says with a supportive smile. "For a marriage to work, you can't be so quick to give up on it."

"He's the one who's giving up on it!" I cry. Then, lowering my voice lest I alert my daughter, "He's the one who walked out on me! Why do I have to do all the work to try to keep our family together?"

"Because," Hope says with a beatific smile, "you're the woman."

Oh Christ. "I need a drink." I stand up. "I think I've got some wine in the kitchen. Do you want some wine?"

"Do you really think you should be drinking at a time like this?"

"You're right. Really, I should be smoking crack." I don't say this though. Hope would undoubtedly take me seriously and plan some preemptive intervention. Instead, I sit back on the couch. "You're right. What I really need is some sleep. I worked a thirteen-hour day and I'm exhausted. Things will probably look a lot more positive in the morning."

"They will," Hope assures me. "And please . . . read at least one chapter of this book. I promise it'll help you understand what Trent's going through."

After I've promised to read several pages of a book designed to help me understand why selfish, pricklike behavior is a God-given right for the entire male species, Hope leaves. Through the front window I watch her taillights disappear down the darkened street, and then scurry to the kitchen for the long-awaited glass of wine. The bottle of chardonnay sitting in the fridge door is half empty. I have no idea how long it's been there, but this is no time to be fussy. With the bottle and a full glass in my hand, I return to the sofa. I try Camille one more time, but she's still not home. For some reason, this fills me with an almost unbearable desolation. It's not like Camille is the only other person I can turn to; I'm on friendly terms with a number of neighbors, coworkers, and mothers of Samantha's friends. But she's the only other person I want to turn to. I'm not ready to admit to the world that my marriage—my whole life—is a failure.

When the bottle of wine and my tear ducts are empty, I head to bed. *Until He Comes Home* sits untouched on the bedside table. I'm too exhausted, too confused, and a bit too drunk to focus on it right now. And I don't even know what I want. Do I want to wait patiently for Trent to realize he loves me and come home? Or do I want him to die in a fiery car crash? Wait—maybe something more horrifying, like being eaten by a shark while he snorkels off the coast of Aruba. Better yet, it should be something really embarrassing, like reacting to the anesthesia during his brow lift. Or maybe a heart attack while lying naked in a tanning bed? With these pleasant thoughts in my head, I drift off to sleep.

Trent

THE ROOM IS dark when the alarm goes off, and it takes me a second to remember where I am. Right. I did it. I left. After months of worrying and stressing, I finally made a move. In the dim light of early morning, it all seems a little unreal. This could easily be a hotel room in Calgary or Seattle where I'm attending a conference, but no. I'm in a hotel in downtown Vancouver, having walked out on my wife and daughter.

Obviously, there's a bit of a negative connotation when it's put like that, but I'm not going to be eaten up by the guilt. Plenty of men reach the same decision that I have: life's too short to be stuck in a passionless marriage. I feel bad for Sam, but she'll get over it. I can still be a good dad to her, and I know Lucy won't let her down. Besides, what kind of example were we setting for her, living separate lives in the same house? She should know there's more to life than that.

I get up and head to the shower. If I don't think about Lucy crying on the sofa, I feel pretty good. I'm a single man again. Okay, maybe one night in a hotel doesn't make me single, but I took a step that needed to be taken. One day, Lucy will see that. Now, it's time to look forward.

My stomach does this weird, nervous, butterfly thing as I think about seeing Annika . . . voluptuous, sexy Annika with those big tits and that wild, curly hair. I decide to jerk off. It's a relief not to have to worry about Lucy walking in on me.

"Yuck! What are you doing?" she'd said when she walked in on me once. Those were her exact words—"Yuck! What are you doing?" Like masturbation isn't the most normal, healthy thing in the world. When did Lucy become so fucking uptight? She used to be fun and sexy, but now . . . I tear my thoughts from my wife and focus on Annika. Now that's more like it.

Lucy

WHEN THE ALARM goes off at 6:00 A.M. I feel confused and extremely thirsty. It would be completely acceptable to call in sick under the circumstances, but I somehow feel the distraction of work might help. After a jarring shower, a piece of toast, and a few sips of undrinkable coffee (Trent always made delicious coffee, but I refuse to let this upset me), I go to my daughter's room. "Knock, knock," I say cheerfully as I let myself inside.

Samantha's sanctuary is an exercise in organized chaos. She's a talented artist, and her walls are plastered with numerous school projects: a surreal self-portrait in charcoal; a scattering of ink drawings featuring stylized, metallic insects; a papier-mâché lantern; and my favorite, a watercolor of sailboats off Jericho Beach that she did when she was only twelve. Interspersed among her artwork are posters of her latest adolescent crush, Cody Summers. Cody Summers, played by the actor

Wynn Felker, is the star of the sitcom I'm working on, *Cody's Way*. The fact that Wynn Felker is not a precocious teenage boy with a knack for getting himself into trouble but a twenty-seven-year-old man with an enormous Hollywood ego does not quell Samantha's affection. She seems to think I'm making it all up just to thwart her first true love.

I perch on the side of her bed. "Morning, honey."

"What?" she growls, pulling the pillow over her head. "What time is it?"

"It's seven. I've got to head to work now, and Daddy—" I pause here, uncomfortable about lying to my daughter. But obviously I can't say that Daddy is at the Sutton Place Hotel finding himself and booking appointments with plastic surgeons. "Your dad had to go away on business. So, can you get yourself off to school on your own?"

She emerges from under her pillow. "Of course I can. Duh? I'm not, like, nine."

"Okay . . . well, that's good then. You should get up now or you're going to be late."

"Fine," she grumbles, throwing off her duvet and stumbling toward the shower.

THIRTY MINUTES LATER, I pull up in front of the *Cody's Way* studio building in an industrial area south of Vancouver. "Hi, Tanya," I mumble to the receptionist as I wander through the inauspicious lobby toward my office at the back. When I enter the small, cluttered space I share with Camille, my friend is already seated at her desk, peering intently at a spreadsheet on her computer.

"Morning," she says, without tearing her eyes from the screen.

"Where were you last night?" I ask, dropping my purse under my desk.

She turns to me then. "Oh god! Are you okay? What's wrong?"

I'm grateful for her sympathy, but a little chagrined by the fact that my having spent the whole night drinking wine and crying is so readily apparent. As I start to explain, I feel the tears welling in my eyes. Before I can speak, Camille grabs my hand. "Let's get out of here. We'll talk in my car."

As we drive toward Burnaby and one of the prop houses, I explain the events of last night. Not surprisingly, Camille says, "That fucking bastard. Does he think he's nineteen? God, men are such weak creatures."

"I know," I snivel into a balled-up tissue, "they are."

"Seriously, you're better off without him if this shows his strength of character. And Samantha's better off too. How's she taking it?"

"Sh-she doesn't know!" I wail. "He hasn't told her yet."

"Oh my god! You're kidding me. He just walked out and left you to deal with the aftermath? Do you see what kind of person he really is? He's a selfish, self-absorbed dick with the emotional maturity of a twelve-year-old. Seriously, you don't need a piece of shit like him in your life."

"He's not that bad," I say, for some reason a little defensive. I was married to the guy for sixteen years. "I told him he needs to come talk to her, and I'm sure he will."

Camille pulls the car into the parking lot outside the large warehouse building and turns off the ignition. "Stay here and get yourself together. I'll go in and look for the stuff we need. I want you to take it easy today, and tonight, I'll come over with some booze and we'll talk this whole thing out."

" 'Kay."

"And remember," she says as she hops out of the Explorer, "in the long run, you'll be glad all this happened. I promise."

Trent

I'M WITH CLIENTS all morning, which is a good distraction. Of course, I can't help but catch a glimpse of Annika as she escorts a young couple out of her office. God, she's sexy. She's a little heavier than Lucy, but in all the right places. And that hair . . . I just want to grab it, pull her head back, and suck on her neck. She glances my way and I wave. It feels juvenile, not to mention unprofessional, to wave at the girl you're hot for while you're advising a fifty-eight-year-old high school teacher on his retirement investments. But when she smiles and gives me a wink, I feel this heat in the pit of my stomach. Thankfully, the high school teacher doesn't notice and continues to peruse the mutual fund brochures I've given him.

At lunch, I'll call Lucy. I'm sure she's still too pissed off to have a civil conversation with me, but I'm concerned about Samantha. Given Lucy's work schedule, I'm usually the one who's home with Sam in the mornings, and often at dinner. She's bound to notice my absence and question her mom about it. I don't want Lucy to explain why I've left. No doubt she'd say something mean like, "Your dad is an immature, irresponsible dickwad who wears funny pants and doesn't love you."

When Mr. Larson leaves at 11:50, I pick up the phone to dial Lucy's cell. I've just punched in the first set of numbers when Annika pops her head into my office.

"Do you have plans for lunch?"

I abruptly hang up the phone. "No, actually, no plans."

"Want to go for noodles? I'm starving."

"Yeah, sounds good."

"I'll go get my purse. Meet me at the front door when you've finished your call."

"No," I say, standing up and sticking my phone in my pocket, "I'll make the call later. Let's go eat."

At lunch, Annika and I sit on tall stools at a tiny round table, bowls of Japanese noodle soup in front of us. We make small talk about work as we eat. I love how she eats. She scoops up enormous heaps of noodles with her chopsticks and shoves them in her mouth. She's not trying to be phony and ladylike. It's great how she can just be one of the guys, like she's completely comfortable in my presence. Unless, of course, that means she just thinks of me as a friend, and isn't interested in me as, like, a man. The thought sends a wave of something like anxiety through my stomach. I set down my chopsticks and take a drink of Coke.

As if she can read my mind, Annika coyly stirs her soup. "So . . . how's your wife these days?"

I refrain from letting out an audible sigh of relief. Her question—or more accurately, her delivery—makes it clear that I'm more than just a coworker to her. Besides, we've been flirting like crazy for months now. "Uh . . ." I clear my throat before continuing. Is it too soon to tell her that I've left Lucy? Will it scare her off? But our eyes connect and I feel the intensity of her gaze. "We've separated. I moved out."

"Oh . . . I'm sorry," she says, placing her hand consolingly on mine.

"I'm not," I say, my voice hoarse. Our eyes are still connected, and I swear to god I could take her into the restroom at the back of the restaurant and do her right now. Except, of course, everyone would hear us and our receptionist is at the counter ordering her lunch at this very moment. Plus, we'd be banned from eating lunch here ever again, and it's the best place to get noodles in the general vicinity of our office.

"Where are you living then?"

"I'm staying at the Sutton Place, just until I can find an apartment."

"Nice hotel," she says, waving to the receptionist as she carries her takeout back to the office. "I love the bar there. It's so fun to have a drink and watch the celebrities."

It's a cue, isn't it? It's not just a simple, celebrity-spotting anecdote. It can't be. Christ, I've been off the scene for so long, I can't tell anymore. But I take the plunge. "Yeah . . . We should meet there for a drink one night. I heard Lance Armstrong was staying there the other weekend."

She looks at me and smiles. It's a playful smile, almost teasing, but not mocking like when Lucy was looking at my skinny-leg trousers. "My friend and I saw Gene Simmons there two months ago. How's Friday?"

When I get back to the office, I can't stop smiling. I feel like an idiot, but I can't help it. I have a date with Annika. Of course, it's not officially a date: it's just two coworkers getting together to have a drink and spot B-list celebrities. But I can feel the attraction between us and I know she can too. It's been building for ages. And who knows where Friday night will lead? It could be the start of something, something new and exciting and unbelievably hot.

I decide not to phone Lucy. She's only going to bring me down with her insults and accusations. I deserve to enjoy this moment of anticipation. It's been way too long. But I haven't forgotten that I owe my daughter an explanation. I busy myself with paperwork until 4:30 when I know Sam will be home from school.

"Hey you," I say cheerfully when she answers the phone.

"Oh, hey, Dad."

"What are you doing?"

"Nothing. I just got home." I hear her opening the fridge, rummaging for her after-school snack. "Where are you?"

"I'm at work," I answer, a little confused by the question.

"Mom said you were out of town on business."

Thank you, Lucy. At least she had the decency to let me tell Samantha in my own words. "Right. Well, I'm back now and catching up on some stuff at the office. But I'll be home around 7:00, 7:30. Will you be there?"

"Yeah," she says, chewing something she found in the refrigerator. "I've got a project to work on for the art show in March."

"Great. Okay, that sounds great."

" 'Kay. See you later."

"Uh . . . Sam?"

"Yeah?"

"When I get home, I'd like to talk to you and your mom . . . Okay?"

"Sure, fine. See you then."

"Bye, honey . . . I love you." But she has already hung up.

Lucy

I TRY TO cling to Camille's words for the rest of the day, but I have trouble believing that, in the long run, I'll be ecstatic that my husband chose to walk out on me and my teenage daughter. Perhaps when Camille comes over tonight with her bottle of vodka she'll be able to convince me. But when I get home from work, Samantha relays a message.

"Dad called," she says, staring at *Access Hollywood* on the TV.

"He did?" I reply, my voice sounding shrill and strained. I consciously affect a more casual tone. "Okay . . . so, what did he say?"

"He said he'll be home around 7:30." Her eyes remain on the television screen. "He wants to talk to us about something."

"All right then," I say cheerfully, going to the fridge and peering inside. "What should we have for dinner?"

"I already had soup," Sam calls.

"Okay, good." Of course, I can't eat. My stomach is suddenly filled with butterflies. Home. Trent said he'd be *home* at 7:30. Could that mean he's come to his senses and wants to apologize to us? Of course, he doesn't really need to apologize to Samantha, since as far as she's concerned he just went away on a business trip. But perhaps he wants to start a new chapter of our life together? Maybe he wants to tell us both that he really treasures us and will start treating us accordingly. I'm a little surprised at how the possibility of his return fills me with elation. As angry as I am, Hope was right. I really do want him to come home and put our family back together.

I suddenly realize I'd better call Camille and tell her not to come over with her cocktails and venom. Thankfully, I get her answering machine and leave a brief message. I don't really want to hear her tell me that I'm married to an immature cocksucker who doesn't deserve a second chance. Now I wish I hadn't even told her. No, as Hope said, Trent just needed a little time alone before he realized that he loves his family and can't bear to give us up. It's normal, middle-aged male behavior. I'm just lucky that it only took one night in a downtown hotel for him to realize it, and not multiple trips to Aspen and the Bahamas.

Suddenly, my daughter lets out an earsplitting squeal. "Oh my god! There's Wynn Felker! You didn't tell me he was going to be at the Teen Choice Awards!"

"I didn't know," I say, closing the fridge and looking at the TV. Sure enough, Wynn Felker is being interviewed at the afterparty by a bubbly Latina with a microphone. "I don't know why he's there. He's hardly a teen."

"Shhhhh!" my daughter insists angrily, leaning closer to the television.

"Yeah," Wynn is saying, "it's really flattering to be voted

Choice Hottie. You know, I've been in the business for a few years now . . ."

I scoff. "Only, like, fifteen or so."

"Mom!" Samantha says angrily, eyes still affixed to the TV.

Wynn continues. "You know . . . it's just really nice to get recognized."

"I can't believe I missed the Teen Choice Awards!" Samantha cries when the program breaks for commercial. "If you had told me that Wynn was going to be on, I would have made sure I stayed home."

"Sam," I say, exercising patience, "I told you, I didn't know. Just because Wynn Felker stars on the show that employs me doesn't mean we're best friends. He barely acknowledges me."

"Well, maybe if you made more of an effort," she says. "Like, why have you never invited him over for dinner?"

"Why would I? What would I have in common with Wynn Felker?" But the sound of a key in the front door stops me. Damn! Trent is here already. I'd hoped to have time to freshen up before he arrived. Not that I intend to completely forgive him for his desertion of us, but it would have been nice to mark his return with a little fresh lipstick and maybe offer him a martini.

"Hi, my girls," he says, walking into the living room with his usual greeting. I can't help but smile as he leans over the back of the couch and kisses the top of Samantha's head. We're a family, even if we are going through a rocky patch.

Sam flicks the TV off. "So what's up? I've got an art project I want to get started on."

"Why don't we all sit down together?" Trent says, looking over at me. Obediently, I move to the TV area and sit next to

Samantha. Trent, sitting on her other side, continues. "Your mother and I would like to talk to you about something."

Sam twirls a piece of shoulder-length blond hair, evidence that she senses this is no ordinary conversation. Automatically, I reach over and squeeze her knee. She looks at me, her eyes full of fear. I give her a supportive smile. *Don't worry,* I try to convey with my expression, *it's all going to be fine. Dad's gone through a little mini-crisis, but he's home now.*

Trent clears his throat. "You know I wasn't home last night."

"Yeah." Sam shrugs. "Mom said you were away on business. So?"

"Well . . . that's not entirely true. I . . . uh . . . Your mother and I have decided that . . . we've reached a stage in our marriage where we need to spend some time apart."

Oh, no, you don't! "Well, Sam, that's not entirely true either. Your father has made this decision one hundred percent on his own." I'd hoped to keep the anger out of my voice for Samantha's sake, but somehow it seeps in. Perhaps it's the rage that is suddenly engulfing me, sending hot, bubbling hatred coursing through my veins. Not only is he not coming home, now he's trying to blame me for half of this!

"Okay, whatever," Trent says, dismissively. "Who decided is irrelevant."

"Irrelevant? Hah!"

"Lucy . . . this isn't helping."

"Oh, I'm sorry," I say, sarcastically. "I'm sure if I just smiled and nodded along, Samantha would have no trouble accepting that her father has decided to leave us."

"Mom!" Sam cries, sounding annoyed at me.

"What, honey?"

"Just let him talk, okay?" And I see her chin tremble with emotion.

Trent shoots me a look of warning and then turns to our only child. "I'm going to be moving out for a while."

"How long?" she asks, suddenly sounding about four years old.

"I don't know. It's not that I don't love you . . . and your mother," he adds, in a tone that could not be more devoid of love. "It's just that I need to spend some time by myself to figure out . . . some stuff."

"What stuff?"

"Uh . . . grown-up, man stuff."

I snort. I know I'm supposed to let him talk, but "grown-up, man stuff"? Pleeeeeze!

Trent ignores me. "I still want to see you, sweetie. And I still want to be a part of your life. I'll still come to your art show in March. And I'm going to get a two-bedroom apartment so that you can stay with me some weekends."

Samantha stands up. "Oh, can I?" she says, obviously having inherited her mother's sarcasm. "That sounds great! I can't wait!" Marching from the room, she growls, "Whatevs."

"Well done," I snipe, moving back to the kitchen. "You've broken two hearts in two days. Good job."

"Enough with the sarcasm," Trent barks. I have to admit that even I am getting a little tired of it. I turn to face him as he continues. "This is not an easy time for any of us. And I know you think I'm being a selfish bastard for moving out, but I'm not Saddam Hussein, for Christ's sake. Cut me some slack."

And suddenly I feel the tears starting to build. Oh no, not again. I'm torn between wanting to cut him some slack and wanting to cut him into several pieces with the paring knife sitting next to the toaster. But of course, a paring knife couldn't possibly cut through a full-grown man. I nod mutely, a single tear trickling, almost poetically, I think, down my cheek.

"Oh honey," he says, coming toward me. He reaches for me but I wisely step away. As much as I want to melt into the familiar comfort of his arms, I know it wouldn't change anything. It would only make it that much harder when he walks out the door.

"Okay then," he says. "I'll check on you girls later."

When he's gone and I've ebbed the flow of my tears, I go to Samantha's room. "Knock, knock," I say, opening the door. "Can I come in?"

"No," she snaps, "I'm working on my art project."

"Can I see?" I ask, as cheerfully as possible.

"It's not ready yet."

"Okay . . . well, if you want to talk about any of this, I'll be downstairs." Silence. "I love you, Samantha . . . more than anything in the world."

There is a long pause before my daughter finally mumbles, "Yeah, whatevs."

THE NEXT MORNING, it's evident that my daughter and I have made an unspoken pact not to mention the fact that we now live in a broken home.

"How are you?" I ask, as she shuffles into the kitchen.

She looks at me morosely. "How do you think?"

"Well, if you're not up to going to school today, I understand. I could take the day off and we could do something. Go to the art gallery or something?"

"Nah," she says, grabbing a banana out of the fruit bowl. "I don't want to get behind. See ya later."

"Have a good day, honey!" I call after her.

And that's how I get through the day: with a forced cheerfulness that's probably bordering on creepy. As I dig through the chaotic prop room looking for pool noodles, coolers, a punch bowl, and various other toys for Cody's end-of-school-year beach party, I let the facade drop. But as soon as I face any of my coworkers, I smile with a ferocity that's almost painful. When I receive a few awkward, almost frightened looks, I wonder if I'm looking a bit like The Joker.

Hope calls me on my cell phone at noon. "I left you four messages yesterday. Where were you?"

"Sorry. I was at work and when I got home, Trent came over and—"

"See?" she says triumphantly. "I knew it was just a phase. That was really quick though. I mean, it took Mike a few months to sort himself out."

I explain my husband's visit. "Oh, Lucy," she says, "I'm sorry."

"Yeah," I say, trying to control the quiver in my voice.

"You and Sam are coming over for dinner tonight and I won't take no for an answer."

"That's nice of you, but . . . I don't know if it's really a good idea for Samantha to be around a happy family right now. It might just make her feel worse about what's going on at home."

"Mike won't be home though," Hope says. "Trent asked him to go for drinks tonight. It'll just be us and the kids."

"Drinks? Trent's going out for drinks?"

Hope laughs. "Don't turn it into some kind of bachelor

party. Trent needs someone to confide in, and Mike's already been through this. You know he's going to tell him to go back home to you and Sam."

"Okay," I mumble, "I'll call you after I talk to Sam about dinner."

"Tell her to come and spend some time with Sarah-Louise. It'll be good for her."

I already know my daughter won't be in the mood for perky, straight-A-getting, trombone-playing Sarah-Louise, but I don't say anything.

I hang up the phone just as Wynn Felker walks past, trailed by one of his obsequious female handlers. As usual, he ignores me and I him. But I can't help but think about Samantha's suggestion that I invite him home for dinner. Obviously, he'd say, "No, thanks. Who are you?" but it's the one thing I can think of that would cheer my daughter up. And even I would rather have dinner with Wynn Felker tonight than with a pitying Hope and her three eerily perfect children.

But Wynn barks, "Debbie, I'm not going to some mall opening in Nebraska. I don't care how much money they're offering."

"I know," Debbie chirps, "but Stephen thinks it would be good to capitalize on your Choice Hottie win. He says you need to get your face out there."

"In Nebraska?"

"I know, but Stephen says your numbers are lower in the Midwest, so it might be a good idea . . . ?"

"I can't do it," Wynn says. "I've got other plans and I can't be in two places at once, can I?"

"I know. Okay, I'll talk to Stephen and tell him your position."

At that moment, Wynn turns and looks through the door-way of the props room. Our eyes meet for a moment, but there is no warmth, no recognition. And there is certainly no "You look like you're going through a hard time right now. Would you like the Choice Hottie to come over for dinner to cheer up your teenage daughter?" I flash him my creepy, Joker-like smile. He gives me a quick, indifferent grin and then continues on his way.

Trent

"YOU KNOW I'M supposed to be talking you into going home," Mike says, sawing off a piece of blue-rare steak and shoving it in his mouth. He's a big, beefy kind of guy and looks really comfortable eating nearly raw meat.

"I'm sure you are."

"So . . . ," he continues as he chews, "are you going to?"

I shrug, sawing at my filet mignon. "I don't know. I went to talk to Sam last night and Lucy was a total bitch. I mean, I still care about her, but it's hard to see us getting back together when she's acting this way."

"Well, take your time and have some fun, if you know what I mean." He moves his eyebrows up and down suggestively. "Who is she, anyway?"

"Who?" I ask, feigning innocence.

"Give me a break. You don't just walk out after being married that long. There's always somebody else involved."

"There's not, really." God, am I blushing? What am I, twelve? The way Mike is laughing and pointing his steak knife at me confirms it. "Okay . . . I am interested in someone, but she's not the reason I left."

"I knew it! Spill."

"I work with her . . . I don't know . . . she's great."

"She hot?" he mumbles through a mouthful.

"Soooo fucking hot."

"Have you nailed her yet?"

"No. We've been flirting for a while but it hasn't gone beyond that. But we're having a drink on Friday at the bar in my hotel. So, you know, hopefully . . ."

"Get busy, man," Mike counsels. "You know Lucy won't wait for you forever."

I shrug, sawing off a piece of steak. "Well, the way I feel right now, I'm not too worried about that. You know . . . maybe this thing with Annika will work out." Mike lets out a snort of laughter. "What?"

"This thing with Annika is not going to work out."

I suddenly feel like punching him in his fat, steak-eating mouth. "How do you know?"

"I've been there, remember? There was a girl, a flight attendant, when Hope and I were going through our stuff. In fact, there were a few girls. I thought I might end up with one of them, but in the end, it was just about sex. It's just the excitement of being with someone new. Your life is with Lucy and Samantha."

"Samantha will always be a part of my life," I say, defensively. "She's my kid. I don't have to be living with Lucy to be a good dad to her."

"No, but it makes it a hell of a lot easier."

"Life's not always easy, Michael," I say, sagely. I wave to the waiter to bring two more beers. "I'll be a better father if I'm happy. And Annika makes me happy."

"Of course she does. I bet she makes you feel young and desirable. She probably makes you want to take better care of yourself, wear hipper clothes, maybe get a little plastic surgery . . ."

"I wouldn't go that far—but yeah, she does make me feel . . . you know, younger. What's wrong with that?"

"Nothing. Except that it won't last."

The big-fat-mouth-punching urge is returning. "Look, you don't know anything about my relationship with her. Just because things didn't work out with you and your flight attendant doesn't mean you know what's going to happen with me and Annika."

"Okay, okay. Jesus, I'm sorry." The waiter approaches and sets down two more Stella Artois. "You're right. Your relationship might be totally different than mine were. I'm just saying what happened to me."

I take a swig of beer. "What happened?"

"Well, Tammy—the first one—was still involved with her ex-boyfriend. Mel, the flight attendant, was just a fling really. She was too young for me, but she was really uh, energetic, if you get my drift. And then I had this flirting thing with a client, but I couldn't cross that line. She was married anyway, so it would have been a big mess."

"Yeah, well, Annika's not a client, she's not too young, and she's not married. So . . . it's totally different."

"Yeah, of course it is. I'm sure you'll live happily ever after."

"Fuck you."

Mike laughs and takes a swig of beer. "So . . . how about those Canucks?"

Lucy

"I'M KIDNAPPING YOU for the afternoon," Camille says when I enter the office Friday morning.

I look over at our boss, Bruce, the props master. "Fine with me," he says, reclining in his chair. "Wynn Felker's gone to L.A. for some party, so they're just shooting green-screen scenes with Adam's character. You'll make the time up next week after the concept meeting on Monday."

"Well, okay then," I say gamely. "What are we going to do?"

"It's a surprise," Camille says, with a devilish twinkle in her eye. I feel my stomach lurch uncomfortably. Oh, please don't take me to a male strip bar or something—not that I know of any male strip bars that operate in the afternoon. Unlike men, women don't really like to watch the opposite sex gyrate around in the nude while they eat lunch. Still, from the look on Camille's face, she's got more in store for me than an afternoon of shopping.

The morning drags but finally, at one o'clock, she finds me on set. "Okay, let's go."

"Sure . . . So, where are we off to? Lunch? Shopping?"

"Let's grab a quick smoothie. I've got us an appointment at 1:30."

The spa! Hurray! Some pampering will do me a world of good. Obediently, I follow Camille out to her SUV and allow her to chauffeur me to the juice place. "So where is this spa?" I ask as we hurtle down Oak Street, sucking on our thick blueberry smoothies.

"On Broadway," she says cryptically.

I try to think of a spa located on Broadway but come up empty. "Is it a new place?"

"No, he's been there for a while." Her tone is dismissive.

"Okay," I say, realizing that she's not going to be any more forthcoming. I sit back and drink my smoothie, thankful for Camille's heated seats in the damp February chill. I take a deep breath and feel myself relax in anticipation of the impending indulgence. Considering that my husband left me only five days ago, I'm handling myself quite well. Not that I have the luxury of falling apart completely. I have my daughter to think about.

Sixteen minutes later we're in a small mirrored elevator traveling up to the eighth floor of a nondescript office building. "There's a spa in here?" I ask. It seems a strange location, but then all the elite spas are probably hidden away in nondescript buildings.

"We're not going to a spa," Camille says, her expression mischievous.

"Where are we going then?" I snap. "My husband just left me five days ago. You better not be taking me someplace weird."

"Dr. Andrews is a licensed dermatologist. We're going to get you a Botox treatment, and it's on me."

"What!" I shriek at the precise moment the elevator doors open with a ding.

"Come on, you big baby." Camille grabs my arm and escorts me into the hall. "You're not afraid of needles, are you?"

"No," I retort, "I'm afraid of looking like a frozen mannequin. I'm afraid of getting a droopy eyelid or a permanent headache. I've heard tons of horror stories about Botox gone wrong. Thanks, but no thanks."

"Come on," my friend cajoles. "I've been doing it for years and I've never had a bad experience with it."

"You have?"

"Yeah! Getting Botox is like dyeing your hair was in the eighties. Everybody does it. They just don't talk about it."

I look at Camille's forehead. It is surprisingly smooth for a forty-two-year-old. Why hadn't I noticed it before? I've always attributed her youthful good looks to the fact that she's never had to juggle the stress of having a family and a career. I'm two years younger, but in comparison I always look a little . . . haggard.

"Let's go in," she continues. "Dr. Andrews will explain all the risks and you can decide then. But just think, in a matter of minutes you could completely get rid of that deep frown line."

"Deep frown line?" My hand flies to my forehead. "Is it really that deep?"

"Well," she says kindly, "if you get Botox now, it won't get any deeper."

Dr. Andrews looks about twelve years old, except for his

receding hairline. He is possibly, but not definitely, gay. He explains that, in his nine years of practice, no one has suffered a droopy eyelid or a permanent headache, and all customers are completely satisfied.

"You'll love it!" Camille chirps. "You won't look so tired and angry anymore. Do it!"

Tired and angry?

"What do you think?" Dr. Andrews says encouragingly. "Should we get rid of those nasty frown lines?"

Oh great. Now a licensed plastic surgeon has diagnosed my frown lines as "nasty." No wonder Trent left me! I'm a hag! Before I break down in a blubbering pool of self-pity, I blurt, "Let's do it."

Dr. A assures me that the needle will feel like a mosquito bite, which is true if you count those giant killer mosquitoes in horror movies. But it's all over in a matter of minutes, and I leave the office with a series of bloody dots on my forehead. As I prepare to exit, the doctor says, "The toxin will take a couple of days to kick in. Try to frown a lot to help it activate faster."

"That shouldn't be a problem," I say. "Thanks."

Camille has already paid the receptionist when I emerge into the lobby. "Next stop, my hairdresser!"

"This is too much," I insist. "Seriously, let me pay."

She leads me to the elevator. "No, I want to do this for you. Besides, it's fun for me. It's like I'm your Pygmalion. I'm going to have you back on the scene in no time."

"Camille!" I look at her in shock. "It hasn't even been a week since Trent left!"

"So? Do you think he's sitting alone in his hotel room looking wrinkly and frumpy? You've got to get out there again."

She has a point, and it would seem ungrateful not to go along with her plan. Camille does have really gorgeous hair, and when we leave her Yaletown salon, so do I.

"Wear something sexy and we'll go for drinks at George tomorrow night," she says, driving me back to the office to pick up my car.

"I can't leave Sam home alone right now." The thought of my daughter has me fishing in my purse for my cell phone. I'd turned the ringer off when I thought we were going to the spa. "Besides, I'm just not ready."

"I'm not saying you should go out and pick up a guy," she scoffs. "But it'll be good for you to get out of the house for a couple of hours."

"Shit!" I say, extracting the phone: two new messages.

"What's wrong?"

I put the phone to my ear. "I just hope Sam didn't need me. She's been upset all week." The first message is from Anthony in the set decoration department. I skip it and move on to the next one. "Oh god," I murmur as my worst fear is realized. "Oh no."

Trent

I DOUBT THAT Annika is the kind of girl who cares if my hotel room is a mess, but I tidy it up just the same. Lucy would laugh if she saw the state of it, saying something like, "How can you make such a mess in a room that comes with its own maid?" Of course, it's possible that Annika won't even come up to my room tonight, but it's just as possible that she will. The thought makes my stomach gurgle. I need a drink.

Going to the minibar, I mix myself a rum and Coke. I'm really going to have to buy a bottle if I stay here much longer. These minibar costs are breaking me. The rum burns in my stomach, a comforting feeling.

Okay . . . Whatever happens with Annika tonight, it's going to be fine. I want her, and unless I'm completely off base, she wants me, too. No, I'm not off base. The sexual tension has been building between us for months. So if we both want each other, then we should be together. Just because I've been making love to the same woman for eighteen years doesn't mean it can't be great with someone new. And I'm sure I'll be able to satisfy Annika, just as I satisfied Lucy. I mean, how different can two women be?

Although . . . Annika definitely has a lot more experience than Lucy. She's probably had dozens of lovers—even hundreds. The thought is a little intimidating . . . in fact, it's almost scary. That reminds me, I don't have any condoms. It's the guy's responsibility to provide protection, right? It used to be, but maybe that's an old-fashioned notion. Annika will probably come prepared. But what if she doesn't? And what if she's had hundreds of lovers and she gives me some horrible venereal disease? And what if Lucy and I get back together and I give her the horrible venereal disease I caught from Annika? I've got to calm down. I down the remains of my drink.

The clock radio next to the phone tells me it's time to get dressed. I strip off my shirt and stop in front of the large, wall-mounted mirror. I stare at my reflection: not bad for forty-three. I mean, other than the fact that most of my chest hair is gray, I could pass for a much younger man. Could I dye my chest hair? Or would that be really obvious? If Annika noticed, she'd think I was trying too hard—and it would definitely buy into Lucy's midlife crisis theory. I turn to the side to take in my profile. I have a definite paunch—it wouldn't necessarily qualify as a beer gut, but it's there just the same. Oh fuck, I can't sleep with Annika. She'll think I'm old and fat and disgusting.

For some reason, I feel another surge of anger toward Lucy. Obviously, all my insecurities aren't her fault, but would it have killed her to show a little attraction to me once in a while? Couldn't she have initiated sex, like, even once in the past three years? If she had, I might not be in this situation right now.

Okay, I've got half an hour until I'm supposed to meet Annika downstairs. Do I shave or am I sexier with a bit of five o'clock shadow? Stroking my chin, I decide to leave it. When I got in I'd showered, but I think I forgot to put on deodorant. I sniff my armpit. I can't really tell, but better safe than sorry. As I head to the bathroom my cell phone rings. The shrill sound in the quiet of the room startles me.

"Hello?" I'm worried that it could be Annika calling off our date, but I try for a casual tone.

"Trent, it's me."

I suddenly feel guilty and a little sick to my stomach. "Oh, hey Lucy. How are you?"

"Not good. I'm not good at all. It's Sam."

"Sam?" Panic makes my knees weak and I sit on the edge of the bed.

"I was out all afternoon and there was a message on my cell phone from the school. She . . ." A sob steals her voice.

"What?" I practically scream. "What is it?"

"Sam and her friend Jordan turned up drunk at school! She cut class and now she's drunk! At school!"

I could almost laugh—not that it's funny that my daughter is turning into a teenage piss-tank, but considering that moments ago I thought she was the victim of some kind of school massacre, it is somewhat of a relief. "Okay, just calm down. Where are you now?"

"I'm driving to Crofton House. I'll be there in about ten minutes."

"Great, okay. Take her home, give her some carbs, and send

her to bed. I'll be over in the morning and we can deal with it then."

"What?" Lucy shrieks. "You expect me to handle this all on my own? You expect me to march through the halls of the city's best private school, pick up my wasted daughter, and apologize to the principal for my shoddy parenting, all by myself? You're the reason she was drinking in the first place!"

"That's a low blow!" I growl. "If we could have handled things my way, she wouldn't be so upset."

"Oh, so I drove her to the bottle by being a little sarcastic," Lucy snaps back. "Right, yeah, of course, that's it. This had nothing to do with you LEAVING US!"

"Calm down," I say, suddenly fearful that she might crash her Forerunner into a power pole. "There's no need to panic. Sam's fifteen. This is pretty normal teenage behavior."

"Don't tell me to calm down, Trent. Our daughter is drunk at school. Would you prefer we wait until she's a crystal meth addict panhandling on Hastings Street before we freak out?"

"No, of course not. I'm just saying—" But my wife cuts me off.

"What have you got going on tonight that's more important than dealing with your daughter's drinking problem? Are you going out with Mike again? Or have you got a date or something?"

"No!" I cry. "Of course not! I just thought . . . I don't know . . . that maybe you could handle this on your own."

"Oh, I'm sorry I'm so weak and incapable," the queen of sarcasm continues. "My husband walked out on me at the beginning of the week, and now my fifteen-year-old daughter's drowning her sorrows in a bottle of gin. But you're right, it's no big deal. I should just toughen up."

I know when I'm defeated. "Fine. I'll be there as soon as I can." Before she can say another word, I hang up and start to punch in Annika's number. Strangely, I feel just the smallest glimmer of relief.

Lucy

"WHAT HAVE YOU got to say for yourself, young lady?" Samantha looks at me, her eyes slightly unfocused. Then she bursts into laughter. "You think this is funny, do you? Well, let me tell you, little girl, this is not funny!"

"Don't waste your breath on her right now," Trent interjects. "She's hammered. We can deal with this in the morning."

I turn on him. "Don't you mean *I* can deal with this in the morning? You'll be at your hotel, maybe having a massage or enjoying the brunch buffet."

"Right, like I'm on vacation."

"Well, it sure as hell beats staying here and dealing with all this shit!"

Samantha finally speaks. "Here you go again," she slurs. "Can you blame me for having a couple gin and orange pops at lunch? God!"

"Don't you try to blame us for this," I snap. "You're old enough to take responsibility for your actions."

"Right," she mumbles. "I'll be responsible . . . like you guys are."

"Watch it, Sam," Trent growls. "Don't say something you're going to be sorry for later."

"Okay," she says. "Can I have some nachos?"

"No, you cannot have nachos!" I scream, finally losing it with her nonchalance. "Go to bed and we'll talk about this when you're sober." The words prompt an uncontrollable swelling of emotion. Trent and I have handled our separation so badly that my fifteen-year-old daughter has turned to alcohol! At lunch! At school! I burst into tears.

Trent looks at me and then puts his hands on Sam's shoulders. "Let's get you off to bed," he says to her, steering her weaving form out of the kitchen and up the stairs.

I try to gain control over my emotions while he's out of the room. I don't need him to know how alone I feel, how defeated and lost. Who would want such a pathetic, emotional wreck of a woman back? It's no wonder he left me, really. I'm a terrible mother and I was probably a terrible wife, too. And now my husband is gone, my daughter's a teenage alcoholic, and it's all my fault.

Of course, this train of thought makes it significantly harder to calm down. When Trent returns to the kitchen I'm still weeping. As he approaches, I grab a paper towel and hold it to my face.

"She'll be fine," he says. "In the morning, she's going to be so hungover that she won't drink again for years."

I snuffle a response into the paper towel.

Trent moves toward me, his voice soft. "This isn't your fault, you know. If you want to blame me, I understand. I guess I could have handled this better . . . with Sam and everything."

My face remains buried in the paper towel, but I manage to shake my head. I don't want to blame Trent for this. I don't want to be angry at him anymore. I want us to join together as a team, to discuss how our daughter has fallen in with a bad crowd, how getting drunk at school is really just a rite of passage, and how we'll all laugh about this one day. For the first time, I raise my face and meet my husband's eyes. Instead of the pity or disgust that could be there, I see only tenderness.

Uh-oh.

Trent

IT WAS PROBABLY a bad idea. It's just that she looked so sad and alone, and I guess I was still a bit worked up because I had that date planned with Annika, and . . . it just happened. I'd only meant to comfort her, so I gave her a hug. And then she was playing with my hair, which she knows perfectly well turns me on, so obviously, she wanted it. Then the next thing you know we were going at it on the living room sofa. It was pretty fantastic, I have to say. If we'd been having sex like that all along, I never would have left.

I ended up staying over, which I'm afraid may have sent the wrong message. Lucy looked kind of disappointed when I left for the hotel that afternoon. But one good fuck on the couch doesn't erase three years of living separate lives. There's no way she could think we were getting back together already. And on the bright side, the sex did make us stop fighting long enough to deal with Sam's drinking, so . . . I guess it wasn't that big of a mistake. As long as Lucy understands that we've still got a lot of problems we need to work on before I can think about coming home. I'm sure she gets that, right?

Annika walks by with a coffee cup in her hand and doesn't even glance into my office. Does that mean she's mad at me for bailing on our Friday plans? Surely she understands that a drunken teenage daughter constitutes an emergency situation. Although, how can I expect her to understand? She's only thirty-two.

Swallowing the remnants of my coffee, I decide to follow her into the kitchen to make sure. Ugh! It's ice cold, but I need an excuse to enter the coffee room. I can't chase after her like some love-struck kid.

Annika is making herself a cup of some kind of herbal tea when I approach. "Hey," I say casually, going to the coffeepot.

"Oh, hi, Trent," she responds cheerfully. She doesn't sound pissed, so I decide to continue.

"How was your weekend?"

"Great. I went snowboarding on Saturday. It was amazing."

"Awesome," I say, as if I actually find snowboarding amazing as well. The truth is, I've never snowboarded, and rarely even ski anymore. I hurt my hip getting off the chairlift a few years back and it still bothers me in the cold. Plus, at my age, a snowboard getup would be laughable.

"How's your daughter?" Annika asks, tossing her tea bag in the trash.

"Oh . . . yeah, she's fine. She went home for lunch with one of her girlfriends and they decided to have a couple of highballs. It was just stupid. She's not a bad kid."

"Of course not," Annika says. "I remember drinking half a

bottle of rye one lunch hour in tenth grade. And look how well I turned out!"

This is a perfect opportunity for me to say something suggestive, like, "Yeah, you turned out great" or "I love the way you turned out," but I hesitate too long and the moment's gone.

"Actually," Annika admits, "I had a few too many on Saturday night. My girlfriend and I went to check out this new club. It's called Mania. Have you heard of it?"

"No," I mumble, stirring cream into my coffee. I suddenly feel like some midlife crisis Michael Caine character. What am I doing? Why am I chasing after a hot young thing who spends her weekends snowboarding and clubbing when I have a perfectly good, age-appropriate wife at home? A wife with whom I had incredible sex not three days ago! Am I really such a cliché?

"It was wild," Annika continues. "But I paid for it on Sunday."

I give a small laugh and prepare to slink back to my office. But before I've gone far she says, "So, how about a rain check for last Friday?"

I stop. "Sounds good," I say. And suddenly, I'm eighteen again.

Lucy

THE BOTOX FINALLY kicked in this morning. I'm grateful I still had the ability to frown over the weekend so that I could show Sam my extreme disapproval over her lunchtime cocktail party. Trent and I were very calm and collected when we talked to her about her behavior the next morning. I'm glad we didn't end up bickering and pointing fingers. I guess having sex helped us reconnect.

I hadn't expected it to happen, but I was upset and he comforted me. One thing led to another and we ended up having sex on the living room sofa. It was really spontaneous and quite risky. Of course, we knew we wouldn't be discovered since the only other person in the house was in an alcohol-induced coma, but we hadn't done it outside of our bedroom for years. It was pretty incredible, I must say. Not that we don't still have issues to work out, but I think it was a step in the right direction.

So whether it's the Botox, the highlights, or the hot sex, I feel really confident today. I spent a little longer on my hair and makeup this morning, and evidently, it's paid off. Even Tanya, the nearly mute receptionist, says "You look nice today" when I walk past her.

Camille is more verbose. "Why, Eliza Doolittle!" she cries when I walk into our shared space. "Don't you look fantastic— if I do say so myself."

"Thanks," I say, giving my hair a little flip as I deposit my purse under the desk. "I had a pretty great weekend."

"You did?" Camille looks shocked. "I thought Sam getting drunk at school on Friday would have set a bad tone."

"Shhhhh!" I look around to make sure no one heard. "Well, of course that part was bad, but we dealt with it really well. Trent came over—"

Bruce pops his head into the room. "Script meeting starting now, ladies. Let's go."

With notepads and pens in hand, we follow him to the boardroom at the end of the hall. Kev, the director, a twenty-eight-year-old weenie who considers himself the next Woody Allen, is already there, eager to dictate his vision to the various departments.

Each week the scripts get less and less inspiring. Our overage teenager seems to find himself in more predictable predicaments as the show progresses. This week he's got to pretend he has a twin brother so that the girl he likes doesn't think he's a complete idiot. Of course, she ultimately finds out there's only one Cody—and that's just the way she likes it. If I wasn't in such a good mood about the positive direction in which my marriage is headed, I might gag.

Bruce is rattling off the props that Cody and his fake twin will need this episode when the door suddenly opens.

"Wynn!" Kev says, jumping to attention as the star of our show enters.

"I need to talk to you," Wynn says, with no regard for the twelve other people in the room.

"Right . . . okay. Take a break everyone."

I watch Wynn Felker as he stands in the doorway, waiting for the director to hurriedly gather his scripts. He's an extremely good-looking guy, but he's too good-looking really, almost pretty. I prefer a more masculine type, like Trent. I look down at my notes and doodle my husband's name. It's juvenile, I know, but he's on my mind. Trent has always been my type, physically. He's aged over the years, of course, but I'm not one to complain about a bit of a belly. It's not like I'm perfect . . . though at the moment, I would have to say I'm pretty damn good.

"Sorry to interrupt your meeting," Wynn says as the director hustles over to join him. There is a general outpouring of obsequiousness.

"No problem at all!"

"Oh please! I'm sure your needs are more urgent."

"Don't worry about it."

I roll my eyes just as Wynn looks at me. Oh shit. But surprisingly, I see a hint of humor in his gaze. He reaches for one of the pastries sitting on a tray in the middle of the table. "You don't mind, do you?" He's saying this directly to me. Obviously, he thinks I'm the person responsible for the pastries instead of Tanya.

"Go ahead," I say coolly. It's not that I'm *above* arranging the morning pastry delivery, but it would be nice if he ever paid attention to what anyone else's job was.

Wynn reaches for a Danish then lifts his gaze to me. Our eyes connect for a moment, and I feel the burning of attraction between us. But that's stupid. Wynn is Choice Hottie, after all, and while I'm feeling rather attractive at the moment, I'm not going to kid myself. Hurriedly, I drop my eyes to the notepad in front of me. I must have got it wrong.

Casually, I look up and our eyes meet again. Oh god, what is with that intense staring? I can't help but blush as I quickly look away. I glance back. In response, Wynn chuckles and, turning on his heel, leaves the room. Oh, I get it. This must be something he does to women who get too full of themselves. Well, he certainly brought me down a peg or two. I suddenly feel exceedingly plain and frumpy.

Camille leans over. "So, tell me about this great weekend you had."

Her words return me to my former glory. "Well, this thing with Sam . . . it really allowed Trent and me to reconnect."

"Reconnect how?"

The disapproving tone of her voice and the look in her eye keep me from admitting that we reconnected on the living room sofa. "We just came together as parents and . . . it felt really good."

"Oh."

"Yeah . . . that's it. And of course . . . ," I lower my voice, "the Botox kicked in. I should have done this years ago! Even when I'm feeling really angry and unhappy, you can't tell!"

"I know. It's great, isn't it?"

"What about lip injections? Have you ever done those?"

The director barges back into the room. "Sorry about that, everyone. Okay . . . where were we?"

Trent

ANNIKA AND I set a date for Thursday night. She suggested George, this trendy Yaletown place. I wish we were sticking with Plan A—celebrity spotting at the hotel bar—but I felt awkward suggesting it. Besides, I've gotta move out of there soon. Lucy's car needs new tires and hotel living costs a fortune. I've become addicted to my minibar Grolsch and Toblerone, and that alone is costing me over twelve bucks a night.

So with my beer and chocolate bar on the bedside table, I call some apartment listings. There are two that would work—both in Yaletown. Yes, moving into that neighborhood will feed into the midlife crisis cliché, but I don't give a shit. It's time I stopped caring about what looks good to everyone else and started caring about what feels right for me. I played that game long enough. This is my time.

I set up appointments to view the apartments tomorrow, and

then decide to grab a burger. That's another reason I've got to get my own place. I need to start eating better—especially if Annika's going to see me in the buff. Christ, even the thought of it makes me nervous. But the rumbling in my stomach makes me think of Sam. I wonder what Lucy's been feeding her? I've always done most of the cooking. It's not that Lucy can't cook, but she always says she's too tired. Or she doesn't get home until eight o'clock and it's too late by then.

I throw on my coat and head downstairs. It's raining, of course; it's February. But I decide to walk to my favorite burger joint. It's only a few blocks away on Davie Street. Lucy and I used to eat there all the time after a night out on the town. Suddenly, I feel my cell phone vibrate in my pocket.

"Hello?"

"Hey. It's me."

It's like she knew I was thinking about her. "Hey, Luce. What's up?"

"Uh . . . not much. What are you doing?"

"Going to grab a bite to eat."

"Oh. I was just going to make something for Sam and me. Maybe . . . enchiladas?"

Lucy knows I love her enchiladas, and it's pretty clear this is an invitation. But I can't go there. "Good. How is she?"

"Well, that's why I called . . . to let you know that she's fine. She's kind of quiet and grumpy still, but that's nothing new."

"She'll come around. It's bound to take her a while to get used to this."

"Yeah . . . and we're still in agreement that it's best not to ground her?"

"I think so. Things are hard enough for her right now."

There's a pause on Lucy's end. Then: "It would cheer her up to see you. I could make enchiladas tomorrow night instead. You could come over for dinner . . . ?"

I sigh heavily before answering. "Tomorrow's not good. I've got a couple of appointments . . . to look at apartments."

"Oh."

"Yeah . . ."

"Some other time then . . ."

"Sure. I'll call her. Maybe take her out for a burger."

"That's a lot of red meat, Trent. Don't forget what your doctor said."

And there's that tone, that mothering, condescending, holier-than-thou tone. I'm talking about bonding with our daughter, and she brings up my fucking cholesterol.

"I gotta go. Tell Sam I'll call her tomorrow." I hear Lucy start to say something, but I hang up.

Lucy

"I INVITED HIM to dinner, and he said no!" I wail into the phone.

"I told you, he's going to need some time," Hope says patiently. "Just like it says in chapter four."

"What?"

"Chapter four in *Until He Comes Home*. Haven't you been reading it?"

"Uh . . . I haven't gotten that far."

"It's all about the elastic band effect. Like, how our men are connected to us by an elastic band, and if you let them pull away, eventually they'll snap back. But if you try to pull them back before they're ready, they'll continue to stretch the band until it breaks."

"Oh."

"Read it, Lucy. It makes so much sense. It's exactly what I did with Mike and now our marriage is stronger than ever."

"Right. Okay."

Hope continues. "And how's Sam? No more hitting the bottle?"

"No," I snap, defensive for some reason. Perhaps that reason is that Hope's daughter, Sarah-Louise, is annoyingly perfect. She's an excellent student, a talented trombonist, and never gets drunk at school—or anywhere else for that matter. Sarah-Louise seems poised to follow in the footsteps of Hillary Rodham Clinton, or some other highly intelligent, extremely successful if slightly drab female. In contrast, Samantha seems poised to follow in the footsteps of Courtney Love.

"Trent and I talked to her and she's learned her lesson. She won't do it again," I say, with more confidence than I feel.

"See?" Hope says. "You're still parenting as a team. In chapter eight, I think it is, Dr. Ladner talks all about maintaining parental unity as a way to bring you back together."

"I've got to go," I say, pulling my Forerunner into the parking lot. "I'm back at the office."

"Okay, hon. Let me know when you and Sam can come over for dinner again."

"Will do." I hang up, and hop out of the truck. Hurrying to open the hatchback, I remove an enormous red-foam lobster costume. Cody has been "tricked" into being the mascot for Central High's basketball team, the Lobsters. It's so ridiculous. What kind of school would name their basketball team the Lobsters? And how can Wynn Felker, a grown man, allow himself to be dressed up in such a stupid costume and follow such a stupid plotline?

I struggle through the doorway, down the narrow halls, and into the props room. Just as I dump the cumbersome costume, my boss, Bruce, appears in the doorway.

"Oh, good, you're back. We need Wynn to try the costume on right away. Bring it to wardrobe."

"A little help here, please," I retort, as Bruce starts to walk off. Would it kill the guy to offer to carry the lobster to wardrobe? I'm already sweaty and disheveled from lugging the fucking thing in here. Okay, and maybe I'm a little crabby since my husband had hot sex with me on the living room sofa five days ago, and now he won't even come for dinner when I'm making his favorite dish.

"Right," Bruce says, realizing it's probably best to help me without comment. "Sorry."

I hold one foam claw as we maneuver our way to wardrobe. Technically, I would have thought a costume would be wardrobe's responsibility, but apparently it falls under props. When we arrive, Wynn is waiting there. As usual, he's surrounded by a number of sycophants whose only job seems to be to make sure he's exceedingly happy every minute of the day.

"Here it is," Bruce says, placing the costume before our illustrious star. "Why don't you try it on?"

Obediently, Wynn steps into the foam lobster. Kelly from wardrobe and a couple of Wynn's assistants begin to pull the costume up around him. They're fiddling with the snaps around his waist when he says, "I don't know about this . . ."

"What's wrong, Wynn?" obsequious assistant #1 asks.

"This costume . . . It's stupid."

"It'll be really funny, though!" Kelly tries.

"It just seems dumb," Wynn continues. "Who would have a lobster for a mascot?"

In the background, one of the production people is urgently calling the director. "Wynn doesn't like the lobster . . . Okay . . . okay. You'd better get down here."

"The basketball team is the Central High Lobsters!" another guy from the production department says nervously.

"Yeah, I know," Wynn snaps. "But, why would a team call itself the Lobsters?"

"It's funny!" Kelly cries.

"Lobsters are quite fierce and aggressive," the first production person says, hitting redial on her cell phone.

Obsequious assistant #2 jumps in. "Wynn's right. It's stupid!"

"What do you think?" It takes me a second to realize Wynn is addressing me.

"Uh . . ." I can feel Bruce's eyes on me. Obviously, it's in all our best interests to talk Wynn into wearing the lobster costume. If he refuses, I'll have to drive back out to Burnaby to look for a tiger or a bear or whatever they come up with next. But I simply can't deny that the lobster-as-mascot idea is retarded.

"It's retarded. No high school basketball team would call themselves the Lobsters. They're bottom-feeding crustaceans."

"Yeah!" Wynn says, extricating himself from the red foam. "It's retarded."

Just then, Kev flies into the room. The stress is written all over his twenty-eight-year-old face. "Hey, Wynn fella, what's up?"

"The whole lobster thing is stupid," Wynn begins.

I take this as a cue to duck out. Bruce is there to protect the lobster costume, and I'm sure I'll be the first person he tells when they agree on a suitable mascot.

On the way back to my office I step into the women's restroom. As I expected, all the lobster-lugging exertion has made my face a little shiny. I wet a paper towel in the sink and dab at my forehead. It seems the lack of expression lines has increased the shine factor. My forehead looks a bit like the side of a porcelain toilet now. But I'm still looking better than I have in months, maybe even years. If Trent had had the decency to come over for enchiladas, he would have seen that. Tossing the soggy towel in the bin, I head into the hall.

I've almost reached my office when I hear, "Hey!" I turn, and am startled to see Wynn Felker loping toward me.

"Uh . . . hey," I say, glancing quickly over my shoulder to make sure he's actually talking to me.

Wynn walks right up. "Thanks for the support back there. I'm Wynn." He holds out his hand.

"Yeah, I know," I say, taking it briefly. "Lucy."

"Nice to meet you, Lucy."

He's smiling at me in that charming Hollywood way, probably expecting me to faint or start crying at any moment. Instead I say, "What did you decide about the mascot?"

"They're taking it back to the writers. All I know is that I'm not gonna be lobster-boy."

"Good for you." I prepare to continue to my office, but Wynn seems in no hurry to leave. He does, however, notice that I seem a bit anxious.

"So . . . do you want to grab some lunch or something?"

Lunch? Is he joking? Why would Cody Summers want to have lunch with me? What would we possibly talk about? Acne medication? What to wear to the prom? Of course, Cody Summers is just a persona, but I doubt Wynn Felker and I would have much more in common. We could discuss various school mascots, but how long would that take? Ten minutes? It would be awkward and strange. "I'm just gonna eat at my desk. I've been trying to get home early for my daughter."

"That's cool. How old is your little girl?"

"Fifteen."

"No!" Wynn says, and he really does look shocked.

"Yes!" I say, imitating his tone.

"It's just that . . . you don't look old enough to have a teenage daughter."

"Well, I am. And she's a big fan of yours."

This prompts the return of his Hollywood cockiness. "Tell her I said hello."

"I will." And I hurry on to my office.

Trent

"ANOTHER ROUND?" THE waiter asks. He's all chiseled and tanned and Ashton Kutcher–ish; obviously, a wannabe actor.

I look to Annika. "What do you think? One more?"

Annika giggles. "I don't know if I should. One more of these martinis and I won't be able to drive home."

"I'll get you a cab."

"Come on," Ashton Kutcher says, giving her a blinding smile. "One more."

"Okay," she says gleefully. "If you two are gonna gang up on me."

The waiter leaves and I lean across the tiny table toward Annika. "What a cheeseball."

"Who?"

"The waiter. Where do they get these guys? Do they grow them in a lab or something?"

Annika peers toward the bar. "He is really good looking, but I thought he was nice."

"He's gotta be an actor," I continue, watching him punch in our drink order. "I think I recognize him, actually. Yeah . . . he was Alien number three in the last episode of *Star Hunter*."

"You watch *Star Hunter*?"

"No . . . I was just joking."

"Oh."

There's a moment of tense silence. Lucy would have laughed at that joke. But if I was with Lucy the joke would never have been made, since we'd never be having drinks in this hip bar with the handsome waiter. It's only 5:30. If I was still with my family, I'd be heading home to make Sam dinner and Lucy would still be at work for at least two more hours.

I look over at Annika, who's fishing a cranberry out of her martini glass with one finger. It suddenly occurs to me that bashing our good-looking server is probably making me look really old and insecure. It's not like I feel threatened by Ashton, but I have to admit, he's probably more suited to Annika than I am. I struggle for something to say . . . something light and fun that will show her I'm not jealous of some two-bit actor. But what? I'm about to mention the upcoming Justin Timberlake concert when Annika speaks.

"So . . . have you talked to your wife lately?" Her eyes are downcast, staring at the last two cranberries in her drink.

"Yeah," I say, affecting nonchalance, "just about Sam . . . making sure she's okay."

Annika looks up. "And is she?"

"I think so. I'm going to see her this weekend."

Her eyes return to the table and she fiddles with her coaster.

"Have you and your wife made any plans . . . about the future?"

I'm not exactly sure what she's asking, but I try to placate her. "We're not rushing into anything, but . . . I rented an apartment a couple days ago."

"That's great," she says, beaming as though I just won the lottery. "Why didn't you say something?"

I shrug. "I just did."

"It's just that . . ." She looks shy suddenly, girlish. She's even blushing a little. "I've been fighting my feelings for so long because you're married, but . . . I really like you, Trent. I just don't want to move forward with this if you're still trying to work things out with your wife."

Fuck. What am I supposed to say to that? I don't see Lucy and me working things out anytime soon, but one day? I can't deny that it's entirely possible. I mean, we have a history together—not to mention a daughter, a house, a couple of cars . . . "I really like you, too."

"I want to fuck you tonight," she says, causing me to choke a little on the last sip of my drink. Annika laughs at me, not in a mean way, but I can't help but feel foolish. It's got to be dead obvious that I'm not used to such an overtly sexual expression.

I clear my throat. "That sounds like a good plan," I manage.

Annika laughs again, just as Ashton appears with two more martinis. I'm thankful for the booze and the distraction.

"Here you go," he says, placing the bright red concoctions before us. "You two have fun now."

"Oh, we will," Annika purrs, suddenly not shy and girlish at all.

Lucy

"OH MY GOD!" Camille squeals. "Wynn Felker invited you out for lunch?"

"Shhhhh!" I peek out the doorway of the props room to make sure no one has overheard. "He said we should grab a bite," I whisper, after confirming the all clear. "It was just casual. He wanted to talk about the lobster costume."

"Yeah, right!" my friend replies, not following my sotto voce lead. "If it was just about the lobster costume, you could have talked about it in the office."

"Maybe he was hungry. Why are you making such a big deal about this?"

"Uh . . . because the Choice Hottie asked you out for lunch."

"The *Teen* Choice Hottie."

"Whatever. Do you know how many women enter radio contests and stuff just to meet that guy for two minutes?"

"Not women," I correct her, "girls. Cody's a teen heartthrob. Grown women are not lusting after him."

"You'd be surprised."

"Trust me. Sam and her friends worship him."

"I still think you should be really flattered," Camille says, digging through a box of plastic creepie-crawlies. "A super-hot TV star is into you. Maybe you should tell Trent about that, next time he's too busy to come for enchiladas."

I can't deny that she has a point. But would Trent care that another man is interested in me? I have a bad feeling not. My husband has been an endless source of disappointment since our pointless couch reunion. He said he'd call Sam and she still hasn't heard from him. It's one thing to blow me off, but quite another to do it to our daughter.

Luckily, I hadn't told Sam that he was planning to take her out for a burger, so she wasn't disappointed. She's been really pouring herself into her piece for the art show in two weeks. I'm at least thankful she has that positive, creative outlet instead of drowning her sorrows in a lunchtime bottle of liquor.

After twenty minutes of fruitless digging, I volunteer to drive out to the Burnaby prop house to look for the plastic frogs we need for Cody's science class to dissect. A glance at my watch tells me it's already 5:30. By the time I get out there, find the frogs, and drive back to the studio in rush hour traffic, it's going to be at least eight. I try to shrug off the wave of guilt that engulfs me, but to no avail. Sam's father walked out on us, and I can't even get home to make her a grilled cheese and a bowl of soup. What kind of mother am I?

As I head to my desk, I combat the tears that are threatening to come. But giving in to self-pity won't help anything. Instead, I decide to channel my emotions into anger. Samantha wouldn't have to be left alone if Trent would step up to the plate. Before my outrage subsides, I call him at the office.

"Hi," his cheerful recorded voice says. "You've reached Trent Vaughn. Sorry I can't take your call right now. Please leave a message and I'll get back to you as soon as I can."

"It's me," I snap. "I'm going to be home late tonight, so I need you to be with Sam . . . When you get this message, call me back so that I know you're going to pick her up or whatever."

When I hang up, I dial my daughter at home. "Hi, honey," I say brightly. "How was your day?"

"Fine."

"Good. How's the art project coming along?"

"Fine."

"I can't wait to see it! You've really put a lot of hard work into it."

I hear her exasperated sigh on the end of the line. "What do you want, Mom? I'm trying to watch TV."

"Okay, well, I'm going to be a little bit late tonight. But I left a message for your dad, and I thought you two could have an evening together. Maybe get him to take you for dinner?"

"I already ate."

"Oh . . . What did you have?"

"Chips."

I almost start crying again. My little, fatherless child is home alone eating chips for dinner! It's like some sad movie about life in the projects. I can't do this. "I'm going to see if Camille can do the Burnaby run. I'm coming home now."

"No, it's okay. I can hang with Dad."

"You're sure?"

"Yes, I'm sure. I've gotta go, Mom."

"Okay, sweetie. Will you do me a favor?"

"What?" She sounds irritable.

"Please eat some carrot sticks or something with some vitamins in it?"

"I will. See you later."

She's fine, I tell myself as I gather my purse and car keys. It will be good for her to spend some time with Trent. He's a selfish asshole, but he's still her father and she loves him.

I'm almost out the door when I hear my name. "Lucy!" The voice is immediately recognizable. But it can't be. I turn and see him striding toward me.

"Hi, Wynn," I say, a little nervous for some reason.

He joins me at the door. "Hey," he says, pushing it open and ushering me outside. "Are you heading home?"

"No, no. I've got to get some frogs for your science class shoot tomorrow."

Wynn rolls his eyes. "Right. So, I wanted to let you know that we're not doing the lobster thing. Bruce says he can get a polar bear costume or something. Still funny, but slightly less nonsensical."

I can't help but be pleasantly surprised that he just used the word *nonsensical*. "And slightly less degrading for you."

"Slightly." We both laugh.

I indicate my car with my thumb. "Well, I'd better get going. I've got a long drive ahead."

"Yeah . . . ," he continues, something hesitant in his bearing. "So, I was just gonna say that we should grab a drink some time . . . you know, when you're not rushing off to buy frogs?"

My face is hot with embarrassment, awkwardness, excitement. Did he really just ask me out for a drink? Did he just sound nervous and not at all cocky or annoyingly Hollywood? He's not nearly as cheesy as I'd originally thought. I mean, yes, he is borderline "pretty," but there's also something manly about him that I hadn't really noticed before, a subtle magnetism that—

But I can't do it. I've only been separated two weeks! Six short days ago, Trent was screwing me on the living room sectional! It's too soon. And while it might be fun to have a drink with Wynn, in my heart of hearts, I know I still want things to work out with my husband. "Thanks but . . . I'm really busy with work and . . . my daughter and . . ." I scramble for one more thing, finally coming up with " . . . my scrapbooking hobby."

"Oh." He sounds taken aback, as though it never occurred to him that I might turn him down. Come to think of it, it probably never did. "Right. Okay, see ya."

He turns, and without a second glance, walks back into the building.

Trent

THE CLOCK RADIO clicks over to 6:45 A.M. In fifteen minutes the alarm will go off, signaling that I should be in the office
in about an hour. If I go in, that is. But I have to go in. I have a
client coming at 9:30. What am I going to do, call in sick? Quit
my job so I don't have to see Annika again? That's ridiculous.
Just because the sex was an unmitigated disaster, I can't hide
out here forever.

I get up and fill the tiny coffeepot with water. Of course I'll
go to the office. It's not like I'm some high school kid who can't
face up to his humiliation. At least if I were some high school
kid I'd have an excuse for the disaster that was last night. But
I'm not a horny teenager who can't control his bodily func-
tions: I'm a middle-aged guy struck down by performance
anxiety.

I stick the prefilled coffee filter into the basket and go take a shower. The beads of hot water do nothing to wash away the guilt, the shame, the embarrassment. The fact that I've had only three hours of sleep probably isn't helping. But how can I sleep when every horrifying second of the night keeps looping through my brain like a YouTube video?

It started out okay. Annika had made her intentions exceedingly clear when she came back to my room with me. There was no room for misinterpretation when she flopped onto the bed and pulled me down on top of her. I'd waited so long to be with her. It was new and yet somehow familiar. I mean, we'd been working together for more than a year, so it wasn't as if we were total strangers. And I had fantasized about having sex with her so many times that it was almost as though I'd been there before, in a way. So, it was all going pretty well—the making out, the clothing removal. The lamp was on, which made me feel a little uncomfortable. It's not that I'm ashamed of my body, but it's been a long time since I've hit the gym. It was really cool looking at Annika though.

It wasn't until she said "Do you have a condom?" that things went off the rails. "Uh . . . yeah," I said, having had the foresight to pick up a pack prior to our date. I crawled off her and walked naked, in the lamplight, to the bureau. I could feel her eyes all over me, a disturbing sensation. I guess I could have been flattered, but I just felt awkward and vulnerable—like I was walking around naked with a boner in front of a coworker. Which, I guess, I was. Grabbing the box of condoms, I hurried back to the bed.

"Get it on," she said, or more appropriately, growled. I hadn't used a condom since 1990, so it was a little challenging, getting the packet open and trying to get the thing on, especially with Annika watching every move like she was doing some kind of research study. And suddenly, all the tension and the guilt just got to me. My dick was just lying there like a sea cucumber.

"It's okay," Annika said, diving on it like a lifeguard intent on bringing it back to life. And it did work, to some degree. But when I made another attempt at putting on the condom, I could feel the nerves getting to me again. Annika tore the rubber disk from my hand. "Forget it," she said. "Just do me . . . now!"

I was pretty uncomfortable with the idea of going at it without protection. Of course, I'd had a vasectomy when Sam was eight and I realized Lucy would never take time out of her career to have another baby. So it wasn't like I could get Annika pregnant. And I'd been completely monogamous for the past sixteen years, but what about Annika's sexual history?

Lucy would say it was poetic justice if I caught some nasty STD off Annika. She'd laugh and laugh when she visited me in the hospital—not that many STDs land you in the hospital, I guess . . . except AIDS. Obviously, this train of thought was not exactly enhancing my performance. But before I could give it any more consideration, Annika took control and we were suddenly fucking.

It lasted all of forty-five seconds, which, on the bright side, is probably not even long enough to catch an STD. On the not-so-bright side, it lasted forty-five seconds and now I have to see her in the office and pretend that I'm not completely mortified by what happened last night. Oh shit. What if she tells someone? Who would she tell? She's not really close to the receptionist or Meg in accounting. Maybe Karen. What if she tells one of the guys? Oh Christ, then I really will have to quit. But until that happens, I've got to act like a man and face the music.

When I arrive at the office, Annika is already meeting with Don, the managing partner. Neither of them glances in my direction as I scurry to my office. Not very manly, the scurrying, but I'm not feeling particularly macho at this point in time. I boot up my computer and check my voice messages: my nine-thirty's running late; and there's a message from Lucy last night, wanting me to be with Sam.

A wave of guilt resembling nausea washes over me. I can't believe my daughter needed me while I was out fucking (if what we did even qualifies as such) my coworker. It's terrible. It's worse than terrible, it's disgusting is what it is. I've really been letting Sam down. Not that Lucy is entirely blameless in this situation. If she could ever get her ass home before eight o'clock at night, none of this would even be happening. Not for the first time this morning, I wonder if I've really done the right thing in leaving my family.

Suddenly, Annika pokes her head inside my office.

"Hey, you," she says flirtatiously.

"H-hi . . . Hey . . ." I strive for a casual tone; fail miserably.

"I had fun last night," she says coyly.

Is she being sarcastic? Or maybe she's talking about the part at the restaurant, where we had the waiter who looked like Ashton Kutcher? Because the sex part of the evening could hardly qualify as fun: maybe in some parallel universe where being eaten alive by fire ants is considered a good time, but not here.

"Uh . . . yeah." I clear my throat loudly.

"So listen," she says, stepping into my office. "I've got a girlfriend coming in from Toronto on Tuesday. Why don't you grab a friend and join us for drinks? I want her to meet you."

"Right. Sounds good."

She lingers for a moment, smiling at me coyly. "Okay . . . we'll talk more later."

"Yes, definitely. Later." And finally, she's gone.

Lucy

"WHAT DO YOU mean, you didn't see your dad last night?"

"He never called me." Sam shrugs, shoveling cereal into her mouth and staring at the *Early Show* on TV.

I try not to lose control, but I can feel the urge to throw a tantrum. "So what did you do all evening?"

She shrugs again. "Watched TV."

"Did you at least eat some vegetables, like I asked?"

"I don't remember." She turns to me for the first time. "If you're so concerned about what I eat, maybe you should try coming home and cooking dinner for once in your life."

"Once in my life?" I gasp. "I've cooked hundreds of dinners, young lady."

Sam stands, takes her cereal bowl to the sink. "Do the math, Mom. Cooking hundreds of dinners over fifteen years of my life isn't that impressive."

"Listen, missy . . ." I start, but trail off. She's right. It's not impressive. It's terrible and neglectful. And now I've driven her father away, the parent who actually did come home and cook dinner for her. Last night I didn't get home until she was already in bed. I'm a failure as a mother, as a wife. The tears start to come and there's nothing I can do to stop them.

"Sam . . . I'm sorry," I mumble, but my daughter is already stalking out of the room.

"Gotta get to school," she mutters as she heads upstairs.

I wait until she's gone to call Trent. She doesn't need to hear the screaming accusations I plan to throw at him.

"Good morning, Trent Vaughn," his cheerful fucking voice answers the phone.

"Why didn't you see Samantha last night?" I hurl.

"I didn't get your message until this morning," he says, at least having the decency to sound guilty.

"I didn't get home until ten. She was alone all night eating chips for dinner."

"Maybe you should try to get home earlier," Trent snaps.

"Last I checked, she had two parents. Or are you planning to cut her out of your life, too?"

"Listen," he says, lowering his voice. "I can't be doing this right now. I'm at the office. If you want to fight, I'll call you later."

Suddenly, I'm crying again. "I don't want to fight! I just want to know I can still count on you to be there for our daughter. My job is busy and unpredictable, and I need your support, Trent. Maybe you hate me now, for whatever reason, but don't take it out on Sam."

"I don't hate you," he says in an emphatic whisper. "I still care about you very much."

"It doesn't seem like it." I sniffle.

"Let me call you later. And tell Sam I'll take her for dinner tonight. I mean it."

I notice that I'm left out of the dinner invitation, but frankly, I'm not in the mood. "Fine," I mumble. "But you can't let her down again, Trent. You really can't."

Trent

I'M FEELING A lot better since I spent some good quality time with Sam. As usual, Lucy had blown everything out of proportion. Sam seems to be doing fine. And she wasn't at all pissed off that I didn't call her on Thursday. She said she watched some TV, ate a bag of chips, and worked on her art project. Lucy made it sound as though she'd spent the evening alone, crying and digging through the garbage can for food scraps.

I picked her up on Friday and we went for burgers at White Spot. As usual, the place was packed with seniors and families with squawking kids. But the place is a tradition for us. We've been going there since she was a little girl, ordering the Pirate Pak. Now she gets a lean and tasty chicken burger, but it still has the same feel.

Conversation was a little awkward, though. There seem to be a lot of "don't touch" subjects at the moment. Neither of us wanted to discuss her mom, our marriage, or if I'm going to move back in. I tried to get her going on her art show, but she just shrugged and said her project was "coming along." Finally, we connected over an old Will Ferrell movie she'd just watched on TV. We both knew the thing practically verbatim, so we threw jokes back and forth until the bill came.

When I dropped her off at the house, I suggested hanging out the next day. "We could do something fun," I said, scrambling to think of something that qualified as fun to a fifteen-year-old girl. "Shopping! I could take you shopping?"

"That's okay," Sam said, hopping out of the car. "I've got to work on my art project." She slammed the door and was gone.

Knowing that my daughter is in a good place allows me to focus on more pressing issues, namely drinks with Annika and her friend on Tuesday. "Bring a friend," she said, like I've got tons of single guy friends free to hit the bar mid-week. In fact, I don't have any single guy friends. Sure, there are a couple of guys in the office, but I can't let them know about Annika and me.

For the first time, I realize that most of my friends are really just the husbands of Lucy's friends. And being the husbands of Lucy's friends, they probably hate me now. Of course, they don't really hate me. Deep down, they probably understand, even respect what I did. I bet they're envious that I had the balls to do what they can only dream about. But to their wives, I'm practically Satan. And no one's gonna let their husband out for drinks on a Tuesday night with Satan.

On second thought, Lucy probably hasn't even told any of her friends. It would tarnish her reputation as Miss Perfect. That would make it even more awkward for me to call up one of the guys and invite him for drinks with Annika and her friend. At least Hope knows we've separated. And of course, Mike has a unique understanding of my situation. He's the only option. I dial the phone.

"You've got to come," I plead, when he says something about quizzing Sarah-Louise for a national spelling bee. "You're the only guy I can turn to."

"Thanks," Mike says. "It's nice to feel special."

"You know what I mean. You're the only friend I have who gets what I'm going through."

"Yeah, I get it," he acquiesces. "It's lonely when everyone takes your wife's side."

"Is everyone taking Lucy's side?"

Mike laughs. "How the hell should I know? I'm just saying how it felt when I left."

"Right." I remember Lucy's outrage when she heard about Mike's exotic optometry conventions. "Can you help a guy out? I'm sure her friend is hot."

There's a pause, and I hope Mike is checking his calendar. "I can come between seven and nine," he finally says.

"Thank you! You're the best!" I'm being over-the-top effusive, but such is my relief at having someone to bring with me tomorrow night. It's bad enough that Annika thinks I've got the sexual skills of a fifteen-year-old. If she thinks I'm a friendless loser too, she's sure to dump me.

"I gotta go. I've got a patient," Mike says. "See you tomorrow."

Lucy

"DRINKS ON A Tuesday?" I say, digging my purse out from under my desk.

"Yes, drinks on a Tuesday," Camille insists, snatching up her car keys. "You've obviously lost your mind and I need to talk you back into some sort of sanity."

I lower my voice. "I can't go out with Cody. He's too young."

"Cody's too young, but Wynn's not. He's twenty-seven."

"And I'm forty! That's too big an age difference."

"Look at Ashton and Demi," Camille says, like this is a really convincing argument.

"Yeah, I'm sure they'll still be married when she's sixty-five and he's like, thirty or whatever."

"Fine!" She caves in. "Don't go out with him. But at least come out with me for a cocktail or two. I worry about you sitting home alone, pining away for that asshole."

I am instantly defensive. "He's not an asshole!" But a moment's reflection makes me reconsider. Trent has been a bit asshole-ish of late. He did finally take Sam out for dinner, but he's made absolutely no effort to work on his "grown-up man problems"—at least none that I can see. "And I'm not pining," I grumble.

"Good. If you're not pining, then you can come out for an after-work martini."

I realize that the only way out of this would be to sprint for the door and barricade myself in the SUV. "Let me call Sam. If she's got plans tonight, I'll come for one."

"Two," Camille presses.

"Don't push it!"

Trent

"THIS IS LEAH." Annika introduces the tall blonde beside her. She's pretty, but a little severe in that successful business-woman sort of way.

I hold out my hand. "Nice to meet you. I'm Trent."

"I've heard a lot about you," Leah says, a knowing twinkle in her eye. Shit. What has she heard? My eyes dart to Annika, but she's smiling happily, almost proudly. Did I imagine the smirking tone? I must have. Obviously Annika's not going to tell her visiting friend that her new boyfriend has erectile dysfunction.

I clear my throat. "This is my buddy, Mike."

Mike turns to Annika first. "Good to finally meet you."

Finally? He'd never heard of Annika until two weeks ago. He makes it sound as though I've been talking about her obsessively for six months. Annika gives a delighted giggle, obviously interpreting his comment the same way. Mike then turns to Leah. "And nice to meet *you*, Leah," he says smoothly.

"Thanks." Leah's eyes flit to Annika's. She looks a little panicked.

"Sit," Annika says nervously, indicating the two low cubes across from them. "Where is that waiter?"

When Mike and I have ordered beers, Annika fills the awkward silence. "So, Mike, Trent tells me you're an optometrist. Do you enjoy it?"

"Yeah, it's not bad. It has its perks." He looks directly at Leah. "There are a lot of optometry conventions in Vegas and Palm Springs. Good times."

Leah smiles tightly.

I jump in. "What do you do, Leah?"

"I'm the human resources director for Shinnegar Thompson."

"And what do they do?"

"They're the largest laminate flooring manufacturer in North America."

"Really?" Mike says brightly. "I've been thinking of tearing up the carpets in the office. Maybe you could come in and show me your samples."

It comes out like "show me your tits." Why is Mike acting like such a tool? I wanted him along so I wouldn't look like a friendless loser. Now I'm thinking that might have been better.

Leah clears her throat. "We have a sales rep here. I'll tell him to give you a call."

"Come on," Mike cajoles, taking a swig of beer, "I don't want some local guy. I want the big shot from Toronto."

She looks at him. "I'm in human resources. I don't sell flooring."

Annika senses this isn't going well. "Honey," she says,

placing a proprietary hand on my wrist, "tell Leah how you love Toronto." She turns to Leah. "Trent loves Toronto."

I do? I mean, I've had some fun times there, I guess. And I've never really understood that whole "Let's all hate Toronto" thing that some Canadians get into. But love it? I guess to smooth things over, I can love it. "Yeah, I love it."

Leah seems pleased. "Have you spent much time there?"

"I've gone for business a few times. And my—" I stop myself. I almost said "my wife and I," which would obviously be the wrong choice of words. I cover quickly. "My daughter and I went out and did the theme parks and museums a few years ago."

Annika snuggles up to me. "Trent has a fifteen-year-old daughter. She's a really talented artist."

Leah is unfazed, but Mike looks at me. Annika made it sound as if she and Sam were the best of friends.

Annika turns to Mike. "What about you? How old are your kids?"

"Fifteen, fourteen, and eleven." He winks at Leah. "That last one was a bit of a slipup."

She looks at him like he's a piece of dog crap sitting on the cube chair. But he continues.

"No kids, Leah?" He stares directly at her breasts. "I can tell."

What the fuck are you doing, Mike? I manage to hold my tongue, but my eyes shoot daggers at him. Why are you acting like such a sleaze? I feel Annika's nails dig into my forearm. It's obviously important to her that our friends get along.

Leah gives Mike a tense smile. "What does your wife think about you hanging out at a bar on a Tuesday night?"

"My wife and I have an understanding."

Leah takes a sip of her martini. "Maybe you only think your wife's at home with the kids. Maybe as soon as you head out the door, she calls a sitter and runs off to see her boy-toy."

"You don't know my wife."

"Maybe you don't either."

Oh shit, this is a disaster. But when I look at Leah's expression, she actually seems to be enjoying putting Mike in his place. And, of course, he probably considers her put-downs a subtle type of flirting.

Annika shifts her cube closer to mine and leans in. "I missed you this weekend."

"Me, too," I say, though, in reality, I was relieved to forget about our disastrous rendezvous for a couple days. "But I had to spend some time with Sam."

"I understand. I can't wait to meet her."

I try not to react. It just never occurred to me to introduce the two. I mean maybe, down the road, if this thing with Annika turns into something more, but Sam's so not ready to be meeting my girlfriend. If Annika even is my girlfriend. Right now, with the way she's cozying up to me right in front of Mike and Leah, I'd have to say she is. "Sam needs some time," I say lamely.

"Of course," she says, kissing my neck intimately. "I'd never pressure her. My stepmom was so desperate for my sister and me to like her that it totally backfired."

"Oh." I take a large swig of my beer. I'm not going to read anything into that stepmom comment. She's just sharing her past, not talking about her relationship with Sam. That would be crazy. Shifting subtly toward Mike, I pick up their conversation.

"You don't know what it's like to have kids and responsibilities. You have to get out and have a few beers and just forget about it all once in a while."

"That's so sweet," Leah says. "If I ever have children, I can only hope they'll have a doting father like you."

"You guys! Stop!" Annika cries playfully. "I don't want Trent to have to break up a brawl."

Mike snorts. "Like he could."

"Of course he could," Annika says, rubbing my biceps. "He's my big strong man." She leans in for a kiss. I feel really weird with Mike watching, but I don't see another option. I kiss her.

Mike says, "He might be able to take me, but he'd never be able to handle this wildcat." He points his beer bottle at Leah, who bursts into laughter.

"How about another round?" I say, suddenly thankful that Mike is here. "Where's that waiter?"

Lucy

I TRY NOT to feel self-conscious as Camille leads me into the martini bar. It's surprisingly busy for a Tuesday. At least, it's surprising to me. I haven't gone out for mid-week cocktails since the early nineties. By the time I finish work, I've always been too guilt-riddled to do anything but rush straight home. But Sam assured me that she was helping with setup for the art show. And obviously, Trent could not care less whether I come rushing home or not.

Camille heads straight to the bar, a dark wood and back-lit glass construction. The bartender, all tanned and smooth-chested, approaches.

"Gin and tonic?" Camille asks me over her shoulder. I nod and she orders, plopping her breasts on top of the bar. With an appreciative glance, the bartender sets about making our cocktails.

"God," I whisper as we wait, "everybody's so ridiculously good looking in here."

"Including us," Camille says confidently.

"Speak for yourself," I mumble. I don't mean to be self-deprecating, but I can't help but feel old and out of place. A woman my age should be home with her daughter . . . and her husband.

"Please!" my friend cries. She pretends to address the crowd. "Anyone in here been asked out by this year's Choice Hottie? What? No one?" She turns to me. "Oh, you have?"

"Okay." I laugh, gathering the G&T that has materialized on the bar. "I'm soooo good looking."

"That's better." Camille pays the bartender and indicates two vacant seats in the corner. "Quick!" she says, already making a beeline for the stools near the window.

I follow along, trying to ignore the gaggle of tanned, breast-implanted twenty-somethings in knockoff Pucci prints. Of course, theirs is a phony, L.A. type of attractiveness, but I still feel plain in comparison.

When we've perched on the Lucite cubes, Camille says, "Tell me the real reason you said no to Wynn Felker."

"I already did," I say, sipping my gin and tonic. "He's too young."

"But wouldn't you at least like to have sex with him? He's so hot."

"He's more like . . . pretty."

"Pretty fucking hot!" Camille takes a sip of her drink. "If I were you, I'd at least go for a drink. I hear he rents this gorgeous house right on the water. You could go back to his place and have sex in the pool."

"Camille!" I say, blushing despite myself. "I barely know the guy!"

"Obviously, you'd use a condom."

"Obviously. But I've said no, so it's irrelevant now."

"No, it's not!" she cries. "You could just tell him you changed your mind."

"I can't," I say, staring into my drink. "It's too soon."

Surprisingly, Camille agrees. "I know you're still emotionally fragile. I'm just saying that you should allow yourself to have a little fun. That's why we're here."

"This place is supposed to be fun? Yeah, it's really fun sitting here comparing myself to a bunch of Paris Hilton clones."

Camille laughs. I continue. "Look at this crowd. Do they grow them in a petri dish or something? Everyone looks the same."

"Not everyone's gorgeous," Camille says, peering into the room. "Look at that guy with the big bald spot over there."

Through the forest of beautiful bodies, I search for Mr. Bald Spot. It takes me a second to spy him. "Okay, so there's one guy here who doesn't—" I stop. "Oh my god. That's my friend Hope's husband."

"Hope the housewife?"

"Yes," I say, shooting her an admonishing look. Camille has always looked down on women who don't work outside the home. "What's he doing here?" I crane my neck to see his companions: a cool blonde, a voluptuous girl with a mane of curly hair, and Trent.

The wave of nausea that engulfs me is terrifying. I honestly fear I might puke all over the backlit glass counter. Frantically, I turn away, afraid to see any more. Is he here with that curly-haired girl? Are they dating? How could he do this to me? Not two weeks ago, he was doing something else to me on the living room sofa. And now . . . Oh god, I think I might pass out.

Camille notices my pale, shaky demeanor. "What . . . ?" She cranes her neck and spots Trent. "Oh shit. Let's get you out of here."

I'm not sure I can stand, but Camille grabs my hand and drags me through the bar. Outside on the uneven bricked sidewalk, I gasp for air. Tears pour from my eyes. I try to speak, but no words will come. I think I'm having some kind of nervous breakdown . . . or an emotional one.

"Asshole," Camille growls, taking me into her arms. And this time, as I sob into her shoulder, I don't contradict her.

Trent

"SORRY ABOUT MIKE," I had apologized as we drove through the darkened streets back to my hotel. "It's like he doesn't know how to act around attractive women. He feels compelled to hit on them."

Annika laughed. "Leah can handle herself. I've seen her put bigger idiots than him in their place."

I should have defended my friend, I guess, but he was kind of an idiot. And maybe I'd been an idiot for inviting him. But what choice did I have?

"But I'm sure she liked you," she said, sliding her hand down my inner thigh. I was no longer wondering if I was an idiot. I was too busy trying to keep the car on the road as Annika proceeded to give me a mini hand job through my pants.

The car foreplay worked, though, and I was able to give a fairly impressive performance in the sack. Obviously, that initial disaster was just first-time jitters. It's to be expected. I hadn't had a first time since I got together with Lucy. In fact, Annika was so impressed that we've spent four of the last six nights together in my hotel room. The sex is so good, I can't get rid of her!

I'm joking of course. It's not like I really want to get rid of her. But our relationship has gotten kind of intense, kind of fast. When I left home I hadn't expected to be spending so much time with Annika. The whole idea was to be alone, to get to know myself as an individual. That's a little hard to do with an over-sexed thirty-two-year-old crawling all over you.

Annika's not really oversexed. I guess I just got used to the routine with Lucy: sex on Sunday mornings, with an occasional Friday night thrown in if we'd had some wine. When I was younger, I wanted it more often, too. I still want it. I mean, Annika is totally hot. But I can't help feeling a little exhausted by her attentions.

I tear my thoughts from my amorous girlfriend and focus on my wife. It's been almost a week since I've heard from her. I've left three voice messages and Lucy still hasn't called me back. I spoke to Sam on the weekend, and we made plans to see a movie on Wednesday. "How's your mom?" I'd asked, striving for a nonchalant tone.

"I don't know. Kind of weird," Sam mumbled.

"Weird how?"

"She's been, like, cooking dinner and stuff. It's weird for her."

I breathed a sigh of relief. I guess one of the positive side effects of my leaving was that Lucy realized she needed to reevaluate her parenting skills. It makes me feel a lot less guilty knowing that she's finally pulling her weight in that department.

But I still need to talk to her. On one of my voice messages

I'd suggested we attend Sam's art show together. Plus, I get possession of my apartment on the fifteenth, and I want to take the double bed out of the spare room. I could use some kitchen appliances, too, and Lucy's got more than enough for both of us.

Maybe email will be more effective? She's plugged into her BlackBerry 24/7, so I'm sure she'll get the message. As I start to type, Annika pops her head into my office.

"Hey, hon."

"Hey." I shift uncomfortably in my ergonomic chair. We both agreed we'd keep a lid on things in the office, but Annika seems to have a little trouble remembering that.

"Why don't you come to my place for dinner tonight?" she continues. "You need a home-cooked meal—not that I'm much of a cook. But I can pick up these really gourmet boil-in-the-bag dinners from this little shop near my apartment. Do you like osso buco?"

"I can't," I say, before I've even thought of an excuse. As tempting as boil-in-the-bag osso buco is, I need to spend the evening alone.

Annika's face immediately falls. "Why not?" she says, sounding a bit like my daughter when we tell her she can't stay out past curfew.

"I've got to see Sam," I lie. "She's having some trouble at school . . . Math . . . you know how it is."

Annika brightens. "Bring her along! I'm great at math. But she probably won't want osso buco. We can order pizza?"

"Annika," I say, my voice hushed. "Sam's not ready to be brought into this . . . relationship." The word sounds almost ominous.

"Well, when will she be?" Annika snaps, making no effort to lower her voice.

"I don't know. One day . . . maybe."

"One day *maybe*?"

Christ! She's practically yelling. What the hell does she expect? That my daughter would want to meet the woman I'm screwing less than a month after I've walked out on her mother? But I calm myself. This is not the time or the place to be having this conversation. "Can we talk about this later?" I grumble.

"When? Tomorrow? At my place?"

"Fine." Thankfully, she leaves without causing any more of a scene. I've always been attracted to fiery women—Lucy being a prime example. But when it starts interfering with my job, well . . . that's another story.

With a heavy sigh, I turn back to the email missive to my wife. Perhaps it's my frustration with Annika, but my words take a harsh tone. Lucy can't just ignore me this way. Whatever is happening with our marriage, we're still co-parents, and she'd better start acting like it. Finally satisfied with my note, I hit SEND. There. Now that ought to get her attention.

Lucy

IN EIGHT YEARS as a props buyer, I've called in sick only a handful of times. Sam got mono once and the babysitter refused to take her. Another time I had eaten some bad shrimp and couldn't bear to be away from the toilet. And then there was last week. While I didn't have the flu or anything clinical, I was absolutely, undeniably sick. I was sickened by Trent's infidelity, his betrayal, his complete and utter shit-headedness. Worst of all, I was sickened by my own gullibility.

I put on a brave face for Sam's sake. (The fact that my forehead can no longer relay any sort of emotion has been extremely helpful in these circumstances.) My daughter's been through so much lately I feared that having her mother fall apart might send her back to the gin bottle. Each morning, I got up and made her toast or oatmeal or some other substantial start to the day that was always rejected in favor of a protein bar or a banana. When she walked out the door to school I would return to my bed, sobbing for hours. Eventually, when I was numb with exhaustion, I'd flick on *Dr. Phil*.

The show served only to confuse me more: all these complete fuck-ups working tirelessly on their train-wreck marriages. Thirty-two-year-old Tammy had been employed as a call girl behind her husband Merle's back, and still, he wanted to work on it. "We have a baby and three ferrets together," Merle said in his southern states twang. "I think our marriage is worth saving."

So what was wrong with Trent and me? I had never been unfaithful, for money or otherwise. We had a child together. Was it our lack of a pet that made our bond so disposable? Would a guinea pig or a weasel have made all the difference? Or was Trent just a selfish, unfeeling prick as Camille suggested?

Hope had been calling ceaselessly as well. "Just wondering if you've got to chapter fourteen yet," she'd chirp into the answering machine. "It's about letting go of the indiscretions that happened when you were separated, and starting a brand-new life when you come back together. I'm not sure if you're ready for it yet, but it really did help when Mike came back home."

I hadn't called her back. What was I going to tell her? That her chipper message had prompted me to rip out chapter fourteen and tear it into tiny pieces that were subsequently flushed down the crapper? Same went for chapter four (Trusting Your Bond), chapter nine (Accepting His Humanness), and chapter twelve (Healing the Wound). Based on Hope's marriage, that book was complete drivel designed to let men cheat on their wives then be welcomed home completely scot-free! Did she know Mike was hanging out at bars, hitting on cool blond businesswomen? Did that goddamn book tell her that was "just something men needed to do"?

But today I'm back in the office. My guilt at leaving Camille in the lurch had propelled me out of bed—not to mention the fact that Sam seemed a little creeped out by my constant presence. Immersing myself in the work buildup is somehow therapeutic. At least it allows me to focus on something other than the sour lump of anger sitting in my stomach. We had our briefing first thing this morning, we've compiled the episode's props list, and now I'll spend the rest of the week racing around the city in search of Cody's remote-control model T-Rex and his fifties-flashback leather jacket. While this routine has become increasingly uninspiring of late, it beats sitting at home watching Dr. Phil counsel Tammy and Merle on how to keep their family together.

So I'm deep in the belly of Toys "R" Us when my BlackBerry vibrates. I could ignore it, but what if it's Bruce with another toy to add to the props list? I don't want to have to make a second trip out here. Extracting the device from my bag, I check the new message.

From: Trent Vaughn
Subject: Your Attitude

Lucy, I've left three messages to which you have not responded. If you're pissed off for some reason, I wish you'd have the maturity to talk to me about it instead of giving me the silent treatment. This juvenile behavior is not good for Sam. We're both still her parents, remember.

Also, I get possession of my apartment on the 15th. I need to get the double bed from the spare room.

Call me ASAP.

Trent

A sour burst of incredulous laughter bubbles up from within me—or is it vomit? He's got to be kidding! He's the one out boozing it up on a Tuesday night with some curly-haired slut, and I'm immature? My behavior is affecting Sam? Oh my fricking god!

Obviously, there is only one way I can react to this missive. Okay, there are two ways. One would be to wait outside his office in my idling SUV and then mow him down in front of all his coworkers. This would be deeply satisfying for me, but hard on Sam. And I'm not sure I want her raised by my mother while I languish in the big house for vehicular homicide. Not that I blame my mom for the way my marriage turned out, but if she'd equipped me with the tools I needed to make better choices in men, none of this would have happened. I want more for my daughter. I will choose option two.

When I'm behind the wheel of my Forerunner, it is more than a little tempting to head to Trent's downtown office. But with an impressive display of willpower I turn back toward the *Cody's Way* set. As I hurtle through the afternoon traffic, I seem to be having some kind of mild stroke. My heart races and the blood pounds in my ears. My hands are shaking and I'm covered in a thin slick of sweat. Surprisingly, I'm not crying, despite the heavy lump of emotion caught in my chest. I drive aggressively, borderline recklessly. But twenty minutes later I reach the office in one piece.

As I get out of the car, my mini-stroke has turned into a different sort of physical sensation. With my labored breathing, trembling hands, and shaking legs, I'm almost feeling a little turned on. Maybe it's the friction of these new jeans, but as I storm into the building I feel on the verge of some kind of mini-mally enjoyable, highly embarrassing orgasm. As I stride past mute Tanya, her widened eyes tell me that even she's noticed something's not right with me.

Without stopping at my desk, I move directly toward the set. It takes only a second to spot him. As usual, he's surrounded by a gaggle of hangers-on, whose purpose in being there is a complete mystery to me. Before nerves can set in, I march up to him.

"Wynn, can I talk to you for a sec?"

The hangers-on gape as though I've just proposed marriage to him. But Wynn says, "Of course," and touches my forearm in a very intimate way. I know it's just my forearm, but in my current heightened state, it might as well be my nipple. When we've moved a suitable distance from his entourage, he says, "What's up?"

"I'd like to go out with you—for a drink with you," I blurt. "If you still want to."

"Yeah, of course," he replies smoothly. "If you're sure you're not too busy scrapbooking."

"What?" Then I remember my previous lame-ass excuse. "I don't even scrapbook," I admit. "I just didn't think it was a good idea . . . you know . . . before . . ."

"Before what?"

I know he's just flirting, but I suddenly feel on the verge of tears. "Before I caught my husband and his fat slut at a bar last week! Before he emailed me and asked for the double bed from the spare room so he and that bitch have somewhere to fuck!" Instead, I shrug, trying to compose myself.

"Are you okay?" His hand massages my shoulder, and it no longer feels sexy. It feels comforting and kind and supportive. Shit! The tears seep out of my eyes before I can stop them.

"No," I mumble, stifling a sob. "I'm not okay."

*   *   *

TRENT AND I met at a party when I was a twenty-two-year-old college student. He was drinking something pink and slushy that turned out to be rum, ice, and pink lemonade crushed in the blender. By way of introduction, I pointed at his drink and said, "Yum." He said, "Want one?" I said, "Sure," and followed him to the kitchen. Three hours and four rum and pink lemonades later, we were making out on a ratty futon mattress in a small bedroom with a Nirvana poster on the wall.

At the risk of sounding like a drunken floozy, most of my dating was done while under the influence of alcohol. I had a boyfriend in high school (I got the nerve to tell him I liked him after I'd had two kiwi coolers before our eleventh grade Halloween dance). Then there were two one-night stands in college (rye and Cokes were to blame in the first instance, Kokanee beer in the second). In my second year, I made eye contact with a guy in my sociology class for three weeks before we ran into each other at a bar. I was on my fourth Corona when we literally bumped into each other and ended up dating for six months. It turned out he was a pompous know-it-all who wore glasses without a prescription and started smoking a pipe at twenty-three, but for a few months, I'd considered him sophisticated. And then came Trent.

Obviously, picking up men while intoxicated has not had a very high success rate. But it was infinitely easier than the position I find myself in now, trying to carry on a sober conversation with a guy I barely know, who is thirteen years my junior and a teen sitcom sensation. While I rarely overindulge these days, I take an enormous sip of the gin and tonic before me. The situation calls for a little social lubrication.

"That lobster suit was so stupid," I say, chuckling lamely. We're in a seedy sports bar in a remote area of Burnaby. Given Wynn's recent Choice Hottie win, he needs to keep a low profile. You can't get much lower than Maxwell's Bar in the Kingsway Inn.

In response, Wynn lifts his mug of beer and twinkles his eyes at me. I'd never thought eye twinkling was a skill that could be done on cue before, but he seems to have mastered it.

"What were they thinking?" I blather on. "The Central High Lobsters. So dumb! I mean, do they really think teens are so stupid that they'd buy that? Are the writers just lazy, or what?"

"How long were you married?" Wynn asks. His eyes have stopped twinkling and are now dark, intense.

"Too long," I grouch, sipping at the straw in my gin and tonic.

"What's he like? Your ex?"

I'll admit it sounds strange to hear Trent addressed as my ex. Even when I saw him in the bar with his chubby girlfriend, I still considered him my husband, present tense. But hearing Wynn refer to him as such flicks a switch. Suddenly, he seems very much in my past. "He's selfish," I say, "and incredibly immature." I'm sure this line of conversation is an enormous turnoff to the young hunk across from me, but he asked. "He's a good father, I'll give him that, but he's a pathetic excuse for a man. He wears eye cream and funny pants. He's a walking midlife crisis cliché."

Wynn chuckles. "I know the type. I think my mom dated about six of him when I was growing up."

"Really?" I ask, but then quickly change the subject. "I don't want to talk about him." I lean forward. "Tell me about you."

"Well," he begins, activating the eye twinkler, "I was cast in a dog food commercial when I was twelve. I've always looked younger, so I played this eight-year-old kid who lost his golden retriever. After that, I did a few plays in high school and really caught the acting bug. So, I moved to L.A. when I was seventeen, and after three months, I got cast as Bruce Boxleitner's son in *The Con Man Next Door*."

"Not your résumé," I say, embarrassed that I'm actually a little familiar with the tale from Sam's teen magazines lying around the house. "Tell me about you."

He looks sincerely confused. "What about me?"

"Where did you grow up? What are your parents like? Do you have siblings?"

Wynn looks a little uncomfortable. "Off the record?" he says, as though I'm a *Tiger Beat* reporter. I nod. He takes a drink of beer then plunges ahead. "I was raised by a single mom in a trailer park in New Mexico. My dad left when I was six and I've only seen him twice since. Of course, now that I'm famous he wants a relationship, but as far as I'm concerned, it's too little, too late."

"Oh," I say, unsure of the appropriate response.

"I have an older brother, Dennis. We were really close but he's been arrested twice for drug offenses—just pot, but obviously, that would damage my reputation as a"—his fingers do air quotes—'teen heartthrob.' "

"Right."

"So I've been advised not to see him. But I see my mom once in a while . . . She's had a hard life and she made some bad choices, but . . . she's my mom, so I guess I have to make an effort."

"You do," I say, reaching for my gin and tonic and taking a

fortifying sip. "She's your mother and I'm sure she did the best she could. My mother wasn't perfect either."

Wynn shrugs. "Did your mother ever get arrested for check-kiting?"

"No."

"For throwing a TV at her boyfriend?"

"Thankfully no, but trust me, there are times when TV throwing is extremely tempting."

He chuckles. "I guess."

I soften my tone. "That must have been pretty rough, though."

"It wasn't so bad. I actually think my upbringing made me stronger," Wynn says, his confident air returning. "I've had to stand on my own two feet for a long time, so I can roll with things that a lot of people can't."

"Maybe," I say, wondering if my Cleaver-esque upbringing had made me soft.

"And I've got lots of good, quality friends."

I refrain from asking how many of these good, quality friends are on his payroll. Instead, I say, "I think you should call your mom . . . and your brother. Who cares if he's smoked a little pot? Sometimes our family disappoints us, but they're still our family."

Wynn looks at me, smiles. "Maybe . . ."

"And don't let your managers make decisions for you. Like you said, you can stand on your own two feet. You're a really strong person."

Wynn looks slightly uncomfortable with the praise as he takes a drink of beer, but I continue. "It's true. Lots of stars would use a background like yours as an excuse to do drugs and pop in and out of rehab." I pat his hand. "I'm proud of you."

As soon as I've said it, I realize how motherly it sounds. Suddenly, I feel like I'm out for a beer with seventeen-year-old Cody Summers. It's sick and wrong. "I should go," I say, starting to stand.

Wynn grabs the hand that just administered the matronly patting. I'm thankful that my wedding ring is sitting in the jewelry box on my dresser. "Stay," he says, giving me an intense look. The twinkling blue eyes are brooding and sexy.

I sit down. "Okay," I say hoarsely. "I guess I can stay a bit longer."

Trent

ANNIKA'S DOOR SWINGS open before I've even knocked. She pulls me inside and kisses me passionately, grinding herself up against me. Just when I'm getting aroused, she backs away.

"I can't believe we had our first fight!" she says, as if it's a celebratory milestone. "I'm sorry, baby."

"It wasn't you, it was me." After almost twenty years with Lucy, I know this is the appropriate response. In reality, I don't know if it was her or me. I don't even know what we were supposedly fighting about.

"No, it was me," she insists and kisses me again. "I pushed too hard. It's just that we're finally together and I want to be a part of your life."

"Okay," I say lamely.

She leads me into the tidy apartment where a small round dining table is set for dinner. A bottle of red sits breathing in the center. Annika pours two glasses, continuing her diatribe.

"I know you said you've been emotionally divorced for years, but I guess there's really no way for your daughter to know that. Like, I'm sure she thinks you and Lucy were totally happy until last month. So I get what you're saying—like, that we can't rush into telling her about us." She hands me a glass of wine.

"Good," I reply, taking a grateful sip.

"Sam and I should absolutely meet as friends first. Then, once she gets to know me, we can tell her that we're in love."

I don't spray the mouthful of red wine all over her pale yellow tablecloth. Instead, I start to choke. She rubs my back, making a shushing noise like I'm a baby choking on mushy peas. When I've stopped sputtering, she says, "Down the wrong tube?"

"Yeah," I croak.

She giggles. "You're so cute. So," she places her glass on the table and fiddles with the buttons on my shirt. "What do you think?"

What do I think? I think I should tell her that I'm not in love with her, that I don't plan to ever introduce her to my daughter. I think I should tell her that this is all about sex for me, about being with someone new after years with the same woman. In that moment, I can hear Mike uttering these words through a mouthful of steak, but I choose to ignore the irony. I should tell Annika the truth about my feelings, but I can't. If I'm perfectly honest, I'm a little afraid to rock the boat. "Sounds good," I manage to mumble. "What's for dinner?"

"Osso buco," she says, dropping to her knees before me. "But I thought I'd have you for an appetizer." And as she unzips my fly, all thoughts of setting her straight suddenly fly out the window.

Lucy

I DID STAY at Maxwell's in the Kingsway Inn for a bit longer. In fact, I stayed four drinks longer. Sam wasn't expecting me home until at least seven, so I had plenty of time. Unfortunately, when seven o'clock rolled around, the five gin and tonics I'd imbibed left me in no shape to drive . . . or walk . . . or think straight.

"Don't worry," Wynn said, rubbing his thumb across mine. We were holding hands now. Somewhere around drink three we started holding hands. "Jamie and Todd will pick us up and drive your car home."

"Are you sure it's no trouble?" I cooed. Somewhere around drink four, I started cooing.

"Of course not." I realized that Jamie and Todd were likely the "quality friends" Wynn kept on the payroll to be at his beck and call. "We'll have you home in half an hour."

As Wynn spoke to Jamie on his cell phone, I struggled into

my coat. I waited patiently as he gave our location, taking in Wynn and my surroundings through blurry eyes. It was such a strange juxtaposition: this gorgeous celebrity in this crappy dive bar. What was I doing here? This was not my life. Or was it? Wynn caught me looking at him and winked. My stomach did a little flip. Camille was right. I deserved to have a little fun. Who was I hurting? And Wynn *was* hot . . . really fucking hot. And I was drunk . . . really fucking drunk.

"They'll be here in fifteen minutes," he said, snapping his phone closed.

"What should we do until then?" I said, taking an unsteady step toward him.

Before Sam was born, copious amounts of gin had been known to turn me into an aggressive nymphomaniac. Apparently, nothing had changed. Wynn was quick to pick up on my not so subtle cues. He slid his hands into my open coat and around my waist. With a forceful tug, he pulled me toward him.

"We'll think of something."

As our bodies collided, I felt an intense surge of desire. This was really happening. I was here, alone, with this beautiful, sexy man who had far more depth than I ever would have imagined. What Camille said was true. He wasn't seventeen-year-old Cody. He was Wynn Felker and he was all man! Our eyes locked and one thought filled my mind: I wanted him. I didn't care if it was wrong and weird and completely unprofessional. In fact, in my inebriated mental state, that just added to the excitement.

Wynn leaned forward and kissed me. His lips were soft and warm and he tasted like beer . . . delicious, yummy beer. My hands flew to the back of his hair as our kissing intensified. A small moan escaped as I surrendered to the feeling of his mouth, the softness of his hair, and his hands roaming my back. For the first time since Trent walked out, I wasn't thinking about my marriage. I wasn't feeling hurt or betrayed or worried about the future. No longer was I Trent's wife, or Samantha's mother, or the winner of the most attractive Christmas lights display on the block. I was just Lucy . . . Lucy Crawford. I was living in the moment, and I was having the time of my life.

Of course, we were not alone. Some perverted chuckling and a muttered "Give it to him, baby" brought our attention back to our location.

"Let's wait outside," Wynn mumbled, grabbing me by the hand and leading me through the dingy pub. I followed obediently, enjoying his take-charge attitude. He was definitely no teenager!

Outside, we were able to resume our make-out session for a few minutes before the irritatingly punctual Jamie and Todd arrived. I gave my car keys to Todd, and Wynn and I piled into the backseat of the Lincoln Navigator.

Jamie's burly presence in the driver's seat cooled our ardor, and as we hurtled down Kingsway I felt myself sobering up. Okay, I was still a long way from sober, but my senses were returning. What the hell had just happened? I was late getting home to my daughter, I was drunk, and I'd spent the last twenty minutes gnawing Cody Summers's face off. It was disgusting. *I* was disgusting . . . also selfish, irresponsible, and slutty.

Wynn leaned over and whispered in my ear, "I had a great time tonight."

"I'm not feeling well," I responded stiffly.

He sat up. "Are you okay? Do you want to pull over? Are you going to be sick?"

Was I? The thought of what had just happened made me feel

sick with guilt. Combined with all the gin sloshing in my stomach and the motion of the SUV, barfing was an appealing idea. "No," I said quietly, "I just need to get home."

Twelve minutes later we pulled into my driveway. The digital clock on the dashboard read 7:27, still a reasonable arrival time. Todd pulled in beside us in my Forerunner and cut the engine. If I handled this right, there was no reason Sam needed to know anything was amiss.

"Thanks for the ride," I called to my driver. I opened the door and exited the backseat. Wynn slid out behind me.

I turned to him. "I've got to get inside."

"Okay." He took a step toward me. "It just seems a shame to call it a night so early."

Did he expect me to ask him in? To parade him past my teenage daughter and up to my bedroom? What kind of woman did he think I was? An alcoholic whore, obviously. I guess I had been sending him those signals. I took a step back.

"My daughter . . . ," I began with a nervous glance over my shoulder. Surely the sound of an enormous SUV idling in the driveway would bring Sam to the window? And what about the neighbors? It looked like I was being dropped off by P. Diddy's entourage.

"I'll walk you to the door," Wynn offered.

"No!" I said, taking an insistent step back. "I'm fine."

But Wynn moved toward me and took my hand. "I'm flying to Nebraska tomorrow, so I won't see you for a few days."

"Nebraska?"

"I have to do a mall opening."

"But I thought you didn't want to go?" If Wynn was wondering how I knew this, he didn't ask.

"I don't, but we've committed. And then we've got some event in Wyoming."

"Well, have fun." I thought I saw the curtain move and felt a bubble of panic in my chest. If Sam saw Wynn here, she'd go crazy. And if she saw Wynn here holding her mother's hand, she'd go on a psychotic killing spree. But Sam's face never appeared and I chalked the swaying curtain up to my drunken loss of equilibrium. Still, I pulled my hand away. "I'll see you when you get back," I said, hurrying toward the house. "Thanks for the drinks."

Now, just a couple of days later, I'm still reliving that evening. It's a combination of drinker's remorse and an aching, longing sort of remembrance. Lust, I think they call it. I vaguely remember the feeling from my early days with Trent. Of course, I've analyzed this yearning to relive, possibly even expand on those kisses with Wynn, and have concluded that they're a product of my intense loneliness and feelings of marital rejection. I must push these lecherous feelings to the back of my mind until they dissipate. And of course, I will never touch another drop of gin as long as I live.

With the Wynn Felker incident firmly behind me, I can focus on my daughter. Sam continues to be sullen and sulky, demonstrating that she needs my full attention. Parenthood is my top priority. Unfortunately, this stupid job continues to suck up far too many hours that would be better spent bonding with my child, but I've got to pay the mortgage. Outside of work, I will be one hundred percent attentive to Samantha. I'm not going to let Trent's midlife crisis affect her happiness and well-being.

Of course it's normal to want to reminisce about that night with Wynn. It was a big, drunken mistake, but that doesn't mean I didn't enjoy myself. I felt so alive and so young and so free—which is an entirely inappropriate way for someone to feel at my age and in my position. No, Sam comes first . . . always. There is no room in my life for gin and kissing.

Wynn's email message was really sweet though. He wrote to me from Nebraska, just to tell me that he'd had a great time the other night and couldn't wait to see me when he got back. For a split second I'd felt a surge of excitement, even possibility, but I quickly came to my senses. It was flattering to receive such a missive, and obviously good for my ego. I mean, how many women my age get asked out by a gorgeous twenty-something? But it doesn't change the facts: 1) Wynn is too young for me. 2) He's a teen heartthrob. 3) My daughter has an enormous crush on him. I could keep going, but those alone are enough.

If I'm being perfectly honest, it feels good to have evened the score with my ex and that curly-haired cow of his. While Trent continues to harass me via email about the spare bed and various kitchen appliances, I continue to ignore him. Tonight he's taking Sam to a movie and wants to "speak to me in person." Obviously, I'll be working late so that I can avoid the confrontation. I love the thought of Trent stewing and stressing over my lack of availability. I can practically see his face turning red each time he checks his email and finds his messages unanswered.

What does he expect? That he can enjoy cocktails with Slutty McSlutterson while I fill a box with steak knives and measuring spoons and individually wrapped plates and coffee cups? That I'll carry the double bed out of the spare room on my back, tie it onto my truck, and deliver it to his new bachelor pad? He probably wants me to go in and put clean sheets on it so that it's all ready for him to screw his fat girlfriend on.

I feel my face getting hot with anger and I'm disappointed

by my physical response. Why do Trent's actions still affect me so much? I just got an email from a TV star who says he can't wait to see me. Why do I still care about that paunchy cliché of a man I was married to for so freaking long? And I realize I've just answered my own question. I was married to Trent for sixteen years. If I stop caring about him a few weeks after he walks out on me, it's as though our time together was all a lie. It wasn't. We've got Sam to prove that. And I've still got this dull ache in my heart.

Trent

WHEN I PULL into the driveway, the first thing I notice is that Lucy's car isn't there. "That bitch," I mutter under my breath, as I turn off the Lexus's engine. A lone light shines in the living room, and I suddenly realize how alone my daughter must feel. A small wave of guilt washes over me, but I push it away. Lucy should be feeling guilty, not me. She wanted to stay in the house and play happy families. She should be the one to step up and take responsibility.

I jog up the steps and try the door. It's locked. The key is still on my ring, but I knock. I don't want to barge in and scare the crap out of Sam. But when she hasn't answered after several seconds, I fish for the key. I'm about to insert it in the lock when the door swings open.

"Hey," my daughter says, with a marked lack of enthusiasm.

"Hi, my girl." I step into the foyer and prepare to give her a kiss, but Sam is already digging in the closet for her coat. I survey the room. It's basically unchanged since the day I left: still formal, pristine, professionally cleaned. Okay, so the house is showing no signs of neglect, but I look at my daughter. As she struggles into her hoodie, I notice the shadows under her eyes and a certain hollowness to her cheeks. Are these new, or did she always look like this? I feel bad that I can't remember.

"So," I say casually, "your mom here?"

"No," she mumbles, zipping into the ridiculous boots she insists on wearing.

I check my watch. "Shouldn't she be home by now? It's almost seven."

Sam rights herself and looks at me. "You lived with her for, like, twenty years. You should know what time she gets home better than I do."

"Watch the tone," I say, asserting some parental control. I get that this has been hard on her, but it doesn't give her the right to be rude. "Show some respect."

Sam's eyes narrow as she stares at me. I'm afraid she's about to say something horrible, and frankly, I'm not sure what I'd do if she did. It's a little hard to enforce punishment when your relationship consists of dinners at White Spot and the odd movie. But thankfully, she bites her tongue. "Let's go," she mumbles, brushing past me and out the door.

Forty minutes later we're slouched in our seats in the darkened movie theater. Sam munches on popcorn, and I worry that it constitutes dinner. But I don't ask. She's obviously in a bad mood and I don't want to set her off again. She's probably getting her period or something. Instead, I take a sip of Coke and turn my thoughts to Lucy.

By now I've figured out that she's trying to infuriate me. You don't spend almost twenty years with a woman without getting into her psyche. Yeah, her avoidance is definitely a way of punishing me. It's normal for her to be pissed, but it's been nearly a month since I left. Lucy has to accept that I need some time to myself. If she thinks her childish behavior is going to make me come running home, she's got another think coming.

I glance at my daughter, her face highlighted by the movie light. She's going to be okay. She's strong and resilient, like her old man. There haven't been any more drinking incidents, and she hasn't dyed her hair green or gotten a tattoo. She's obviously throwing her teen angst into her art. As long as her mother's petty avoidance act doesn't segue into neglecting Sam, she'll come through this all right.

The movie was a stinker, but Sam seemed to like it. She is borderline animated on the drive home. Well, as animated as a premenstrual teen whose parents have just split up can be. "I'm looking forward to your art show on Saturday," I say as we turn onto our street.

Sam clams up suddenly, shrugs. "Yeah," she mumbles, staring out the window.

"Don't be so modest," I say, as we approach the house. "You've got real talent."

"Whatevs," she mutters.

I'm relieved to see the Forerunner in the driveway and a couple of lights burning in the house. The dashboard clock reads 9:18—pushing it, even for Lucy. As I put the car in park, Sam is already reaching for the door handle. She pauses, looks at me. "Are you coming in?"

She might as well have asked, "Are you going to show up at my school tomorrow naked?" I realize she's not in the mood for a scene between her mother and me, and frankly, neither am I.

"No," I say, letting the car idle. "I'll see your mom at the art show."

There is no hiding her relief. "Okay, bye." She hurries off to the house.

As I watch my daughter fiddling with the front door, it suddenly swings open. I catch a glimpse of her mom as she ushers Sam inside, and I wave. It's instinct, common courtesy, but Lucy ignores the gesture. The door slams and I feel the anger bubble up inside me.

"Fine," I mutter, banging the car into reverse. "You want to play it that way then we'll play it that way." As I gun the car down our quiet, tree-lined street, I growl into the darkness. "See you Saturday, Lucy."

Lucy

I AM ONCE again buried in the props room, searching for microphones for the Central High talent show, when Camille bursts into the cataclysm. "You've got to come back to your desk."

"Why?" I ask, my stomach lurching with panic. If Crofton House has called to tell me my daughter's plastered again, I don't know what I'll do.

But Camille's exuberance makes it evident that it's not bad news. "Just come!"

I see the bouquet of flowers before I'm even in the room. Since it's about the size of Jupiter, it's hard to miss. In fact, a small crowd of women has gathered to gush over the lily, peony, and hydrangea extravaganza.

"That's a two-hundred-dollar bouquet," someone murmurs.

"I've never seen one that big."

"I have, on TV. I think it was at Anna Nicole Smith's funeral."

"Who's it from?" Camille asks as I reach for the card. It has to be from Wynn. The size and expense of the arrangement screams Hollywood. And he did email again to say he'd be home in a few days and was looking forward to seeing me.

But there's also a slim chance that the bouquet is from Trent. He's stopped harassing me about the spare bed, and I wonder if this signals a change of heart. A floral arrangement this enormous might be saying: "Please forgive me. I'm so sorry I left you for that fat frizzy slut and now I'd really like to come home to you and our daughter." Despite my anger toward my husband, I feel a small glimmer of hope that this is the case. I tear open the card.

I'll be back in Vancouver Sunday. Can't wait to see you.

Wynn

The swell of disappointment takes me aback. I'd expected the note to be from him, so why am I so chagrined? Did I really think Trent would come around that easily? That he'd suddenly realize the error of his ways and come home to the family fold? No, I didn't. But I'm surprised how much I wanted it.

"Who's it from?" Camille squeals.

"It's anonymous," I say coyly, smiling at the gaggle of women encircling me. With a groan, they disperse back to their offices, but Camille gives me a wink. It's obvious she's knows they're from Cody Summers.

LATER THAT EVENING, I drive home with the flowers in the back of my SUV. They significantly lower my visibility and force me to rely on my side-view mirrors. Thankfully, I arrive without incident.

"Oh my god," Samantha says as I stagger through the doorway with the gigantic bouquet. "Where'd you get those?" She's lounging on the couch, as usual, watching *Entertainment Tonight*. Obviously, I can't tell her they're from the teen heartthrob whose photos are wallpapering her bedroom. In fact, telling her they're from any man could be upsetting. And if I say they're from her father that would needlessly get her hopes up.

"They're for you," I say, pasting on a bright smile. "Just to say break a leg for the art show tomorrow—or whatever you say in art show circles."

My daughter gets off the couch and approaches the floral monstrosity. She fingers a lily, sniffs a peony. My hand reaches to my back pocket, feels Wynn's card safely tucked away. Sam looks at me for a moment, her expression unreadable. "It's huge," she finally says.

"Well, tomorrow's a big night for you," I reply.

"Right," she mutters, heading back to the couch and her television program. "Hope called for you."

"So, that's it?" I snap. "No thank-you or anything?" Technically, I'm re-gifting this enormous bouquet to her, but she doesn't know that. When did my only child become such a spoiled brat?

Sam's eyes stay fixed on the TV. "Thanks," she says, coolly.

I go upstairs to change my clothes and fume about my daughter's reception. She's lucky I didn't shell out two hundred dollars on those flowers, or I wouldn't be letting her off the hook so easily. Is this what happens to children of broken homes? They're given carte blanche to act like selfish little monsters because Mommy and Daddy feel too guilty to discipline them? I experience another surge of anger toward Trent. If only those flowers really had been from him, then I wouldn't have had to lie in the first place. The logic around this train of thought is a little sketchy, but blaming Trent does make me feel slightly better.

Going to the phone, I finally return Hope's call.

"How are you?" she asks, her tone pitying.

"Fine," I reply. "It's getting easier."

"You don't have to pretend with me, pal. I know how it is, remember?"

"I'm not pretending," I snipe. "I'm fine, really." I suppose she means well, but I can't help but feel Hope wants me to be a sniveling mess so that she can swoop in with her cookies and self-help books.

Hope senses that it's time to change the subject. "I just called to tell you that Sarah-Lou and I will be coming to the art show tomorrow night."

"Oh . . . okay." I'm surprised and a little confused, but my friend elaborates.

"We want to show Sam our support. Plus, I know Trent will be going and I thought you might like to have a friend there."

I suddenly feel guilty for doubting her motivation. She's right. After the strained silence between my husband and me, our face-to-face meeting is bound to be tense. It will be nice to have Hope there for support.

"Thanks, Hope," I say, my voice wobbling a bit.

"I'm here for you, you know."

"I know."

"Okay, we'll pick you up tomorrow at seven."

Trent

ANNIKA AND I spent the day trolling through Ikea. She insisted on lending me her "design eye" for my new place. Fifteen hundred dollars later, we returned to the small apartment and began the arduous task of assembling my furnishings. When we were done, I surveyed the room. I had the distinct feeling that I'd just graduated from college all over again. The one bedroom and den was a sparsely furnished sea of unfinished pine, brightly colored pillows, and flat couches with weird names.

We had sex on the Karlstad three-seat sofa bed (Annika insisted we christen it) then grabbed some take-out sushi from the restaurant downstairs. And now we're sitting in my car in the darkened school parking lot. I stare straight ahead at the building, peering into the few lit classrooms. A stream of parents heads in through the main doors. I haven't spotted Lucy yet. She's either already there, or running late.

"Okay," Annika says from the passenger seat, "I'm just a

friend from work who's really interested in art. There's nothing romantic going on between us, but we are good friends."

"Right."

"I can't wait to meet your daughter," she says. "This was such a good idea—like, to have us bond over her art first."

I turn to her. "What about my wife? Can you wait to meet her?"

Annika places a consoling hand on mine. "Don't worry. If I'm just an art-loving friend, how can she get mad?"

Oh, she can get mad, I think, but don't say. In fact, the whole purpose in bringing Annika here is to make Lucy mad. And as I enjoy these last moments of peace, I can't help but wonder: what the fuck was I thinking? Do I really want my wife and my girlfriend to collide at my kid's art show? My relationship with Sam is strained enough. What the hell is wrong with me? Sure, Sam might buy the "art-loving coworker" bit, but there's no way Lucy will. Annika's way too sexy to be just a friend.

I ponder Lucy's reaction. Will she assault Annika with a piece of art? I can't see her embarrassing Sam that way. Besides, Annika's got at least twenty pounds on Lucy. She could take her down in a second. I allow myself a quick visual. If I wasn't so stressed out, I'd be turned on right now.

Annika's voice brings me back to the present. "Let's go in, babe." She leans over and licks my ear. Somehow, it's simultaneously erotic and annoying. She sits back in her seat. "From this moment forward, you are nothing more than my good friend and coworker who was kind enough to invite me to his daughter's art show."

She's trying for levity, but it falls flat. "Let's go," I mutter, getting out of the car.

As we enter the bustling studio, I decide not to search out my wife. Let her stumble upon us. It'll be even more shocking that way. Christ, when did I become such a prick? But I remind myself that Lucy asked for this. She's been a complete bitch since the day I walked out. She's been cold and stubborn and shut off from me—except for that night when I fucked her on the couch. It seems like months ago, but I suddenly realize that, other than the brief glimpse in the doorway, that was the last time I saw her. I turn to Annika.

"This was a bad idea."

"What?" she asks, peering at a pastel drawing of kids building a sand castle.

"This," I say, tugging at her arm. "This isn't the right place for you to meet my family."

Annika turns on me, hands defiantly on hips. "We discussed this. You said it was the perfect place to meet your daughter."

"But it's too hard on Lucy." I reach in my pocket and hand her my keys. "Take the car home. I'll catch a cab."

She lets out a bitter, humorless laugh. "You think I'm going to leave, just like that?"

Oh fuck. What have I done? I glance nervously around the room for Sam or Lucy. Oh Christ, what are *they* doing here? Hope and the chipper Sarah-Louise are already headed toward me.

"Hi, Trent," Hope says, giving me a perfunctory hug. As usual, when I embrace Hope I can't help but think of my rather large Aunt Marilyn.

"Hi," I say cheerfully. "Hi, Sarah-Louise."

"Hi, Mr. Vaughn."

"You must be very proud," Hope says.

"I just got here, actually. I haven't seen Sam's pieces."

"I haven't either, but I'm sure they're great."

Annika steps forward. Of course, it would have been too much to ask that she continue to unobtrusively stare at the sand castle picture. She holds out her hand.

"I'm Trent's friend and coworker, Annika."

Hope takes her hand briefly, her eyes darting to my face. "Nice to meet you," she says coolly.

"I love art," Annika continues, "especially young people's art." She reaches out and touches Sarah-Louise's arm. Of course, being a robot programmed for only pleasant responses, Sarah-Lou smiles sweetly.

"Trent, Lucy is just getting a glass of wine." Hope points toward a table set up in a far corner. "I'm sure she'd like to admire your daughter's artwork together."

"Great!" Annika smiles. "We'll be right over."

I feel like punching a hole in the wall. What the hell is wrong with me? Have I lost my fucking mind? Was I that enraged at my wife that I wanted to humiliate her like this? I'm a monster, a fucking monster. Lucy was right to shut me out. I'm subhuman.

Hope and Sarah-Louise scurry back to Lucy, obviously trying to warn her. I turn to Annika. "We can't do this."

Annika smiles sweetly. "Don't worry, pal." She slips her arm through mine; I fight off the urge to shudder.

"It's going to be a disaster," I plead.

"No," Annika says, already pulling me toward the wine table, "it's going to be fine."

Lucy

I'VE JUST TAKEN a sip of red wine when Hope and Sarah-Louise rush up to me. "I just saw Trent," Hope whispers, as Sarah-Louise continues to smile agreeably.

"I'm glad he made it. He's let Sam down too often over the past month."

"He's got someone with him," she says through gritted teeth.

"Who?"

Hope turns to her daughter. "Honey, go find Sam's artwork for us, would you?" When Sarah-Lou has obediently departed, she continues. "It's a coworker . . . some woman who 'loves young people's art.'"

My stomach lurches and I know. Even before Trent materializes with that frizzy cow hanging off his arm, I know. Hope places a calming hand on my forearm. Or perhaps it's just to keep me from chucking my glass of wine in his face.

"Hi, Lucy," Trent says, his voice thin and reedy. "Nice to see you."

I am actually thankful now that I'd spotted the two of them at the bar last week. Instead of fainting or crying or throwing up, I am composed. Well, as composed as you can be when you realize the man you were married to for sixteen years is the biggest shithead on the face of the planet.

"Hi, Trent," I say, with a forced cheerfulness bordering on the psychotic. "Who's your friend?"

Trent's pallor goes from pale to ghostly. He clears his throat. "This is my coworker Annika. She loves young people's art, so she thought she'd tag along."

"Nice to meet you." Annika sticks out her fat hand and I force myself to touch it, briefly.

"I'm Lucy, Trent's wife. But you probably already know that."

Annika looks nervously to Trent, who is now peering around the room.

"Have you seen Sam's pieces?" he asks, not having the balls to actually look at me.

"Not yet," I say. "So Annika, do you like all young people's art, or just my daughter's?"

"I love checking out the art of teenagers," she says, sounding like a Miss America contestant. "It's a real window into the soul of the next generation."

I can't suppress a snort of vicious laughter. Hope steps in. "Where is Sarah-Lou? I'm dying to see Sam's stuff."

"Did Sam come in with you?" the cowardly lion asks, eyes looking everywhere but at me.

"She came in early to help set up." I turn to Annika again. "Tell me, how long have you been dating my husband? Was it before he left me, or just after?"

"We're not dating," Trent cries. "She's a work friend."

"I saw you, asshole," I growl, leaning menacingly toward him. "At Chill."

"Shit."

Hope tries once more to intervene. "We're all here for Sam, remember? You can talk about this later."

"That's right," Trent says, sidestepping away from me. "This isn't the time or place."

"Right. You're so concerned about your daughter's feelings that you brought a date to her art show," I spit. "I nominate you father of the year."

"Oh, here we go!" Trent says. "The queen of sarcasm reigns again."

"That's rich, coming from the king of insensitivity—make that the emperor!"

Trent lowers his voice. "Maybe if you'd responded to any of my messages, we could have talked about this before."

"Talked about what? That you're dating Miss Piggy a month after you deserted us?"

Annika steps up. "Watch it, you scrawny bitch."

Hope turns to Trent. "You're going to let her talk to the mother of your child that way?"

"She called her Miss Piggy!"

I step back. "If the size ten–wide shoe fits . . ."

"You're totally right, Trent," Annika snarls, "she's a real monster."

"Oh, you just wait, porky! You think you're happy now, but soon he'll be telling you he needs to sort out his grown-up man stuff."

"That is crossing the line!" Annika cries. "You definitely have an eating disorder or something."

"You're unbelievable," Trent barks at me.

Sarah-Louise walks up to her mother. "Samantha's not in the art show," she says calmly.

"What?" Trent and I whirl on her.

"I couldn't find her paintings, so I asked the teacher. She said Sam pulled out two weeks ago."

"Oh my god," I say softly, the anger seeping out of me like a leaky balloon. It's quickly replaced by a feeling of utter, inconsolable sadness.

Hope puts her arm around me. "It's okay. She'll be okay."

"But where is she?" I cry. "I need to see her."

Trent is already dialing his cell phone. He listens for a minute then says, "Voice mail."

I sag a little into Hope's shoulder. "Let's get you home," she says. "She'll turn up sooner or later."

Trent

"I'M COMING WITH you," Annika insists as I speed toward her apartment.

"No, you're not," I grumble. "You've done enough."

She misses the sarcasm completely. "But I want to be there to support you. It must be scary not knowing where your daughter is, or what she's been doing for the last two weeks when you thought she was working on her art projects."

She is so not helping. "Lucy and I need to handle this on our own. I'm taking you home."

"Fine." She settles back in her seat in a pout. "I just wish you'd let me start participating in this family."

What the fuck is she talking about? We went on our first date just two weeks ago. We've had sex precisely nine times—okay, nine and a half times if you want to count that first disaster. Yeah, we've worked together for a year and we've been flirting heavily for much of that, but that doesn't make her a part of my family! I'd set her straight, but I don't have the energy to get into it. I've got to get over to the house and deal with my daughter.

I pull up in front of Annika's Fairview apartment building, leave the car in drive. She steps onto the curb then pokes her head back into the car. "Call me when you've found Sam. I'm really worried about her."

"Right." I'm inching the car forward before she's even finished talking.

Seventeen minutes later, I'm at Lucy's door. Using my key, I let myself inside.

"Sam?" My wife comes rushing toward me, her tear-streaked face hopeful. "Oh." Her expression crumples with disappointment.

"Has she called?"

Hope appears behind Lucy. "No, we haven't heard from her."

"Did you check her room?" I'm already heading for the stairs, passing a floral arrangement fit for Sinatra's funeral. Normally, I'd make a crack like "Who died?" but under the circumstances, it seems inappropriate.

Hope says, "Good idea. Maybe she left a note?"

"Oh god!" Lucy cries, taking a nosedive off the deep end. "What if she . . ."

I stop on the staircase. "Don't be ridiculous. But she obviously knows that we're aware she dropped out of the art show by now. Maybe she left a note to explain."

As I continue up the stairs, Lucy calls, "Check for drugs while you're there!"

Ten minutes later I return to the kitchen. Hope is making tea. Lucy is sniffling at the table. "No note, no drugs. But I see she's still obsessed with that Cody Summers kid."

"He's not a kid," Lucy snaps. "He's twenty-seven."

"Even more reason she shouldn't be obsessed with him," I bark.

Hope interjects, "Sarah-Lou has a crush on him, too. It's harmless."

I take a seat next to Lucy. I'm tempted to take her hand and comfort her, but after the events of this evening, I'm not sure she'd welcome it. She stares at the table, blows her nose. "She'll be okay," I say.

Lucy looks up at me, her eyes red and puffy. "What if she's not?" she says. "What if we've hurt her so badly that she's off drinking herself into oblivion? What if she's taking ecstasy or snorting coke or whatever kids do these days? What if she just wants the pain to stop?"

I know she's being melodramatic, but I'm suddenly overcome with guilt. "I'm sorry," I mumble, my voice quivering with emotion. "I'm a fucking idiot."

Lucy starts to bawl. "Yes, you are," she cries. Her voice holds no anger, only regret. "You're such a fucking idiot."

The kettle whistles and Hope hurries to the stove. "Do you want tea, Trent?" she asks coldly.

"Yes. No." I look at Lucy. "Is there any beer in the fridge?" She shakes her head. I call to Hope. "Okay, I'll have tea."

And that's when Sam walks into the room. She stands there sullen and defiant, in a pair of skin-tight jeans and a tiny T-shirt. She's a little pale, her eyes are a bit red, but she doesn't appear to be drunk or high on coke. Lucy rushes toward her and embraces her. "Thank god you're okay," she cries, kissing her hair. Sam stands stock-still, not reciprocating, but not pulling away either. I approach, wait for my turn.

"We were so worried," I say, wrapping my arms around my little girl. "Don't ever do that to us again."

Sam pulls away. "Don't ever do what again?" she snaps. "Not show up? Not be where I'm supposed to be?"

Lucy and I stare at her, unsure how to respond. I'm suddenly wishing I'd bought a book on dealing with kids during a marriage breakup. Is it okay for her to be rude and surly toward us? I mean, she's right, after all. We—and by *we* I mostly mean Lucy—have been really unavailable lately. But does that give her the right to torture us this way?

No, it doesn't. We are still her parents. We still feed her and clothe her and pay for the private school Lucy insists she attend. When she was a baby, we changed her diapers and got up with her three times a night until she was five. We deserve some respect, goddammit. "That's right, missy," I say, asserting my parental authority. "You're fifteen. You don't get to call the shots."

"Trent!" Lucy snaps, having obviously decided to go the permissive, guilt-riddled parent route. "She's upset."

"I get that," I snap back. "It doesn't mean she has the right to disappear and worry us half to death. Where were you?"

"At my friend Randy's house."

"Randy? Never heard of her."

"Randy's a he," Sam says defiantly. "He's a friend from school."

"You go to an all-girls' school!" I roar.

"Yeah," she bites back, "he's my friend's brother." She plays with one of the long gold chains around her neck. "He's got his own apartment and sometimes we hang out there."

"How old is this Randy?" Lucy manages to say.

Sam shrugs. "Nineteen."

"And there was a group of you there?" My wife's voice is hopeful.

My daughter looks me directly in the eye. "No, just me and Randy."

The kid is so transparent. She's obviously trying to push my buttons. Unfortunately, it's working. I can feel my blood starting to boil and heat fills my face. I can't blow up and lose it on Sam now. The split has been difficult on her, and exploding in anger isn't going to help our bond.

"It's no big deal." Sam shrugs. She seems to find watching me struggle to contain my rage slightly amusing.

Suddenly, Lucy grabs Sam's chin, forcing her to meet her eyes. "You're high!"

"Oh my god!" This from Hope, who's been busying herself with tea in the kitchen.

I can't believe I didn't notice. I thought she looked tired and pale, but upon further inspection, her pupils are enormous. "What are you on?" Lucy demands. "Junk? Smack? Blow?"

Sam lets out a snort of laughter. "Mom, do you even know what those are?"

"Enlighten us, cool drug user," I snap. "What did you take?"

"Calm down! I smoked a little crystal and then had unprotected sex with Randy and his best friend. It's no big deal."

"Oh my god!" Lucy shrieks.

"What!" I boom.

"Oh lord," Hope says, and I really wish she'd leave.

Sam giggles maliciously. "I'm kidding," she says. "I just smoked some pot."

"You're sick!" I jab my finger at her. "Don't you ever do anything like that to us again."

At least Lucy and I are on the same wavelength about Hope's presence. Lucy turns to her. "Thanks so much for being here, but I think our family needs to be alone right now."

"Are you sure?" Hope says, looking from Lucy to me to Sam.

"I'm sure," my wife says. "But thanks and . . . please, let's just keep this quiet."

Even in the throes of a crisis, Lucy's worried about her precious reputation. It's shallow and superficial, but to be perfectly honest, I'm kind of glad she said something. I don't exactly want it advertised that my fifteen-year-old daughter has been getting stoned at some guy's apartment.

Hope gives Lucy a hug. "You'll be okay," she says. "You'll get through this."

"I know. Thanks."

My wife and I stand silently, waiting for Hope to exit. Sam walks to the fridge, peers inside. When I hear the front door close, I say, "Shut that fridge and get over here."

With much eye-rolling, Samantha does as she's told. "What?" she says, hands on hips.

"What?" Lucy cries. "How can you ask us that?"

I roar, "You dropped out of the art show! You're stoned! You're dressed like a slut and you're hanging out with some nineteen-year-old pothead!" I guess the litany of Sam's transgressions is too much for Lucy. She drops her face into her hands and sobs. "Look what you've done to your mother," I growl.

As soon as the words are out, I realize my mistake. My daughter's eyes narrow and I know what's coming next. "Look what *I've* done to her? What about you? Jordan called me. She said you brought some sexy date to my art show."

Lucy's head snaps up. "Sexy?" She snorts. "More like chunky."

"She's a friend from work who likes . . ." But my voice breaks. Finally, I finish lamely, "Young people's art." My wife and daughter scoff in unison.

"Okay," I fess up. "I've been dating Annika. It's still casual and it was stupid to bring her, but I'm the adult here. You're the kid. You have no right to question my actions."

"Oh, sorry . . . Joseph Stalin."

"Honey." Lucy comes to my aid. "He's not as bad as Joseph Stalin."

Gee, thanks for the ringing endorsement, Lucy, but I focus on the situation at hand. "No more smoking pot and no more seeing this Randy character."

"Who's going to stop me?" Sam looks at Lucy. "You're too busy working." Then she turns on me. "And you're too busy fucking your new girlfriend."

Lucy gasps. "Sam, please . . ."

I could smack her right now, I really could. And maybe that's what she needs, some old-fashioned corporal punishment. On the other hand, who knows what the girl is capable of? She'd probably call some child abuse hotline and have me put away for beating her. I struggle to find a response, but no words are coming. Thankfully, Lucy steps up.

"I know we've handled our split badly, but we're still your parents and we still love you more than anything in the world."

For the first time, Sam looks like my daughter again. She takes a ragged breath and her eyes shine with unshed tears. But when she speaks, her voice is cold. "I'm going to bed."

I step forward. "Not so fast, young lady."

"Let her go," Lucy says, resignedly. I look at her, surprised. When Sam was drunk on gin, Lucy had been the one insisting we try to reason with her. Now that she's smoked a little weed, Lucy seems to think she's too compromised for rational conversation. I'd disagree, but I suddenly don't have the energy. A wave of sheer, utter exhaustion engulfs me. As I look at Lucy, I can see she feels the same.

Sam leaves the room, and suddenly the house is eerily quiet. My wife moves to the sectional sofa and sinks into it, defeated. I stand stupidly in the middle of the kitchen for a moment then notice the teapot on the counter where Hope left it. "Tea?" I ask.

Lucy shakes her head. "I'd like you to leave now."

I move to the couch, sit facing her. "We need to talk about this. Samantha is obviously messed up and we need to deal with it."

My wife looks up and our eyes meet. "I'll never, ever forgive you for this," she says softly.

"This isn't my fault . . ." I start, but there is such finality, such resolve in her eyes and in her words, that I stop. Lucy stands up.

"Lock the door on your way out." And I am left alone in what was once my living room.

Lucy

SURPRISINGLY, I FELL into a deep, dreamless sleep. But as the morning sunlight seeps through my sheer curtains, I wake to the sobering realization that my life is a shambles. I lie there, the pale spring sun warming my face, and allow myself to reflect. It would be easy to blame this all on Trent, but obviously, I went wrong somewhere.

I had been so careful. I'd married a good man by all assessable criteria. He had a degree and a career and excellent hygiene. He made me laugh when we were first together, and the sex was playful and exciting. I had truly loved him, and in turn, he'd loved me. So what the hell happened?

When I was pregnant with Sam I'd taken my prenatal vitamins and stayed away from caffeine. Okay, I'd had a small glass of champagne on New Year's Eve, but surely that couldn't cause all this? I'd nurtured Samantha's artistic talents, paid for dance classes and piano lessons and the best private school in the city.

And I had loved her, unconditionally. I still did! But now she'd turned against me.

No, this is my husband's fault, the fucking bastard. Make that my "soon to be ex-husband." As soon as the thought is formed, my anger is replaced by a feeling of loss. For the first time, I realize that my marriage is irretrievably broken, my relationship with Trent beyond repair. No apology could make me accept his selfish behavior. No amount of time will let me forget the heartache he's caused. And no self-help book could persuade me to forgive what he's done to our family.

I dab at a tear seeping out of my eye with the corner of the sheet. I have lost my husband. It hurts, but I can accept it. What I can't accept is losing my daughter. That is simply not an option.

Wrapping my robe around me, I pad to Samantha's bedroom. Before I fell asleep last night, I'd already decided my parenting strategy. As opposed to Trent's bluster and threats, I'm going to show her how much I love her. I'm going to open up and reconnect with her. She needs to know that I love her, even if she is smoking pot or having crystal meth orgies (she was only kidding, thank god, but I'd still love her). I knock gently, then try the door. It's locked. "Sam, honey," I call through the thick wood. "Open up."

There is no response. "Sam?" I knock again. "It's almost ten. Time to wake up." Still, there is no sound from within. I knock again, harder this time. "Sam?" Panic makes my voice shrill. What if she's not there? What if she sneaked out the window to go do drugs with old Randy? What if she's taken an overdose of smack or crank or whatever and she's in a coma? Or worse! I pound the door with my fist. "Sam! Sam!"

It swings open to reveal my daughter, disheveled and still

half asleep. "God!" she grumbles. "Stop yelling." I follow her inside as she flops back into bed. She curls up with her pillow, her back to me. I perch on the side of the bed, hesitantly patting her leg under the comforter. "How are you feeling?"

"Fine," she mumbles into her pillow.

"That was pretty nasty last night."

No response.

"I think your father and I have some growing up to do."

An affirmative snort.

"But you've been acting pretty childishly, too, Sam. I know you probably think drinking and doing drugs is really grown-up, but it's not. It's irresponsible and immature."

Silence.

I sit for a moment, patting her leg and looking around her room. Wynn Felker's handsome, boyish face smiles down at me from his multiple poses on her walls. There he is in a striped T-shirt, his hair blow-dried to perfection. He's jumping off a ladder in the next one, wearing overalls and holding a can of yellow paint. And in this poster, he's in a leather jacket, his hair short and spiky. He smolders in the photo next to it, his chin resting on his bare shoulder.

"Maybe we should paint your room?" I blurt. "That would be a fun project we could do together."

Sam turns back, pulling the comforter from her face with a swift movement of her arm. "What do you want, Mom? I'm tired."

"I want to talk," I say, as a lump of emotion forms in my throat. "I want you to know that I love you more than anything in the world, and I don't want us drifting apart."

"Fine," she growls. "I love you, too. Now can I get some sleep?"

"No," I say. "We need to communicate, Sam. I'm worried about you. Tell me why you dropped out of the art show."

She sighs dramatically. "I don't know. I just didn't feel inspired anymore. I'm bored with art, okay? It's no big deal."

"It is a big deal. You're so talented."

"Right, like I'm going to be the next Picasso. Get real, Mom."

"I am real. There's so much you could do with an art career. Besides, it's always been such a great outlet for you. You can't just drop it because things have been a little rough at home." Sam snorts again and rolls onto her side.

"I'm going to work less," I say. "I'm going to talk to Bruce and see if we can set some more realistic hours. Maybe they can hire a junior buyer to pick up some of the slack."

"Right." It's obvious she doesn't believe me.

"Listen to me, Sam. You are way more important to me than that stupid job." At that precise moment, from somewhere downstairs the theme song to *Cody's Way* starts to play. It's my BlackBerry. I pointedly ignore it. "And your father's moved into his apartment now. We'll get you a room set up there so you can spend more time with him."

"Him and his hot babe."

"Sweetie," I admonish, "she's not that hot. She's just young and has curly hair. If you saw her you'd probably think she was quite fat."

Sam sits up. "Your phone is still ringing. Will you please just go answer it?"

"Honey, we're talking."

"I don't want to talk now, Mom!" she shrieks. "I want to sleep. We can talk later, okay?"

It has been rather torturous letting the phone go unanswered.

"Okay," I acquiesce, hurrying out of her room, "but we're definitely talking when you wake up."

I charge down the stairs only to have the ringing cease the minute I hit the floor. "Shit," I mutter, heading to the kitchen to put on a pot of coffee. But before I've even reached the sink, Cody's theme, "Be True to Yourself," is playing again from the confines of my purse. I hurry to answer it.

"Hey, Lucy," a male voice says brightly. "It's me."

Me? Who is me? I briefly run through the list of male callers who defy introduction: Trent, Bruce, my brother perhaps . . . But it's none of them. I glance at the monstrous bouquet perched near the front door. It's got to be Wynn Felker.

I'm about to say "Hi, Wynn," but I stop. What if it's not him? What if it's Trent disguising his voice? Not that Trent would disguise his voice, I suppose, but maybe he just sounds a lot different now that he's having sex with some overweight whore? It could be someone else entirely—Trent's brother-in-law Seamus, or Hope's Mike. I can't risk exposing our relationship with a "Hi, Wynn"—not that we have any sort of relationship. It was just a bit of kissing. Still, I don't want to end up in the tabloids: Elderly Single Mother of Drug Addict Romancing Teen Heartthrob.

Finally, I say, "Hi there."

"It's Wynn," he says. "I'm back."

"How was your trip?"

"Long. Boring. Nebraska sucks."

"It can't be that bad!" I say with a girlish titter. It comes out completely flirtatious and I suddenly realize my cheeks are hot and my heart is racing. It's disgusting to be flirting with a guy mere seconds after you've stared at his posters plastering your daughter's bedroom wall—especially the one where he's jumping off the ladder in his overalls. I've got to get a grip.

"Thank you for the flowers," I say coolly. "You shouldn't have."

"Glad you liked them," he replies, then, "I want to see you. I have something exciting to tell you."

I start to decline. My focus has to be on my daughter now. But she did request some time to sleep. And it would be more courteous to explain to Wynn, in person, that our drinking and necking session was a big mistake that cannot be repeated. "How about a quick coffee?" I hear myself suggesting.

THANKFULLY, WYNN JOINS me at my neighborhood coffee shop and doesn't insist we meet in some obscure location in the suburbs. He's wearing a baseball cap pulled low over his eyes, but there's no denying his star quality. As he approaches, a few heads turn, but given that the clientele is largely retired couples in their sixties, no one makes a scene.

"Hi," he says, kissing both my cheeks. It's sweet and sort of European and highly unexpected. "You look great."

"So do you," I say. He's unshaven and uncombed, but he still does look great. I suppose it's impossible to look anything but with those features.

"Can I get you a coffee?"

"Please," I say. "I'll have an Americano."

I watch him surreptitiously as he walks to the counter and orders. God, he's hot. The whiskers and ball cap detract from the prettiness, making him almost rugged. It's hard to believe that the man before me is the same cheesy actor featured in

Sam's poster collection. Unbidden, the image of Cody jumping off the stepladder with his can of yellow paint flashes in my mind. I shake it off. I'm here to talk to Wynn Felker, the adult, not his precocious teenage doppelgänger.

When he's returned with our coffees, I immediately say, "What's your big news?" It may be abrupt, but I'm a little nervous. Last time I saw Wynn I was drunk on gin and chewing on his tongue most of the time.

"I called my mom!" he says gleefully. "And my brother. I'm flying them out to Vancouver."

"That's great," I say, truly pleased.

"I thought about what you said, about how your family is your family, even if they're not perfect. And I just thought: why am I letting my managers keep me from seeing my own brother? It's stupid . . . stupider than a lobster mascot."

I burst into laughter. "You're right."

"So what if Dennis is a bit of a stoner. He's my big brother and I love him."

"That's so great." I'm tempted to reach for his hand in a show of support, but it might send the wrong signals. Despite my enthusiasm for Wynn's familial reunion, I can't forget that I'm here to end things with him. Hands on my coffee cup, I say, "They must be so happy."

"They are." Wynn reaches for my hand, obviously having no such qualms. I'm surprised by the physical reaction his touch invokes, but I keep my cool. "And so am I. And I've got you to thank for this."

"Oh . . . no . . ." I look down shyly. "You'd have had the same revelation on your own . . . eventually."

"Yeah, but it could have taken years! I want to thank you," he says. "Can I take you for dinner one night?"

Now is the time to tell him that our make-out session in the Kingsway Inn was an anomaly. I am not the kind of woman who normally drinks five gin and tonics and sucks the face off her much younger coworker. In contrast, I am a devoted if slightly over-wrought mother who was feeling lonely and neglected and made a serious error in judgment. "The other night . . ." I begin, but I'm interrupted by a sudden presence at Wynn's side. A teenage girl in head-to-toe yoga clothes has approached without our noticing.

"Oh my god!" she squeals. "Cody Summers! I mean, Wynn Felker. I love you, like, I love your show." She glances over at me then. "Oh . . . Hi, Mrs. Vaughn."

I snatch my hand from Wynn's. "Uh . . . hi, Jessica," I stammer upon recognizing the interloper. She's grown since I last saw her, but there's no denying that the gawky teen in Lululemon garb is Jessica Watkins from Samantha's former dance class. "How have you been?"

"I'm okay, Mrs. Vaughn. How are you?"

I wish she'd quit saying "Mrs. Vaughn." Given that I'm sitting here with Wynn Felker, she may as well be calling me Grandma Moses. "I'm fine, thanks. Are you still dancing?"

"No," she says. "I'm too busy with school and I'm really getting into yoga."

"Well, good for you," I say dismissively, but Jessica misses the intonation. She turns to Wynn.

"So, what's going to happen when Cody graduates high school? My friends and I hope that you do a show called *Cody's Way: The College Years.*"

"Maybe," Wynn says, "but I don't think I want to play Cody Summers for the rest of my life."

"Yeah, but you have to do a college show!" Jessica squeals. "Pleeeeeze?"

Suddenly, Ava Watkins's angular frame appears and drapes a lithe arm around her daughter's shoulders. Shit! It hadn't occurred to me that she'd be here, too. Just because my daughter would never consider going for coffee with me, I shouldn't assume that's the case with everyone. Ava and Jessica are even wearing matching yoga outfits. They've obviously just been to a mother-daughter-bonding Ashtanga class.

"Who have you found over here?" Ava says, eyeing Wynn.

"It's Cody Summers!" Jessica says excitedly. Then less so, "And Mrs. Vaughn."

Ava gapes at me for the quickest of seconds before composing herself. "Hi, Lucy."

"Hi, Ava."

"Sorry to interrupt your . . . uh . . ."

"Meeting," I jump in. "I work on Cody's—Wynn's show. We were just having a quick meeting."

"Oh, you TV types." Ava laughs. "Always working, even on a Sunday morning when most of us are having family time."

Jessica says, "Could I have your autograph, Cody?" She giggles. "I mean Wynn!"

"Sure," Wynn says, patting his jacket pockets. "Does anyone have a pen?"

"I'll get one from the barista," Jessica says, rushing off.

Ava watches her lanky daughter skip to the counter then places a bony hand on my shoulder. "I just wanted to say how sorry I was to hear about everything."

"Thanks," I reply awkwardly.

"It was bad enough when Trent left you, but then all the troubles with Sam." She mimes drinking from a bottle and then makes a "drunk face": eyes rolling, tongue lolling. "And then this latest fiasco with the art show," she finishes, pityingly.

I can't look at Wynn—if, in fact, he's still sitting across from me. He's probably left, mortified by this mother/daughter assault. And he's undoubtedly wondering why he ever asked me out, a woman who obviously drove her husband away and turned her daughter into a teenage alcoholic. But I can't think about that now. I'm too busy devising ways to kill Hope for betraying my confidence.

"If you need anything," Ava is saying, "feel free to call. Robert and I are both here for you."

Jessica returns with a pen and a paper napkin. "Okay," she squeals, placing them in front of Wynn. "Could you write: 'To Jessica, Love from Wynn Felker, aka Cody Summers'?"

"Sure," Wynn says, scribbling on the napkin. He hands it to her. "There you go."

Jessica looks at the paper, kisses it. "Thank you!"

Ava smiles. "We'll let you get back to your meeting." Then she adds quietly, "You call me if you need me, okay?"

"Right," I grumble. Then I watch mother and daughter exit the coffee shop hand in hand.

Trent

IT MUST BE nice to be Lucy. Okay, maybe not *nice*, but I wish I had someone to blame this whole mess on. I'm sure she's cursing me up and down, bad-mouthing me to our daughter and the entire neighborhood. By now, she's probably called a lawyer and is planning to take me for everything I'm worth. Not to mention that she'll obviously go for full custody of Sam. And once she tells the judge I brought Annika to Sam's art show, she'll undoubtedly get it. I still don't know what the fuck I was thinking.

Not that Annika's presence at Crofton House was the catalyst for Sam's problems. She dropped out of the art show two weeks ago. But clearly it did nothing to heal our family. And it provided a perfect scapegoat for Lucy, or as she would probably say, scape-pig. God, she's nasty. Obviously, she's not going to love Annika, but all the Porky Pig stuff was really going too far. Annika's right, she's probably got an eating disorder or something. I just hope it doesn't rub off on Sam. She's got enough problems.

I look at the clock on the DVD player: 12:45, and still no word from Lucy or Sam. I left them both messages this morning, but I'm not going to harass them. They want space, I'll give them some space. They just have to remember that I'm still a part of this family and therefore need to be kept in the loop.

I turn my attention back to the football game, making a concerted effort to forget about the women in my life. It doesn't work. Lucy can't keep blowing me off like this. I know she's pissed, but we have things to discuss. Sam might need drug counseling, or at least some sort of counseling. And Lucy and I could probably use some professional help sorting through our problems, too.

At that moment the intercom rings. It's Annika. It has to be Annika, since she's the only person who even knows where I live right now. I fully intend to give my new address to Lucy and have Sam come spend the weekend, but it's a little hard to do when they won't even return my freakin' calls. I reach for the phone and buzz Annika up without even saying hello.

Moments later, she knocks on the door. I haul myself off the couch and let her in.

"I really should get a key," she says, hurrying inside with several shopping bags. I shut the door and she turns to me. "How are you?" She kisses my lips before I can answer.

"I'm waiting to hear from Lucy and Sam," I grumble, making my way back to the Karlstad three-seater.

"They still haven't called?" Annika says, taking her load to the small round dining table. The bags crinkle as she withdraws her purchases, nearly muting her voice. Unfortunately, the bags aren't quite loud enough. "I can't believe you were married to that monster for so long. I mean, she's obviously extremely unhappy with herself. You can see that just looking at her. She's got body dysmorphic disorder for sure. But I can't believe she's trying to shut you out of your own daughter's life. Samantha obviously needs her father right now."

"Mmm," I mumble, staring at the football game.

"Trent," Annika says, blocking the TV. She's holding a large, plush dog. "He's a Shar Pei. Isn't he cute?"

"Sure," I say with a shrug.

"He's for Sam," Annika continues, "to cheer her up. I thought maybe we could take her for dinner tonight and give it to her. What do you think?"

I think my daughter is fifteen, not three. I also think having dinner with Annika and me could send Sam off on a crystal-meth-fueled orgy for real. But I don't bother saying any of this. Explaining to Annika why her idea is stupid—make that ludicrous—seems too exhausting. "I still haven't heard from her," I say.

"We'll just wait then," she says, returning the stuffed dog to its bag. She flops on the couch beside me. "We could have sex," she says, playing with my belt, "to take your mind off things?"

I move her hand away. "I'm not in the mood," I say, eyes on the TV.

"Okay." She snuggles up beside me, her curly head resting on my shoulder. "I'll just keep you company."

"You don't have to," I say. "Really . . . Why don't you go enjoy your day? I'm just going to watch the game."

Annika sits up and looks at me. "I'm not going to leave you alone at a time like this." She kisses my forehead, a strangely maternal gesture. "I'm here for you, babe."

She settles back in beside me and we stare at the TV. My mind's not on it, but it beats rehashing the events of last night. Apparently, Annika disagrees. "Your ex-wife is such a critical person that I'm sure Sam feels constantly judged. It's no wonder she dropped out of the art show."

Without any forethought, I hear myself defending Lucy. "She's actually a really good mom."

"Honey, her hands-off parenting style is just asking for trouble."

I sit forward. "She doesn't have a hands-off parenting style. Yeah, she works too much, but it's not like she doesn't care about Sam."

"But to a teenager, the long hours at work must seem like a choice, like she's choosing work over her daughter."

"Until I left, Sam was a happy, well-adjusted kid."

"You can't put this all on you," Annika says, giving my knee a sympathetic squeeze. "If Lucy's going to be the primary parent, she needs to compensate for your absence. And she obviously hasn't done that."

"And you're a parenting expert now, are you?" I snap.

"I'm a child of divorce," she says sagely.

Flopping back onto the couch cushions, I stare at the game. I don't know who's winning. I'm not even sure who's playing. And I'm definitely not sure why I'm feeling so defensive of Lucy. Annika's probably right: Lucy should have cut back her hours after I left—even temporarily. If she'd spent some time helping Sam deal with our split, none of this would have happened.

But even as I say it, I know it's bullshit. It was me who walked out. It was me who was screwing Annika when I should have been spending time with my daughter, showing her that, just because things didn't work out with her mother and me, I still love her more than anything. Maybe Lucy let Sam down, too, but this is on me. No matter what Annika says, I know that.

Annika looks at me, reads the chagrin on my face. She leans on me. "Don't worry. When we have kids, we'll do things a lot differently."

The anger builds quickly, rising to a crescendo in mere seconds. I jump up. "What?" I bellow.

"What?" Annika says, looking a little frightened.

"Are you suggesting I write my daughter off? That it's too late for her, so I should just start over?"

"N-no."

I stab a finger toward her for emphasis. "Because I will never give up on Sam. That girl means more to me than anything . . . than anyone."

"I understand," Annika says, her tone placating. She stands up and leads me back to the couch. "Of course you love Sam and want to help her. I do, too. I'm just saying that maybe we'd do things a little differently—"

I'm off the couch again. "We are not going to have kids!" I boom. "We barely know each other."

"Of course we know each other." She actually sounds annoyed now. "We've been friends for over a year."

"Coworkers," I say, "not friends. Besides," I add, my voice venomous, "I've had a vasectomy. I couldn't have more kids even if I wanted them."

Her face crumples and I almost feel guilty. But I quickly snap out of it. "I think you've been expecting more from me than I'm able to give," I say. "I'm not looking for a new relationship, Annika. I'm not even sure my relationship with Lucy is over."

"Oh my god!" Annika shrieks. She is instantly off the couch

and charging at me. "You're not looking for a new relationship? Well, what the hell do you call this? We fuck practically every night. We furnished your apartment together. You took me to your kid's art show—"

"That was a mistake," I interrupt her. "I was angry at Lucy and trying to teach her a lesson."

"For a year you've been stringing me along, making me think we'd have a future together if only your wife was out of the picture. So now she's out of the picture and you tell me you don't want a relationship with me?"

"I didn't mean to string you along. I was attracted to you. I *am* attracted to you. That doesn't mean I want you buying stuffed dogs for my daughter and decorating my apartment and planning how we're going to raise our kids together!"

Annika just glares at me. Her chest is rising and falling with the heat of her anger. If this were a movie, she'd slap me across the face and then I'd throw her over the Karlstad and screw her brains out. It's an appealing possibility, but somehow I think it would be a mistake.

"You fucking asshole," she finally says, marching toward the door. She struggles into her coat and boots. "You don't give a shit about me at all."

A small part of me thinks it would be wise to let her storm out under that misconception, but old habits die hard. "Of course I give a shit about you," I plead. "You've been great, really. I'm just under a lot of pressure with Sam and everything. I didn't mean to make you feel bad."

"Well, you did," Annika snivels, retrieving the plastic bag and its canine contents. "You made me feel like a fool and an idiot and . . . a whore."

She's full-fledged crying now, and I feel like crap. "I'm sorry. I didn't mean to . . . Look, just forget what I said. I was venting and—"

She cuts me off. "Good-bye, Trent." In a rustle of plastic shopping bags, she's gone.

Lucy

I'VE MANAGED TO avoid the office completely today. It would be too awkward seeing Wynn after our disastrous coffee date. All that "So sorry to hear about your booze-guzzling daughter and philandering husband, *Mrs. Vaughn*." Plus, it's St. Patrick's Day and everyone's wearing green and pretending they're half Irish and talking about getting drunk. It's annoying.

Thankfully, Cody's summer job at a dude ranch has required I spend the entire day at a farm supply store in Cloverdale. By 2:50 P.M. I've spent two thousand dollars on feed buckets, rope, and horse tack. With my purchases safely stowed in the back of my truck, I head to Crofton House School.

As I fly down the freeway, I dial my cell phone. It rings on the other end and I pray for voice mail. This is not going to be an easy conversation. Bruce is a reasonable man, but he's a props master first and foremost. He hired me to work my ass off during filming and to rest on hiatus. It would never occur to him that a props buyer would allow her personal life to interfere.

But I meant what I said to Sam. I'm going to cut back on my hours, whether Bruce likes it or not. Of course, it's completely realistic that he might fire me, but I would rather be an unemployed single mother collecting welfare than a neglectful, worka— Bruce answers.

"Hi," I say, chipperly. "It's Lucy."

"How's it going out there?" he asks.

"Great! I've got everything for the dude ranch shoot."

"Good work. You coming in now?"

My voice wavers a little, but I plunge ahead. "No, I'm going to pick up my daughter from school."

There's a silence on the other end that I feel compelled to fill. "She's been having a difficult time lately—with her dad and me splitting up. I told her I'd talk to you about cutting back on my hours."

"What do you mean by 'cutting back'?"

"Well," I say, mustering all my courage, "I'd like to finish at three every day so I can pick her up from school."

There's a noise on the other end—possibly laughter. "Why don't you come in so we can talk about this in person?"

"I can't. I'm going to pick her up right now."

"Lucy, you can't just spring this on me. We're in a time crunch because Wynn's taking some time off in a few weeks. His family's coming in from Arizona."

"New Mexico," I correct him.

"Wherever. You need to come in."

"I can't, Bruce," I say, defiantly taking the Willingdon exit. This is the fastest route to my daughter's school and tangibly marks my intention. "I told Sam I'd be there and I can't let her down."

"But it's fine to let me down—to let the whole production down?"

He's angry now, and I sense I could be on the verge of getting fired. "I'll be in early tomorrow. We can talk about it then." Quickly, I hang up and turn off the ringer.

Despite my best efforts, I'm still fifteen minutes late to pick up Sam. I fly into the parking lot and slam the vehicle into a space. Jesus, I'm all worked up. I take a deep, calming breath before jumping out of the car. I just hope Sam doesn't think I've forgotten to pick her up. I picture my daughter riding the bus, staring forlornly out the window at the afternoon traffic. "I guess my mom isn't going to change after all," she'd mumble to herself. When she arrived home, she'd let herself into the cold, cavernous house. "I'll make myself a snack," she'd say, "or maybe I'll just have some crank or blow."

I'm about to dial her cell phone when I see her standing with a group of girls at the corner of the playing field. "Sam!" I call, relief making my voice jubilant. "I'm here!" My daughter's posture changes slightly, but she doesn't exactly run toward me. She and her friends watch me as I traverse the soggy field. Their teenage inspection makes me feel self-conscious.

"Hi, girls," I say as I approach.

"Hi, Mrs. Vaughn." It's Carolyn, a pretty Korean girl who somehow manages to make her conservative school uniform look slutty.

"Hey, Mrs. Vaughn." Oh good, Sam's drinking buddy Jordan is here.

"Hi, there." This comes from a pale blond girl I've not seen before. "I'm Tara."

"Hi, Tara. I'm Sam's mom." I turn to my daughter. "Sorry I'm late."

She shrugs. "I forgot you were even picking me up."

"Well I am . . . from now on."

"Whatevs," she says. Then, addressing her friends: "Text ya later."

"Bye," I say. "Nice meeting you, Tara."

"You, too."

Sam is already making her way across the soggy field and I hurry to catch up.

"How was your day?"

"Good," she replies indifferently.

"Tara seems nice. Is she in your grade?"

"Yeah, she just transferred here. She got kicked out of public school but her dad knows the dean of Crofton."

I look at her to see if she's just pushing my buttons. It's hard to tell, but I'd have to assume yes. Crofton House is not the type of school to pick up delinquents from the public system. But it would be antagonistic to call her on it.

"What should we do now?" I say instead. "I'm off all afternoon. We could go shopping or to the art gallery?"

"Aren't you going to get fired?" Sam mumbles as we approach the parking lot.

"No," I say as convincingly as I can. "I told Bruce that I need to rework my schedule so that I can be available for you. He understands."

Sam makes a sort of snorting noise, but the subject is dropped. We get into the vehicle and I back carefully out of the parking lot.

"So," I say, as we turn onto bustling Forty-first Avenue. "Where to?"

"Home," she mumbles, staring out the window.

"Okay. Do you have a lot of homework to get to?"

"Not really. I just don't feel like traipsing around the mall holding my mommy's hand."

She's being a rude brat, but what else is new? I decide to let it slide. "Fine. Home it is."

Fifteen silent minutes later, we pull into our driveway. When the car stops, Sam hops out and heads for the door.

"You're welcome!" I call after her.

"I said thanks," she grouches. "You just didn't hear me."

Inside, I find myself alone in the kitchen, Sam having declined my offer of popcorn and a movie. "I'm tired," she'd said, trudging up the stairs. I decide to sort through the day's props purchases. This way, though I'm not officially working, I'll be slightly less behind when I arrive tomorrow. When I've unloaded the back of my SUV, the living room floor is a sea of plastic bags. I extract the halters, the feed buckets, the ropes, and the kilogram bags of oats, removing tags and preparing them for use. Then I grab the enormous armload of plastic bags and stuff them in the broom closet. It takes some effort to get the door closed again, but I manage. With that complete, I decide to check my voice messages.

Under different circumstances, having messages from three men would be flattering. Unfortunately, one wants to berate me, another wants to coerce me into going for dinner with him when it's simply not possible, and the third wants to fire me.

Trent's message was significantly calmer than the one he left yesterday, though. In fact, he sounded almost apologetic. I listen again.

"Hi, Lucy, it's me. I just wanted to say that I hope things are okay with you and Sam. I'm probably the last person either of you wants to see, but please tell her that I care about her—about you both. When Sam's ready to talk . . . or if you want to talk, give me a call." There is a pause before he hangs up, almost as if he wanted to say more then decided against it.

I can't deny that his plaintive tone tugs at my heartstrings. But as usual, Trent's timing is all wrong. It was only yesterday that I had an epiphany about our relationship: it's over and there's no going back. So why do I want so badly to call him? Why do I crave the sound of his voice telling me everything will be all right? Force of habit, I guess. For almost half my life I've been turning to him for support. And now, when I need it most, I can't.

To counterbalance the nostalgia, I replay Wynn's message, too.

"Hey, Lucy, it's me. You ran out so quickly after our coffee yesterday that we didn't get to plan dinner. I'd really like to take you out to thank you for your advice and . . . well, I'd really like to take you out. If you're in the office, come find me on set. Or else call me, okay? . . . It's Wynn Felker, by the way."

When the message ends I realize I'm smiling like an idiot— or more like an adolescent girl who just got asked out on a date by a teen heartthrob. I can't go, obviously. My life's a mess and Wynn would only complicate things further. But he really is sweet—and hot of course. And his persistence is a great salve to my battered ego. But I can't go out with him. Can I?

I realize my messages are still playing when I hear Bruce's voice. "I think you need to get in here and talk to me face-to-face. You can't just spring something like this on me over the phone. When one of my props buyers informs me she's going to be working half-days, that impacts the productivity of my department and that could screw up the whole shooting schedule."

"Half-days," I snort under my breath as I delete the message. Only in the TV industry would working seven hours be considered a half-day. But I can't deny that it was unprofessional of me not to mention this before. Of course, before I didn't know that my daughter was teetering on the brink of becoming a teenage alcoholic/drug addict/slut. I need to make Bruce understand my situation. And I need to do it in person.

Once again, I find myself hovering outside my daughter's locked bedroom door. "Knock, knock," I call over the sounds of Good Charlotte or one of those sound-alike bands.

The door swings open and Sam faces me with a sullen glare. "How's the homework coming?" I chirp. I'm just making conversation, but my daughter seems to take it as some sort of assault on her work ethic.

"I can't relax for like, ten seconds after I've been at school all day? It'll get done, okay? God!"

"I just—" But there's no point explaining. "I've got to run to the office for half an hour. Will you be okay?"

"I'll be fine," she snaps. "It's not like I haven't spent the last two years sitting alone in this house till seven o'clock at night."

"Those days are over," I say forcefully. "I just need to sort some stuff out with Bruce and then I'll be home to make dinner. How about spaghetti?"

Sam snorts. "I don't eat pasta." She says the word *pasta* like she's saying *human eyeballs*.

"Fine. I'll make something else." I try to kiss her cheek but she pulls away. "See you soon," I say, keeping my voice steady, though my emotions threaten to overtake me. My husband may be gone, but I can't lose my daughter. I won't.

Trent

THERE'S A REASON why companies have policies against office romances. And as I watch Annika stride, make that stomp, past my office, I wish mine did. If Shandling & Wilcox had had such a policy in place, this mess could have been avoided. On the other hand, it's possible, even likely, that I would have ignored the rule and still gone to bed with her. My dick definitely had control over my brain for a while there. But now it seems my brain has overthrown my dick in a military coup, restoring order and reason. Unfortunately, this allows me to see all too clearly what a bad fucking idea it was getting involved with a woman I work with.

So I would have nailed Annika even if there was an office policy, but at least we would have had to keep it a secret. Annika always acted as though it was common knowledge we were together. She almost seemed proud of it. But now that things have gone sour she's huffing around like this is ninth grade and her boyfriend forgot her birthday. Obviously, the whole god-damn office knows we were together in the first place, and that we've now broken up.

I hear Annika's laughter from down the hall, devoid of mirth and entirely self-conscious. It's obvious she's laughing at me. She's probably telling Karen from accounting that my daughter's a teen-age drug addict or that my wife has an eating disorder. I hear a return titter from Karen, and a heartier laugh—Dave maybe? Oh god, what if Annika's so mad she's telling the staff I'm bad in bed? I mean, I totally redeemed myself after that first fiasco, but hell hath no fury. I can only hope all my coworkers get so pissed on green beer tonight that they'll have forgotten about it by tomorrow.

I try to focus on paperwork, but it's hard. For the sixty-eighth time today I check my cell phone for messages. None. I vowed not to harass Lucy or Sam, but they seem hell-bent on torturing me by exclusion. They act as if I gave up all rights to the family when I left—or more accurately, when I started dat-ing Annika. And that thought just hammers the point home: Annika was a huge mistake.

For just a moment, I allow myself to reflect. Why did I feel the need to leave Lucy and Sam? Were things really that bad? I was bored, there's no denying that. Lucy worked too much and our sex life had become rote. But was walking out the right answer? Couldn't I have asked her to cut back on her hours? Brought home a French maid's costume for her to wear or something? Sure, Lucy might have been pissed off. We probably would have fought about it and there would have been tension and harsh words. But is what I have now really better?

And I realize that what I have now is exactly nothing. Oh, I've got a one-bedroom-and-den apartment full of practically fluorescent Ikea furniture. I've still got my job—although my coworkers think I'm a laughingstock. I've got my car, and I do love my car. But what do I have that really matters? Fuck all. No wife, no girlfriend, no daughter. I need to take a piss.

I've just stood up when she appears in my doorway. "Hello," she says coolly. "Going somewhere?"

"To the bathroom," I say lamely.

She steps into my office. "Were you ever going to come and talk to me, or did you think our problems would just miraculously solve themselves?"

I sigh heavily. "Look, Annika, I'd rather keep our problems out of the workplace, if you don't mind."

"It's a little late for that. Everyone knows we're going through a rough patch, but they totally support us."

"Oh."

"Karen was just saying that she thinks we make a great couple and that what we have is worth working on. What do you think?"

What the hell am I supposed to say? "Look, there's a lot going on in my life right now and . . . I really have to pee."

"It's a simple yes or no answer, Trent." Her hands are on her hips and her voluptuous size suddenly seems downright menacing.

"I don't know," I say, shifting my position to try to staunch the urgent need to take a whiz. "I guess so."

"Good. Because I think what we have is too precious to throw away. If I'm willing to do the work and you are, too, then we'll be fine."

"Fine," I say, attempting to push past her. She stops me with a hand to the chest.

"Take this." She passes me a piece of paper. I look at it. It reads:

Yasmine Wheeler
Relationship Coach
10:00 A.M., March 24
2300 West Georgia

"This was not an easy appointment to get," Annika continues. "But a friend of my cousin's knows Coach Wheeler. We're lucky she could squeeze us in."

A relationship coach? Why the hell do we need to see a relationship coach?

"If we're going to have a future together, we obviously need professional help," Annika explains.

"Professional help?" I'm about to say that Lucy and I were together for eighteen years without professional help, but then I realize that might just prove Annika's point.

"I'm not going to harass you about this, Trent. If you show up at the appointment on the twenty-fourth, I'll know you're serious about us. If you don't, then I'll consider it over."

"Okay."

"In which case, you'll have to find a new job."

"What?"

"It would be too awkward for us both to be working here, and I've already talked to Don about it. He agreed that I have more clients and am better for the corporate culture and staff spirit even though you have more seniority."

Oh my god. Is this fucking happening? I think the urgent need to urinate has caused renal failure leading to hallucinations. "Whatever," I grumble, forcing my way past her.

I charge down the hall, avoiding the sympathetic eyes of my female coworkers and the repressed smirks of the males. Bursting into the bathroom, I rush to the urinal. Ahhh . . . relief:

physical relief at least. Mentally and emotionally, I'm still tortured. How the hell did this all happen to me? My wife hates me, my daughter has shut me out, and now Annika's threatening my job if I don't go to relationship counseling with her. We've been dating for a fucking month!

I zip up my pants and turn to the sink. As I wash my hands I stare at my reflection. That eye cream I bought was a complete waste of money. I look older and more haggard than ever. It's the stress—that and the physical toll of having marathon sex with a nymphomaniac four nights a week. I can't keep this up. But what are my options? Unemployment? Welfare? Angrily, I rip a piece of paper towel from the dispenser, wipe my hands, and toss it in the garbage can. I miss, but I don't pick it up.

As I charge out into the hallway and back to my office, I resolve to put all this shit out of my mind. At least I can focus on work for another seven or eight hours. Returning my attention to a mutual fund spreadsheet, it seems to be working—except for one lingering, disturbing thought: the mess I'm in is all my own fucking fault.

Lucy

"YOU NEED TO understand my position," I said, as I faced Bruce across his cluttered desk. "I'm a single parent now, and I need to be there for my daughter."

"You need to understand *my* position," Bruce countered. "I've got a show to do, and that requires a full-time props buyer. And I hired a full-time props buyer two years ago when I hired you."

"What about bringing on a junior buyer?" I suggested. "I could train him in the mornings, and then he could take over in the afternoons?"

"Good idea." Bruce's voice dripped with sarcasm. "So you'll be half as productive in the mornings, and then you'll swan off at three o'clock and leave some kid to do your job."

I struggled with an overwhelming desire to tell him to fuck off, but then remembered something about burning bridges and how it's a small industry. Still, it seemed a better option than bursting into tears, which was also a tempting possibility. "It wouldn't be like that," I managed to mumble.

"It's not going to work," Bruce said, taking a sip from his coffee cup. "I'm not going to pay two salaries so you can have your afternoons free. You work here a full day or you don't work here at all. I'm sorry."

"Fine," I said, hanging on to my righteous anger. If I let it go for even a second, I'd dissolve into a puddle of emotion. "If you can't respect my family, then I guess this isn't the right place for me."

"I guess it isn't."

I stood up. "All right then."

"All right."

Change your mind, I willed him. *I'll stand here for ten more seconds.* But Bruce turned to his computer and I was effectively dismissed.

That was forty-two hours ago. Now I find myself, once again, curled up on my sofa weeping for all that I have lost. You'd think there'd be a limit to the amount of saline the body can produce, but apparently not. I've easily cried seventeen times my body weight in tears over the past month. All this grief is probably aging me, the water loss turning me into a wrinkled prune. No amount of Botox can help me now! I have no husband, no job, and I look like I'm seventy years old. This must be what's known as "rock bottom."

I'm on the verge of a fresh emotional breakdown when the phone rings. I'd leave it, but the way my life is going lately, it's probably Crofton House calling to tell me Sam's been caught having lesbian sex in the music room.

"Hello?"

"Lucy, it's Hope." It's like she has some kind of homing device for misery. "What are you doing home?"

I can't tell her. Based on my run-in with Ava Watkins, Hope can't be trusted not to blab my misfortune to the entire neighborhood. "Sore throat," I say coldly.

"Oh dear," she says. "Do you want some soup? I've got homemade chicken stock in the freezer. I can whip up a soup and run it over to you for dinner?"

"No, thanks."

"Are you sure?"

"I'm sure," I snap. I'm really angry with her, but I don't have the emotional energy for a confrontation. "I'm going to have a nap now."

"Okay, I just wanted to find out how things went with Sam. I've been so worried."

"She'll be okay."

"It's so sad to see her crying out for help like that. I mean, divorce is devastating to kids. If there's any way you and Trent can hold on to your marriage, at least for Samantha's sake . . ."

I jump in. "There's not."

"I know it's hard to forgive; I've been there, remember? But Mike and I have made a commitment to stay together to give our kids a stable, loving home. It's really allowed them to blossom these past few years—especially Sarah-Louise. She was always shy and awkward, and now she's in the national spelling bee and the junior band. They've just been invited to play at the pregame warm-up show for a professional soccer game in May. I don't know if all that would have happened if she'd come from a broken home."

"Maybe," I grumble.

"All I know is that dating is not the answer, Lucy. As much as you feel the need for attention and affection, you can't give up on the years you and Trent spent together."

"What are you talking about?" But I already know.

"Ava said she saw you with Wynn Felker."

"That was a meeting!" I say shrilly. "And why do you and Ava Watkins feel compelled to discuss every detail of my personal life, even when I specifically asked you to keep it quiet?"

"It's not like that," Hope pleads. "Ava came to pick up Jessica at our house shortly after I left you and Trent. I was upset and she was concerned. We weren't gossiping. We were talking about you as caring friends."

"Right, okay. So if I called Ava and told her I was concerned because I saw Mike out at a bar with some hot blonde—that would be okay?"

"What?" Her voice tells me I've hit a nerve.

I shouldn't do this now. I'm angry and overwrought and could say something cruel and hurtful. On the other hand, I've lost my husband and my job, and my relationship with my daughter is hanging by a thread. I may as well lose my best friend, too.

"I saw Mike at the bar a couple of weeks ago. He was there with Trent and that chunky tart of his. And there was a blond woman with them too. Mike seemed to be enjoying her company quite a lot."

Hope's voice is weak. "What are you saying?"

"I'm saying that you shouldn't go around spouting off about your great marriage! It's not great. Mike's a selfish asshole and he totally takes you for granted. You stay at home cooking and cleaning and sewing while he's off gallivanting around the world with other women!"

"That's in the past."

"Right. You go on believing that so you can keep up the façade of your perfect little life. Well, it's not perfect. Before you start judging me, you should take a long look in the mirror."

"I never said my marriage was perfect," Hope says, her voice shaking with repressed emotion. "But I've made a choice to do what's best for my family."

"Really? So I'm a selfish bitch because I don't want to be treated like a doormat? So, it would be better for Sam if I let Trent walk all over me and have affairs while I wait patiently for him with a big stupid smile on my face?"

There is a long pause. A line has been crossed, and neither of us knows what to say next.

"I'm sorry you feel that way," she finally says.

"Well, I'm sorry you feel the need to judge the way I'm living my life."

"I was trying to be supportive."

"By telling Ava Watkins that Sam's been drinking? By whispering about my so-called date with Wynn Felker? By giving me a stupid book that tells me to let my husband treat me like shit because it's better than being alone?"

"Fine," Hope says, and I can hear the tears in her voice. "I tried to be there for you, Lucy, but don't worry. I won't interfere in your life again."

The finality in her tone makes me panic. "Hope . . ." I say plaintively, but she's not hearing it.

"Good luck with . . . everything." And she hangs up.

As I replace the phone on the receiver I now know for sure: this is definitely what they mean by rock bottom.

Trent

"HELLO?"

I hadn't expected her to answer. Lucy's never home at 4:30. "Oh, hey Lucy. It's me. I didn't uh . . . expect you to be home."

"Well, I am," she retorts. "Did you want to speak to Sam?"

"Yeah, but . . . could we talk for a sec?" Why do I sound so fucking nervous? It's like I'm fourteen and calling a girl I have a crush on for the first time.

"What have we got to talk about?"

Is she kidding me? We've only got everything to talk about: our daughter, our marriage, our future. "We need to talk about Sam," I say, containing my annoyance. "How's she doing?"

"She's fine," Lucy snaps, "since you're suddenly so concerned."

I stay cool. "What's that supposed to mean?"

"I don't know. I just thought you might be too busy banging your fat slut to give your daughter much thought."

That's it. "Can you grow up for five seconds and act like a parent?"

"Oh, I'm sorry. Why don't I follow your lead and be the mature, responsible one for a change?"

Why does she always have to be so sarcastic? I was actually missing her ten minutes ago. "Look," I say, "I'm sorry that I hurt you. I feel like shit if it makes you feel any better."

There is a pause. "A little."

I can't help but laugh. To my relief, I hear Lucy laugh, too. When we've stopped there's a long pause. Finally I say, "How did everything get so fucked up?"

"You left us, that's how." Any trace of humor is gone.

"I was an idiot. I'm starting to see that now."

It's quiet on the other end of the line, and I think I hear her crying. Finally she says, "I'll get Sam."

"Lucy—" I begin, but she's already put the phone down. As I wait for my daughter to come on the line, I think about what I could have said, what I should have said. At the very least, I should have asked if we could get together as a family. Maybe we could all go for dinner? Or to a movie? I should have told her that Annika and I broke up. At least I think we did. But maybe I should wait until I know for sure, before I mention it to Lucy. I wouldn't want to get her hopes up.

"Hello?" The voice is sullen and devoid of expression. It's obviously Sam.

"Hi, honey. How are you doing?"

"Fine."

"Good. I've been worried about you. I wish you would have called me."

She snaps back, "I've been busy, okay? Jeez."

Busy doing what? Having pot parties with thirty-year-old

dope fiends? I want to say it, but I think again. "Is school going okay?"

"Yeah."

"Good . . . good." A panicky sensation takes over me. Christ. I don't even know how to talk to my own kid anymore. "I want you to come for a sleepover this weekend," I add quickly. "I've got a sofa bed for you. We can order pizza, rent a bunch of movies . . ."

"That sounds like a blast, Dad, but I've got other plans."

She's quickly turning into a mini version of her mother. "Sam, you're my daughter. It's important that we spend time together."

"Maybe you should have thought about that before you moved out of the house. I've got my own stuff going on. I don't have time to go on sleepovers."

Unsure of how to respond, I grumble, "Put your mother back on the phone."

Without a word, the line goes quiet. I wait . . . ten seconds . . . twenty . . . thirty . . . Finally: "She's in the bath. She'll call you tomorrow."

It's a lie; I know it is. But what can I do? Insist Lucy get on the phone? My family seems to consider me a blustering bully at the moment, and making demands is not going to help. "Okay. Well, I hope to see you this weekend. At least for dinner?"

"I told you I'm busy, Dad."

"But you have to eat!" Before I've finished speaking, there's a click and the line goes dead.

I hang up. If I had the energy, I'd punch the wall in frustration. Instead, I go to the fridge for a beer. When I return to the couch, I flick on the TV. I stare at the programs blindly: a rerun of *Friends*, a hockey game, a reality show where two adults are standing idly by watching a nine-year-old have a temper tantrum . . . I turn the set off and let the silence envelop me. But it's not silent. As I nurse my beer, I hear the sounds of my neighbors going about their lives. A soft bang signals a cupboard door closing. Somewhere a faucet turns on. There's the dull thud of the bass on someone's stereo.

This is what I wanted: time to be alone, to sort out the rest of my life. So why does it feel so strange and sort of lonely? I'm not used to it, that's all. I went from spending all my time with Sam and Lucy to spending all my time with Annika. And now the solitude stretches out before me, days, months, even years of isolation. If this is what I wanted, I must have been out of my fucking mind.

But I may as well use this time productively. I need to develop a strategy for getting my life back on track. In the span of a month I've lost everything: my wife, my home, and my daughter. Yeah, I wanted a change, but it wasn't supposed to be like this. I need to treat this as a business scenario: identify my objectives and develop a plan to achieve them. What's so hard about that? Nothing—except that what I really want is to rewind my life back to the night before I walked out.

Lucy

SAM FOUND ME curled up under a blanket, watching a home renovation show. She was holding the phone, her other hand over the receiver. "Dad wants to talk to you again."

My shoulders sagged with exhaustion. "I don't have the energy to deal with him."

"So . . . What? Am I supposed to tell him that?"

"Tell him . . . I'm in the bath. I'll call him tomorrow."

My daughter stalked out of the room, her retreating form speaking into the phone. "She's in the bath. She'll call you tomorrow."

As stupid as it was, I felt almost guilty lying to Trent. He just sounded so alone, so genuinely remorseful. But I had to remember all that he'd done to Sam and me. He'd lied and he'd cheated and he'd deserted us. He'd driven my daughter out of the art show and into pot-smoking Randy's apartment. To feel anything resembling pity for him was ludicrous! To feel bad for rejecting his phone call was insanity!

By no means spurred on by my misplaced guilt, a bath did seem like a good idea. I called to Sam. "I'll be in the tub!" Not surprisingly, she didn't respond. She was probably hoping I was off to slit my wrists. If I were a less responsible parent, I'd be considering it about now.

But immersing myself in warm, lavender-scented water was an excellent idea. I'm able to savor this moment, this small luxury that reminds me that life really is worth living. There will be other jobs, and maybe there will be other men. I allow myself to think about Wynn Felker for a moment. While the intensity of my reminiscences is starting to fade, I still feel a little thrill when I recall the feeling of his mouth and his hands roaming my back. Obviously, a repeat performance with "Cody Summers" is out of the question, but it's comforting to know that I'm not completely dead inside. Despite the hurt and betrayal I've suffered, I can still derive some pleasure from a warm bath and a remembered kiss.

I decide to shave my legs. It's been days, perhaps a week. There hasn't seemed to be much point lately. As the pink razor cuts through the piglike bristles that have sprouted all over my shin, I think about Hope. Maybe I was too hard on her? It couldn't be easy hearing that your husband is out flirting with women while you're home quizzing your genius daughter on spelling words. I didn't want to hurt her, but she's living in a fantasy world. She sits at home sewing placemats and baking butter tarts while Mike runs around snorkeling and flirting and getting plastic surgery. And she has the nerve to judge my crumbling marriage? My pot-smoking daughter? On the other hand,

Sarah-Louise didn't fall off the rails during her parents' marital crisis. God, maybe Hope's really on to something?

Suddenly the bathroom door bursts open, startling me. I fumble the razor, causing it to slice cleanly across my ankle bone. I look down to find the wound has produced a surprising amount of blood. "Shit," I say, dropping my foot in the water to rinse it away. As soon as I remove it, the torrent continues. Christ, could I have hit an artery? Then I look up at my daughter, and suddenly, bleeding to death is the last thing on my mind. Sam's face is alight, animated . . . happy!

"Oh my god, Mom! Thank you so much!"

"What? What did I do?"

"I heard a car in the driveway, so I looked out and I was all like, 'Who do we know that drives a Porsche,' and then he got out and he has flowers and he's at the door right now!"

It takes me only a second to process the information, but apparently that's too long. In that minuscule span of time, Samantha has fluffed her hair in the mirror and hurried to answer the door.

"Sam! No! Wait!" I scream, jumping from the tub. Water pours off my body, soaking the bathmat and the floor, but I don't pause to dry off. Grabbing the nearest towel, I wrap it around my nakedness and fly down the stairs.

From my vantage point on the stairwell, I watch my child open the door as if in slow motion. The bouquet of flowers is visible first, its expensive blooms almost concealing his face. But there's no mistaking that it's him. The battered leather jacket, the thick brown hair not covered by a ball cap this time. Sam jumps up and down girlishly for a moment before composing herself. "Hi, Wynn," she says.

"Hey," he replies smoothly. "You must be Sam."

"Yep!" she says, dissolving into a nervous giggle. "Umm . . . come in."

He steps into the foyer. "So . . ." he begins, and I know I have mere nanoseconds to react.

"Wynn!" I scream, as I barrel down the staircase in my towel. I'm still soaked and blood pours from the severed ankle artery, but I can't stop. If I don't intercept their meeting, I'll lose Sam forever.

"There you are," he says, his handsome face relaying his confusion.

"Here I am," I pant, skidding to a stop in front of them.

He points at my ankle. "Are you okay? You're bleeding."

"Mom!" Samantha says, mortified. Jesus, Sam, I'm bleeding on the floor, not *peeing*.

"I'm fine." My eyes bore into Wynn's. "Thanks so much for popping by to cheer up my daughter. She's always wanted to meet you, and she's been going through a rough time lately."

"Mom!" Sam cries louder. Apparently, revealing her troubles to Wynn Felker is more embarrassing than bleeding or peeing on the floor.

"What?" I turn to her. "Sorry."

Wynn seems a little slow to catch on. "Actually, I wanted to talk to you about what's going on at work."

"Right, sure, we can do that. But you brought Sam flowers! That's so nice of you."

I give him a deranged look that says, If you don't hand those flowers to my daughter this instant, I will slash your throat with a Daisy razor.

A little nervously, he hands the bouquet over. "These are for you, Sam."

She giggles again. "Thanks!"

"Don't just stand there," I say to her. "Go put them in water!"

"Okay . . ."

"And trim the stems on an angle. They'll last longer. But don't cut yourself."

"Okay . . ." She reluctantly walks away.

When she's safely out of earshot, I hiss, "What are you doing at my house?"

"I can't believe Bruce fired you. He can't do that."

"He can and he did. That doesn't mean you can show up here like this. My daughter is in a precarious state right now. If she thinks there's something going on between her mom and Cody Summers, who knows what she'll do."

Wynn looks at me coyly. "Is there something going on between us?" His finger reaches out and just barely touches the corner of the towel I'm wearing. I gasp, blush, and become instantly aroused. It's a small gesture, but given that I'm standing naked, mere inches away from one of the hottest men I've ever encountered, it's a little intense. I'm a terrible mother. I step back. "There can't be," I say. "It's way too complicated."

He steps forward. "It doesn't have to be."

God he's sexy. But I will not be swayed. It's true that our drunken make-out session has been the sexual highlight of the last four years of my life (I refuse to give credit to my post-split fornication with Trent on the couch), and that a surge of primal, animal lust is making my groin tingle and my legs feel weak, but I am a mother first and foremost. I take a large, adamant step back. Unfortunately, I am unaware that approximately a liter of ankle blood has pooled behind me. I slip and fall unceremoniously on my ass.

Wynn reaches for me, but it's too late. "Shit!" he says, thankfully not laughing. "Are you okay?"

The crash has brought Sam scurrying from the kitchen. "What happened?" she cries, the paring knife still in her hand. "Mom!" But there is no concern in her voice, only . . . disgust. "Your boob," she finishes more quietly.

Instinctively, I reach for the towel and find that she's right. In the tumble, my left boob has seen fit to pop out—or more accurately, *flop* out, given the state of my forty-year-old breasts. I suddenly wish Camille had bought me implants instead of a Botox treatment.

"Oh no!" I cry, quickly covering myself.

"God!" Sam says. "Gross!"

Wynn reaches a hand out to me. "Let me help you up."

As I raise my hand to meet his, I'm convulsed by uncontrollable laughter. I'm hysterical, obviously, but suddenly it all seems so goddamn funny! I'm sitting on the floor in a pool of blood, wearing only a towel. My left boob has just fallen out in front of the Choice Hottie. My teenage daughter thinks I'm an embarrassment and disgusting and she's probably right. I've lost my job, my best friend, and the only man who wants anything to do with me is known to the world as a seventeen-year-old boy! With Sam and Wynn watching me helplessly, I lean back on my elbows and laugh until the tears come.

Trent

"I NEVER SAID I'd choose Annika over you," Don Spencer is saying. His lithe runner's frame reclines in his leather office chair. He seems to be taking this whole thing rather casually. "She came barging into my office crying that she didn't think she could work with you anymore. I had to say something to calm her down."

"Okay," I say, leaning back in my own chair as relief washes over me. "I'm sorry you had to get involved in this."

"Me, too. And I'm sorry you don't have enough sense not to sleep with a coworker."

I nod sheepishly. "It was a mistake. I can see that now."

"Is it over between you two then?"

"I think so. I don't know. She wants us to go to a relationship coach."

"A relationship coach?" He sits up. "After you've been banging her for a month?"

I mirror his action and sit forward. "I know. She's gotten way too serious. It's scary."

Don chuckles quietly. "I'm sorry Trent, but you've really dropped yourself in it this time."

"Yeah."

"I mean, Annika's very attractive, but she's always come across as a little . . . desperate, you know?"

No, I don't know, asshole. Otherwise I never would have slept with her. But I nod and shrug.

"How's Lucy doing with all this?"

"How do you think?" I say. "She's pissed."

"And Sam?"

I think about Lucy's entreaty to Hope to keep our daughter's pot-smoking, drop-out behavior quiet. But I suddenly realize I haven't talked to anyone about our situation in months. My world has turned upside down, and I'm dealing with it utterly alone. Don's my boss, so not exactly the ideal confidant, but what choice do I have?

"She's had a hard time," I say, horrified to feel a lump of emotion forming in my throat. "She's angry and hurt and . . . she's rebelling."

"What's she been doing?"

"She dropped out of her art show and . . ." My voice breaks. "She's been drinking."

"That's a pretty normal reaction," Don says knowingly. He has two sons, now in their twenties. "But kids are resilient. She'll get over it."

I realize that if I speak, I run the risk of bursting into tears. It's weak and pathetic, but I can't help it. Maybe I'm depressed?

Don stands and moves around the desk to pat my shoulder heartily. "Why don't you take some vacation time and sort yourself out?"

I shrug, nod. Shit. A tear just leaked out of the corner of my eye.

"Your job is safe, okay?" Don says. He probably thinks I'm about to have a nervous breakdown or something. He might be right. "And maybe you and Annika should see this counselor?"

My head snaps up to look at him. "What? Why?"

He continues. "A professional should be able to make her see that this was just a roll in the hay that got blown out of proportion."

He's right. Why didn't I think of that? I guess that's why he's the boss. "Thanks," I croak, clearing my throat loudly as I stand.

Another hearty pat on the back. "Take a few days." It's a command now, not a suggestion. "You'll get through this."

I start to walk out of his office and then stop. "Thanks for understanding." My voice cracks and I make some weird snorting noise—a repressed sob, I guess. I hurry away before I start crying like a baby.

Lucy

AFTER WYNN LEFT, I tried to ignore Sam's excited phone calls to all her friends and acquaintances.

"Oh my god! Wynn Felker just came by to see me! . . . I don't know—my mom told him about me so I guess he wanted to meet me. And he brought me flowers . . . That's what older guys do when they meet a woman . . . Well, guys with *class*."

I noticed that she didn't mention the possibility that Wynn's was a pity visit prompted by her mother's telling him Sam had been having a hard time with the separation. She also left out my boob flashing and mini meltdown.

But by Friday, the commotion caused by Wynn's surprise visit has given way to an eerie sense of normalcy. I get dressed for work and send Sam off to school. When I'm alone, I change out of my work clothes and into a pair of track pants with an old cardigan, and begin my day of shuffling around the house aimlessly. This is my new normal, I guess: without love, without purpose, without employment. I'm in the middle of making a subpar pot of coffee when the phone rings.

"I'm outside your house," Camille says excitedly. "Can I come in?"

Moments later, I usher her inside. She looks at my ensemble and quickly covers her expression of distaste with one of pity. "Oh, hon," she says, giving me a quick hug. But when she releases me, she brightens significantly. "You'll never guess what happened at work yesterday!"

Obviously, I'm not really in the mood to hear work stories. Although I guess it's not that obvious to Camille. "Let's have coffee," I offer, leading her to the kitchen.

She follows me, chatting animatedly. "Okay, so I've been totally swamped since you left. I worked fourteen hours yesterday and the day before, and I still wasn't able to get everything for Cody's keg party that goes awry."

I fill two cups. "What did Bruce say?"

"He's trying to hire someone, but the city isn't exactly crawling with experienced props buyers. He called Miranda Ross, but she's working on that sci-fi series with the grandpa who's an alien."

"He should have been more flexible," I retort. "But I'm sorry this is all falling on you."

"Listen to this," she says, positively gleefully. "So I'm in Bruce's office telling him that it's physically impossible for one person to provide all the props for a series like this, when who should storm in?"

I already know, but she proceeds. "Ainsley, followed by Wynn Felker!"

"Really?" I say, feigning surprise that Wynn and the show's

producer, stout powerhouse Ainsley, had paid Bruce a visit. "What did they want?"

"Ainsley was all over Bruce. She went on and on about how this is a family show, so how can we, as a production, not support employees with families. Wynn just stood there, looking pissed off—and gorgeous, of course."

"Really?" I can feel myself smiling. I can't seem to help it.

"By the end of the conversation, Bruce was apologizing and promising that he was going to hire you back and get a junior buyer in so you can knock off early for Sam."

"Wow." It's all I can think to say.

Camille looks at her watch. "He'll be calling you any minute. I'd better get back on the road. Somehow, I don't think Wynn and Ainsley would storm in to fight for my job." She gives me a mischievous wink.

I walk her to the door and give her a big hug. "Thanks for coming by," I say. "It's really sweet of you."

"I can't wait until we're working together again. I've totally missed you—and I don't just mean you taking back half my workload."

I force a tight smile. Unfortunately, my friend notices. "What?" she says. "Aren't you happy to be coming back to work?"

"Of course!" I say. "I'm desperate to be working. It's not like I can afford to lounge around here all day doing nothing." I shrug. "I'm just tired and overwhelmed, that's all."

"Have you talked to Trent?"

I suddenly remember my promise to call him today. But I don't necessarily have to abide by that, do I? I mean, he promised to love me until death did us part, so he's not really in a position to judge. "Just briefly," I said. Behind me, the phone rings.

Camille jumps. "That'll be Bruce! You may as well ask for a raise while he's begging you to come back."

I shut the door and head for the phone. My blasé response to the impending conversation surprises me. Of course I want my job back. I need the money and the sense of purpose. And the thought of updating my résumé and starting the whole job hunt over again is wearying. But there's also no denying that buying props for Cody Summers has become less and less stimulating. Cody himself has become infinitely more stimulating, but driving all over the lower mainland in search of his skateboards, Rubik's Cubes, pool noodles, and remote-control dinosaurs all seems so meaningless.

So my voice is less than enthusiastic when I answer. "Hello?"

"Lucy, it's me."

"Trent?" I'm surprised and a little annoyed. First of all, I said I'd call him back. Of course, it's entirely possible I wouldn't have, but he didn't know that. Second of all, he's tying up the line so that Bruce is unable to offer me my uninspiring and pointless job back. "Why are you calling?"

"I need to talk to you."

His voice breaks and it almost sounds like he's crying. Trent's never been overly emotional or sentimental, but I suppose Sam's rejection has weakened him. "This isn't a good time," I reply coolly.

"Please," he begs, and this time there's no doubt. Trent is crying, and hard.

"What's wrong?" I demand. Surprisingly, I feel annoyed by his unfettered display of emotion. I don't have the energy to soothe him, to prop him up and help him cope with what he's done. It's no longer my role to play wife to him. That's Petunia Pig's job now.

"Everything's wrong," he sobs. "I miss Sam. I miss you. I miss you and Sam."

It's satisfying, I can't deny it. But still, he's tying up the line. "I can't force Sam to see you, Trent. But I'm sure she'll come around eventually."

I hear him take a deep breath. "I thought maybe we could do something together, the three of us?"

"I don't think Sam's ready to meet your"—I stop myself from saying *whore*—"girlfriend. She's still adjusting to our separation."

"Not with her," Trent says, "with you. The three of us, together again, like a family."

It's the trigger that stirs the emotion in me. My throat constricts as I'm gripped by a nostalgic longing for the way things were. If I could make the last month of our lives disappear, I would, but I can't. We'll never get back what we had. Sam and I will never look at Trent the same way again. "It's too late," I say softly.

"It's not too late," my husband insists. "I fucked up, I know that. But we can't throw away eighteen years over one bad month."

"One bad month?" I screech. "You brought your whore to our daughter's art show! You've driven Sam to booze and drugs! You've continually neglected us both, and now you think we can just go back to the way we were?"

"We'll start fresh," Trent pleads. "Lucy . . . *please*. I need you."

"Really? I thought you needed time alone, to sort out your grown-up man stuff."

My sarcasm usually trips the switch on his anger, but not this time. His voice is quiet, resigned, when he says, "I was wrong."

His tone defuses my rage. There's a long moment of silence as I try to think of what to say next. But what is there to say? I want to forgive him, I really do. I just don't know if I can.

"It's over between Annika and me," he says, "in case you were wondering."

"Not really."

"She wants us to go to counseling, if you can believe it."

The thought of the two of them working on their relationship makes me want to throw up. I remain mute as Trent continues.

"I don't want to go, but Don made a really good point. If we do talk to a professional, then she can make Annika see that it's really over between us."

I am incredulous. "So it's over between you two, but you haven't bothered to tell her that?"

Trent obviously realizes how ridiculous this sounds. "Well, I tried but she's just having a little trouble accepting—"

I slam the receiver down. How could I have been so naive? So gullible? Trent is still the same selfish prick who walked out on Sam and me, the same bastard who brought a date to the Crofton House art show. His tears and remorse don't change a thing. I can't forgive him. He doesn't deserve it. The phone rings again. He obviously hasn't gotten the message.

"What?" I scream into the receiver.

"Uh . . . Lucy?"

Oops. "Yes."

"It's Bruce. I was wondering if we could talk about you coming back to work?"

Trent

YASMINE WHEELER IS a striking, forty-something brunette with really arched eyebrows. She sits with her legs crossed, listening to Annika explain our relationship.

"We were friends for almost a year before we started dating, which I think is a good way to start off a relationship."

"It can be," Yasmine says then turns to me. "But you were married for most of the friendship, right?"

"Yeah," I mumble.

Annika jumps in. "Nothing physical happened until he left his wife. It was more of an emotional and spiritual connection."

What is she talking about? I thought she was sexy and I wanted to bone her. There was nothing emotional or spiritual about it.

"And then when he chose me," she reaches over and gives my knee a squeeze, "we took it to the physical plane."

I clear my throat, simultaneously sitting forward and pulling my knee away from her hand. "That's not exactly right. I didn't choose Annika over my wife. I needed a break from my marriage and I wanted to spend some time on my own. This thing with her was just . . . a fling that got out of hand."

Annika gives an incredulous snort. "Right. So we've been sleeping together practically every night for a month, and it's just a fling to you?"

"Yeah."

"So when we went shopping to furnish your apartment? And when you took me to your daughter's art show? That meant nothing to you?"

Oh Christ, here we go again. "Sorry," I mutter.

Yasmine interjects, "So what I'm hearing is that you're in the same relationship, but with different objectives?"

I look over at Annika. We both shrug.

Annika turns to Yasmine. "But the fact that we're here means we're willing to work on it." She looks over at me and mouths, "Thank you."

"Not really," I say, eyes fixed on our coach. "I'm actually here to make Annika understand that this is over. I'm sorry if I gave her the impression that we had some kind of future together, but we don't. I need to focus on my family."

I was hoping Yasmine would turn to Annika and say something like, "Got the message?" Instead she says, "That must be very hard for you to hear."

"It is," Annika says, grabbing a tissue off the large, dark wood desk. "And the worst part is, I know he doesn't mean it."

"Yes, I do!"

Annika ignores me. "His daughter has been drinking and doing drugs and he's blaming himself. He thinks that if I weren't in the picture, she'd miraculously become his sweet, innocent little girl again. And that's not going to happen."

Yasmine turns to me. "This must be a hard time for you."

Duh? How much are we paying this woman to state the obvious? "Of course it is," I snap. "I'm worried about my daughter. I feel like I let her down and I'll do anything to help her get back on track. I can't do that if I'm stuck in a relationship I don't even want."

"I have been nothing but supportive," Annika shrieks. "All I want is to be there for you and for Sam, but you won't let me! I'm a child of divorce! I could help her if only you'd give me a chance!"

Surely this outburst will get us kicked out, but the relationship coach is nodding along. "Uh-huh. Uh-huh. Trent?"

As both their eyes fall on me, I feel the intense need to get the fuck out of here. I stand up. "This is pointless." I look directly at Annika. "It's over. I don't want your help, I don't want your support, and I don't want to be your boyfriend. Okay?"

Yasmine says, "Trent, please sit down so we can finish the session."

"You don't need me for the session," I grumble, moving toward the door. "You can spend the rest of the hour convincing this nutcase that I just broke up with her."

"Trent!" Annika cries, but I'm already hurrying into the hall.

Lucy

"WELCOME BACK, LUCY!" Ainsley rushes into my office and greets me effusively.

"Thanks," I reply, trying to hide my cynicism. Ainsley had barely said two words to me before Wynn went to bat for my job.

"I hope Bruce is making you comfortable," she says, shooting a warning look at Bruce hovering in the doorway.

"I was just about to call some junior buyers to help her out," Bruce chirps.

"Great," Ainsley says. "This is a family show, so obviously, we've got a lot of respect for families." Given that forty-something Ainsley's family consists of a shih tzu poodle named Grier, she'd never seemed too concerned with how my work schedule affected my daughter. I know Wynn is behind this.

I smile tightly. "Obviously."

She claps her thick fingers together. "All right then. We'll let you get to it."

When they've departed, Camille rolls her chair over to me and whispers, "All this special treatment and you haven't even slept with him yet."

"True," I whisper back, "but I did flash my boob."

"What!"

"It was an accident," I explain. "The towel slipped."

"Towel?" But before Camille can grill me, Bruce is calling for her to join him in his office. Left alone in the room, I sense the perfect opportunity to slip away. Even though the work has backed up during my dismissal, I won't be able to focus on anything until I talk to Wynn.

When I reach the set, the assistant director is overseeing the filming of a fundraising car wash. Teen actors throw wet sponges, squirt water from hoses, and cavort among the soap bubbles. "Cody" isn't in the shot, so I make my way to his dressing room. A number of his hangers-on mill about the hallway and give me the eye as I approach. But I am on a mission and can't be swayed. With a fortifying breath, I knock.

The beefy designated driver of the Lincoln Navigator opens the door. "Hey, Lucy," Jamie says, sounding rather familiar.

"Hi, can I see Wynn for a second please?"

Before I've finished speaking, Wynn's head peeks over his friend's enormous shoulder. "Come in," he beckons me. I enter and Jamie exits, leaving us alone.

"How are you?" Wynn says, perching on the back of an overstuffed chair. His dressing room is sumptuous but without warmth—like a professionally decorated showroom.

"Fine," I say as I assess his ensemble. He's wearing a

fluorescent green T-shirt and a pair of jeans rolled up to his knees. His feet are bare—obviously in preparation for the fundraising car wash. I decide to dive right in. "First, I wanted to say thank-you for getting me my job back."

"My pleasure," he says, eyes twinkling. "I'm glad you're back."

I move farther into the room. "Well," I continue, not looking at him, "the second thing I wanted to say . . . to make clear . . . is that this can't happen."

Wynn stands and moves toward me, a sexy grin on his face. "What can't happen?"

I feel the pull of attraction and decide to focus on his rolled-up jeans and bare feet. This juvenile outfit helps solidify my decision. "I can't have dinner with you," I say firmly. "I'm flattered that you're interested in me but . . . I've just split up with my husband and it would be hard on my daughter if I was to start dating again so soon."

He's standing mere inches from me now. "I understand," he says, his voice soft and kind. I stare at his toes. "I wouldn't want to upset Sam."

"Thanks." His feet are clean and perfect. He obviously gets pedicures.

"But I also don't want to miss out on a great thing just because the timing isn't ideal. I think you're really amazing, Lucy. I've never met anyone like you."

I shrug, smiling despite myself. "I'm not that great."

"Yes, you are. I meet so many phony people in my world and you're so real and honest and wise."

I shift uncomfortably. *Wise* is just a more flattering way of saying *old*, I think.

Wynn puts a finger under my chin and tilts my head up. "That night at the bar was really hot." His voice is husky. "I haven't stopped thinking about it."

"Me either!" I want to cry. "It was incredible and sexy and I haven't felt so alive in years!" But I bite my lip to keep the words in.

"It could be our secret," he says. "Sam doesn't have to know. We'll keep it out of the press. It'll be just ours."

"I can't . . ." I croak helplessly.

"Come on . . ." He leans forward and I smell his minty-fresh breath, the magnetic force of his proximity. And suddenly I think: what the hell? After all I've been through, I deserve this. Trent flaunted his girlfriend in front of me—not to mention a significant portion of the Crofton House parent population. This will be like my revenge—or more accurately, my reward for surviving the humiliation. Besides, it's just a kiss . . . a simple, meaningless, incredible kiss. I lean forward and feel the warm, moist caress of his mouth.

There's a loud banging on the door. I jump back, startled. "Five minutes, Wynn!" someone yells from the hall.

The commotion brings me back to reality. "No," I say, stepping away and composing myself. "This is wrong and inappropriate. My daughter has a huge crush on you, and obviously, she'd find us being together disgusting."

"But she doesn't have to find out," Wynn pleads.

Determinedly, I head for the door. "I said no."

"Okay," he acquiesces, catching my hand as I pass. "Just do me one favor, okay?"

I start to refuse, but he's so goddamn cute. "What?"

"Let me make you dinner." Before I can object he cuts me

off. "As a thank-you. I'm reuniting with my family because of you. I feel like a new person—more grounded and healthy. And I owe that to you, Lucy."

"I don't think so."

"Please. Come to my place on Saturday. I'll cook my special pasta. We'll have a nice quiet dinner and no one will ever know."

It's as though he can sense me waffling in his favor because he says, "Just this once, okay? And then, I promise, I'll respect your boundaries."

The door opens and a girl with a headset pokes her head inside. "We need you on set, Wynn."

Wynn looks at me, his blue eyes plaintive. "All right," I say, "just once."

Trent

ON TUESDAY I go back to work. Don told me to take a couple of days off to sort myself out, and I did. I feel a hell of a lot stronger than last week, and I'm more than a little embarrassed that I was so emotional in his office. But there's no point dwelling on it. I'm moving forward now. I've ended things with Annika and I'm going to get my family back. It feels good to have a clear-cut goal again.

But as soon as I walk into the building, I hear it. It's faint, coming from the other end of the hall, but it's unmistakable. It's crying. More precisely, it's Annika crying.

"Fuck," I mutter, heading to my office. I knew she'd have a hard time with this, but she's got to accept it. Like Don said, it was a roll in the hay that got out of hand. Annika's young and beautiful and she's got her whole life ahead of her. Why is she being so goddamn clingy? Maybe if she went on a vacation or something, she could get herself together.

I'm booting up my computer when Karen from accounting walks in. "Annika's really upset," she says, stating the obvious.

"I can hear that."

Karen puts her hands on her hips, a distinctively judgmental posture. "So . . . what are you going to do about it?"

"What am I going to do about it?" I scoff. "I've been straight with her. It was a mistake and now it's over. She's got to deal with it."

Karen gasps, as if I've just said a punch in the face might set her straight. She turns on her heel and hurries back to comfort Annika.

There are no messages from Lucy or Sam, but I refuse to get discouraged. I dial Lucy's cell. It goes straight to voice mail, so I leave a message. "It's me," I say, affecting a cheerful tone. "I'd like to take Sam out this weekend . . . both of you, if you're up for it. Maybe dinner and a movie? I don't want to pressure you, Luce . . . I just want . . ." I scramble for a benign way to say: I want my family back. I want us to be together again. I don't want to die alone in some crappy apartment and have no one show up at my funeral.

Finally, I come up with, " . . . to spend some time as a family. It will be good for Sam."

I'm hanging up the phone when Don sticks his head in my doorway. "You want to come to my office?" His face is tense: not a good sign.

When I close his office door behind me, Annika is already seated in front of his desk. She is sobbing quietly into a tissue. "Sit," Don commands, indicating the chair next to Annika. I obey. Annika shifts her body away from me, cries slightly louder.

"Okay," Don begins, "I looked the other way when you two started seeing each other, which may have been a mistake."

I'll say—but I don't.

"But now that things are over between you, I'd like your assurance that you can handle yourselves in a mature and professional manner while in the office."

"Of course," I say. Annika snivels.

Don continues. "I know this is a difficult time, but things will get easier. And you're both valuable employees. I want to make sure that you two can continue to work productively together."

"We can," I say, nodding emphatically.

Annika looks up from her tissue. "I don't think so."

I turn in my chair to face her. She's still snuffling into the Kleenex, but I sense a grim determination in her expression. That fucking bitch. She's going to destroy me.

Don clears his throat. "I hope you'll reconsider."

She looks up. "I don't think I can work with someone so heartless and cruel."

"What?" I boom.

But Annika keeps her eyes on Don. "He made me think we had a future together. I invested myself, heart and soul, in our relationship. And then suddenly," she snaps her fingers, "just like that, he announces that I meant nothing to him."

"That's not how it was!" I cry.

Annika continues. "He came to see a relationship coach with me, only to verbally abuse me in front of her and storm out of the session."

Don looks at me. "It w-wasn't like that," I stammer. "It was a misunderstanding."

Annika faces me. "You led me on for almost a year. You introduced me to your friends. You let me decorate your apartment. And now you want to go back to your wife and I'm left with nothing!"

Oh Jesus! My armpits are sweaty and my heart is starting to palpitate. I look at Don pleadingly. "That wasn't my intention. I-I wanted to make her see . . ."

Don leans forward in his chair. "Look, your personal problems are your business. But if they're going to affect the productivity in my office, then something's going to have to change."

I lean back in my seat. It's harsh, Annika getting fired over our relationship, but it's for the best. We obviously can't work together if she's going to carry on like Glenn Close. And frankly, she deserves it if she can't grow up and take her knocks like an adult.

Annika says, "I understand your position, Don. That's why I've consulted a lawyer friend of mine. I know these situations often don't work out in the woman's favor . . ."

I nearly fly out of my seat. Was that a threat? I look from her face to Don's. He's composed, but a vein is throbbing near his temple and he's breathing deeply through his nostrils. Looking back at Annika, I see that she's no longer crying. Her expression is sheer determination and menace.

Don speaks. "I'd prefer that this was worked out without involving lawyers."

Annika shrugs. "Me, too, but I'm afraid it's too late for that."

"No, it's not," I interject. "Annika, please . . . can we talk about this?"

She stands up. "You've made your position clear, Trent. I don't see how we can continue to work together." She looks at Don. "I'll be taking the rest of the week off. I'm emotionally exhausted and would prefer not to come back to work until this"—she points her thumb at me—"is sorted out." Turning on her heel, she strides out of the office.

I turn to Don, my expression one of panic. He promised me my job was safe. I've been a loyal employee for seven years. Yeah, I've fucked up recently, but before that, I was pretty much perfect. He can't turn on me now. "Wow," I say with a nervous laugh. "She's mental."

"Yeah," Don replies dismissively. He's already reaching for the phone. "I need some privacy, Trent."

I stand obediently. "I'll talk to her. It'll be okay."

Don pauses, looks at me. "I think you should stay away from her for now."

Lucy

SOMETIMES THE STARS just align and you know you've made the right decision—like having dinner with Wynn. Despite my doubts and fears, circumstances fell so easily into place that I knew it was okay. Trent had phoned and practically begged to spend time with Sam this weekend. I decided that it would do her good to be with her father. Yes, he has hurt and disappointed her, but he's still her dad and can't be shut out of her life completely. So I arranged for her to spend a night with him at his apartment. And that night just happened to be Saturday, leaving me free to see Wynn.

So now I find myself, glass of red wine in hand, staring out the floor-to-ceiling windows at the expanse of the Pacific. In the distance, the lights of Vancouver twinkle in the darkness. "Beautiful view, isn't it?" Wynn says. His body is close behind me and I can feel his breath on my neck.

"Gorgeous," I say huskily. Turning, I indicate the whole

room with a sweep of my arm: the gleaming walnut floors, pale, modern furnishings, and expensive, strategically placed ornaments. "The whole place is just . . . incredible." The whole place, in fact, looks like a professionally decorated photo spread from *Dwell* magazine. There's a marked lack of personal touches: no books, magazines, or framed photographs. It's a home fit only for a movie star—or in this case, a teen sitcom sensation.

With a gentle hand on my elbow, Wynn leads me to the sofa. We perch (with its expansive seat and low back, it's a piece designed for perching) on the edge. "I'm glad you came," he says.

"Me, too." I smile at him. "Dinner was fantastic. Where'd you learn to cook like that?"

"An old girlfriend taught me that dish."

Strangely, I feel a twinge of jealousy. It's ridiculous and I shake it off. Besides, he's not old enough to have had any significant relationships. "Well, it was great."

Wynn sets his glass of wine on the coffee table and then takes mine. I try to remain calm as he places it next to his. I know what comes next: a kiss. And then, if all goes well—and there's absolutely no reason it shouldn't—we will move to his bedroom. Or, possibly, we'll do it right here on this expensive settee. No, I'd prefer the bedroom. Those enormous windows would make me feel too exposed. Once we've kissed for a few minutes, I'll suggest we move upstairs.

This premeditation does detract from the spontaneity of the moment, but I can't pretend I haven't been thinking about it since our encounter in his dressing room. I've made a conscious decision to reward myself. In the last few weeks I've suffered the loss of my husband, the estrangement of my best friend, the alienation of my daughter, and the indignity of being fired. And I've survived it all with my sanity intact, more or less. I deserve to feel loved again. And by "feeling loved again," I mean the temporary high of sex with Wynn.

I'm under no illusions that it will erase the trauma of the past. And it's not meant to change the emptiness of the future. It is a gift I am giving myself: the physical manifestation of weeks of lust. A sexual release and balm to my damaged ego. I deserve it, goddamn it. I deserve to have sex with the Choice Hottie.

Wynn turns to face me, a sexy smile on his lips. My stomach flips nervously as I wait for him to make a move. The anticipation is killing me. Get on with it, I silently will him, but he doesn't seem to sense my urgency.

"You're really beautiful," he says, gently stroking my cheek with his fingers.

"Thanks," I say, leaning closer to him.

"I've never met anyone like you, Lucy. Seriously, all the actresses and pop stars I've dated . . . none of them compare to you."

Enough with the compliments. I lean in and kiss his lips. It is every bit as strange and wonderful and exciting as the first time—even more so, given that I'm not completely hammered. I have had exactly a glass and a half of red wine: enough to lower my inhibitions and calm my nerves, but not enough to affect my sensitivity . . . or judgment. I know exactly what I'm doing. I am waxed and ready.

"Wow," he says, pulling away for a moment.

"Yeah," I growl, gripping the front of his shirt and dragging him back to me.

We kiss for a few more minutes, the intensity building steadily. I run my hands over his broad shoulders, his strong arms, and the outline of his pectorals. His hands are buried in my hair, then moving on my back, down to the waistband of my pants. "Let's go to your room," I say, already scrambling off the couch.

"Wait," Wynn says.

"What?"

"Are you sure about this?"

"Super sure," I say, reaching for his hand and attempting to haul him up the stairs.

"Slow down," Wynn says with a good-natured chuckle. "I just don't want you to regret this tomorrow."

"I won't," I assure him, unbuttoning my shirt. I know he's already seen my left breast, but I'm still hoping the sight of the pair of them in my lacy push-up bra will be enticing. "I'm not thinking about tomorrow. I'm living in the moment and I really want to do this." I pull my shirt off and toss it on the floor. "I want to make love to you, Wynn. Just this once . . ." Leaning down, I kiss him passionately to emphasize my point. To my surprise, he is less than responsive. I pull away, look at him.

"It sounds like you're using me," he says.

I have to laugh. He's kidding me, right? Wrong.

"I really like you, Lucy. I feel like there's something special between us, like maybe we could have something . . . I don't know . . . real. I just don't want to ruin it or cheapen it by having sex before we're ready."

I suppose I should feel flattered, but instead, I'm pissed. "I've been straight with you from the beginning. We don't have a future together. I'm here because I'm attracted to you, and I feel a connection and I want to have sex with you. Is that so wrong?"

"It's kind of . . . sleazy."

"Sleazy?" I snap. "You're an actor." I narrow my eyes. "Are you religious or something?"

"No," he says, "but I'm turning over a new leaf. I want to live a better life. I'm reconnecting with my family. I'm looking for more challenging acting roles. And I don't want to have another one-night stand. I want more than that."

"Great," I say sarcastically, snatching my blouse up off the floor.

Wynn stands up. "I have you to thank for this."

"Oh, you're welcome!" I struggle into my blouse and, with my buttons still undone, head toward the door.

"Don't go," he pleads.

I turn back to face him. "I'm humiliated! My husband just dumped me for some overweight floozy. And now I offer myself up to you on a silver platter and you turn me down!"

"Not because I don't want you," Wynn says. "Because I want more of you . . . more than just sex."

Looking at him, I am tempted. Sure, I could go back to the uncomfortable sofa and chat about his family, *Cody's Way*, and climate change. We would kiss a bit more before I demurely said, "I should go." We would continue to see each other in secret, hiding out in Wynn's luxurious home when Sam was with Trent. After about six months, we'd "make love"—poignant, emotional love. One weekend, we'd sneak off to New Mexico so I could meet Wynn's mother. Our relationship would build slowly, until the day when Sam walked in and found us midcoitus. "Mom! Stop molesting Cody!" she'd scream.

Gently, we'd explain that I was not molesting seventeen-year-old Cody, but having an adult, consensual relationship with twenty-seven-year-old Wynn. Sam would storm from the room in disgust, hurrying to find the gun that pot-smoking Randy had told her was a "good idea." She'd come back and shoot me, then Wynn, then herself. Or worse, she'd overdose on crank, leaving me to live with the guilt. This is obviously the worst-case scenario, but still . . . No, thanks.

I pick up my purse from the floor. "Sorry, but I've made my position clear." Wrapping my unbuttoned shirt around me, I head out the door.

Wynn follows behind me. "Come back in," he calls as I storm to my car. "We can talk about this."

"There's nothing to talk about!" I scream, moving purposefully to my vehicle.

"Yes, there is!" He catches up to me, grips my arm. "We can sort this out."

"No, we can't. You won't have sex with me, so there's nothing more to talk about."

"I will have sex with you," Wynn says. "I just want to make sure it's meaningful and special. You deserve that."

"I deserve to get fucked by the Choice Hottie!" I scream at the top of my lungs.

Suddenly there's a blinding flash of light, then another. I turn toward it, shielding my eyes, my shirt flapping open in the sea breeze. Behind me, Wynn says "Shit!" and grabs me by the wrist.

"Hey, Wynn!" a male voice calls. "Who's your lady friend?"

Another male voice says, "Not much of a lady with that mouth."

"What's your name, darling?" the first voice asks. But before I can answer, Wynn is dragging me back inside amidst a hail of flashbulbs.

Trent

"HOME SWEET HOME," I say, opening the door for Sam to enter my apartment. I see the place through her eyes, as if for the first time. It looks small and cluttered. I tidied up, but forgot a couple of newspapers on the floor beside the sofa. There's a beer bottle leaning against the leg of the coffee table, too. The furniture is too modern, the pillows are too bright, and the TV is way too big. The place screams "single dad trying to impress estranged daughter." I look at Sam. It obviously isn't working.

"The pizza should be here soon," I say, taking her bag and dropping it in the empty den. I'd called Domino's on my cell phone on the drive over. It had seemed a good way to fill the awkward silence in the car. But now I'm wishing I had something to fill the awkward silence in the apartment. "So . . . what movies should we rent?"

"Whatevs," Sam says, flopping onto the couch. She takes the

remote and turns on the TV. Within seconds she's immersed in a music video.

I try to busy myself in the kitchen, pouring two glasses of Coke, wiping invisible spots off the counter. It's sad, sort of, how uncomfortable I feel around my own kid. She's still the same little girl who I taught to swim, carried around on my shoulders, and took on her first roller-coaster ride. Except that she hates me now.

The phone rings twice, signaling the front door. I rush to answer it. "Pizza's here!" I say jubilantly. I'm positively ecstatic for the sense of purpose. "Yello?"

Through the intercom I hear her voice. "Trent, it's Annika. We need to talk."

I could puke, seriously. I look at Sam lounging on the sofa and a fierce protectiveness overtakes me. "I'll be right down," I growl.

"Something's wrong with the door downstairs," I explain as I head out of the apartment. "I'll be right back, honey." She makes no move to acknowledge that she's heard me, or cares that I'm leaving.

I take the stairs two, three at a time. Annika can't just show up here whenever she likes—especially now that Sam's agreed to spend time with me. This could ruin everything.

I see her through the glass, standing at the front door, her posture defiant. For the first time since I've met her, I don't think about fucking her. Right now, I'm too busy willing her to evaporate like one of those *Star Trek* characters. But no such luck. I open the door.

"What are you doing here?"

"We need to talk," she says, pushing past me into the lobby.

"It's not a good time."

"Really?" She turns around to face me, a bitchy smirk on her face. "I thought you cared about your job."

She's such a cunt. How could I have been so blind?

Annika continues. "If it comes down to getting rid of you or me, you know Don will choose me."

"What makes you so sure?"

"My lawyer says we'd have an excellent case for unfair dismissal. Don won't want to go through a nasty court case if he doesn't have to. And I'm sure you wouldn't want that either." She moves slowly toward me, hands on the belt of her raincoat. "Things could come out in court . . . embarrassing things."

"I've got nothing to be embarrassed about," I snap.

"Oh no?" Annika says, shifting her weight onto one leg. "Erectile dysfunction . . . Dressing up in my underwear . . . Asking me to spank you . . ."

"I never did that!" I roar.

"Only you and I know for sure."

A bubble of panic rises in my throat, but I take a deep breath. I've got to play this right. "Look," I say with a forced calm, "I don't see why we can't still work together."

"We can't," Annika snaps. "You can't just use me and then dump me and expect everything to go back to normal."

"I understand that you're hurt," I try, my voice gentle. "But sometimes things just don't work out. It doesn't mean we can't still be friends."

"Friends?" she squawks. "Why would I want to be your friend?"

"We had some great times together. We, uh . . ." I trail off. She's right. We had nothing in common besides sex. Now that that's gone, there's nothing left. But I've got to try. "I still care a lot about you, Annika."

She snivels, "It doesn't seem like it."

I take a step toward her. "I do. And I wish things could have been different. But . . . it just wasn't the right time for us. I'm too messed up over my marriage and my daughter."

There's an almost imperceptible shift in her posture, and I sense her softening. I've got to keep going. "I know I can't give you what you want, as a man. I'm too fucked up and . . . not emotionally capable of being in a relationship. But I really treasure the time we spent together, and I don't want to lose your friendship."

She stares at me, eyes shining with tears. "I want to stay in your life, too, Trent, but I think it would be too hard. What if you and Lucy get back together?"

"That's not gonna happen," I lie—although, given Lucy's attitude toward me, I'm probably telling the truth.

"Do you promise?"

Now she's getting all psycho-possessive again. I look at my watch. I've been downstairs too long already. "I can't talk about this now. Sam's upstairs. She's spending the night."

"Oh," she says softly. "I'm glad you're getting to spend some time with her."

"Me, too."

"I want the best for you, Trent . . . for you and for Sam."

"Thanks," I say dismissively. "I've got to get going."

She steps forward and places her hands on my chest. "I can wait, if you want."

"For what?"

"For you . . . for us . . . I don't mind waiting as long as you can give me one hundred percent of your heart, when you're ready."

"Annika, it's over," I say firmly. "You need to get that through your head."

She takes a step back. "Fuck you!" she spits out at me. "You fucking bastard! You think you can treat me like dirt and get away with it?"

Oh my god, she's totally nuts! I suddenly feel a little fearful. I'm not dealing with a sane woman here.

"Get out!" I say, pointing at the door. Despite my commanding tone, I think my hand is shaking a little.

"Oh, I'll go," she snaps, backing toward the exit. "But you have not heard the last of me."

"That's fine," I grumble, "just stay away from my family!"

She stops and fixes me with this creepy, self-satisfied smile. "Deal," she says in a really menacing tone. Then she turns and hurries out the door, nearly crashing into the pizza guy on his way up the walk.

Lucy

"COUGAR ATTACK!" THE headline reads. It's one of those small, tabloid-style newspapers devoted to more superfluous news stories. I'd picked it up from one of those free newspaper boxes dotting the city like a teenager's acne. The headline had grabbed me. I was really concerned that someone in the area had been attacked by a cougar. Not so.

Underneath the tantalizing headline is a photo of Wynn and me. My body is angled toward him, my shirt flapping open to reveal my lacy black bra. Wynn appears to be backing away from me, though I know this wasn't the case. My eyes stare at the camera, my expression one of anger and confusion (well, as much anger and confusion as you can express when your forehead is frozen). Wynn's eyes are on me, his features contorted in chagrin that the paparazzi have found us. Unfortunately, this chagrin is easily mistaken for fear, giving the impression that

I'm attacking him and he's frightened. Yes, I am the cougar; Wynn is my prey.

The rustling of multiple plastic bags alerts me to Camille's approach. I toss the paper under my desk as she comes barreling into the office.

"Phew!" she says, dropping her purchases on the floor. "I've got everything for the bake-sale shoot. Are you going to be able to get the roller disco stuff?"

I start to answer but my face crumples with emotion. Camille hurries toward me and puts a consoling hand on my shoulder. "What's wrong?"

Without a word, I reach for the newspaper and hand it to her.

"Oh my god! Was someone attacked by a cougar?" Then she looks at the photo. "Shit," she mutters.

"Sam's going to kill me," I cry, tears flowing freely down my cheeks. "She's going to leave me and move in with Trent."

"You're her mother and she loves you," Camille soothes.

"I'm on the front page of the paper attacking the boy she's in love with!" I wail.

"Everyone knows that the media always get these things wrong."

"My tits are hanging out!" I cry.

"Listen," Camille insists. "This is some little rinky-dink free newspaper. I'm sure no one's even seen it."

That's when Wynn walks into my office. Under his arm I notice folded copies of the city's two largest newspapers. He clears his throat nervously. "Could I talk to you for a sec?"

Camille gathers her shopping bags. "I'll be in the props room." With a pitying glance at me over her shoulder, she hurries away.

"I take it you've seen the photo?" Wynn says, closing the door behind him.

"I saw it," I reply, trying to hold myself together. "Is it in the *Sun* and the *Province*, too?"

"In the entertainment section. And my publicist has already had calls from *People*, *Us Weekly*, *In Touch*, and *Hello*."

"Fuck."

"I know."

"How do we stop this?" I ask pleadingly.

Wynn lets out a puff of breath between his lips. "We just have to ride it out. You know how these things go . . . You're all over the tabloids one week, completely forgotten the next."

I jump up. "I can't just ride this out!" I screech. "I can't be all over the tabloids. I have my daughter to think about."

Wynn's youthful face looks stressed. "You guys might want to get away for a while . . . So you're not harassed . . ."

And then, like a jolt of electricity, the magnitude of the crisis hits me. What if Sam sees the photo before I've had a chance to explain? What if Ava Watkins runs into her and says something like, "Oh sweetie, I'm sorry to hear that your mother tried to rape your teenage crush." What if the press is at Crofton House this very moment, asking Sam to comment on how she feels about her mother flashing her boobs at Cody Summers?

I grab my coat and purse. "I've got to go."

"I'll come with you," Wynn stupidly offers.

"No," I growl at him. "You will not come with me. You've done enough damage."

Trent

"SHE SAYS YOU gave her crabs," Don says.

"No!" I cry. "I didn't!"

"She has a letter from a doctor."

"Maybe she has crabs, but she didn't get them from me!"

Don continues, "We need to sort this out, Trent. She's threatening legal action against the firm."

"So what are you saying?" I snap. "That you want me to resign?"

Don reclines slightly in his chair. "I could offer you a transfer to the Coquitlam office."

I jump out of my seat. "*She's* crazy and I'm being sent to work out in the boonies?"

"It's not the boonies. It'll take you forty-five minutes tops."

"No," I say, placing my hands on the desk and leaning across it. "I'm trying to reconnect with my family. Adding an hour-and-a-half commute to my day is not going to help any."

His response is cool. "Maybe you should have thought about your family before you started banging that psycho."

"I made a mistake!" I boom. "I admit it. But would you rather keep a crazy bitch like Annika in the office than a solid, loyal employee like me?"

Don sits forward, a gesture that puts me back in my seat. "You don't want this to go to court, Trent. She's saying things . . . It's not just the crabs."

"I never asked her to spank me!" I shout, then lower my voice. "She's making all that shit up."

"She says you like to be peed on."

"Oh my god!"

"And dress up in women's lingerie."

"I don't!"

"I believe you. Some won't."

Oh god. Annika will stop at nothing to destroy me. What's next? Boiling Sam's hamster? Thankfully, the hamster died over a year ago of natural causes, but I suddenly realize what I'm dealing with here. I clear my throat.

"I need some time to think."

Don seems glad to get rid of me. "Sure. Why don't you take the rest of the day off. You can give me your decision tomorrow."

Outside, the spring sun is peeking through the buildings, warming the west side of the street. I cross Hastings and move onto the sunny side of Richards. It's grown on me, this walking back and forth to work. I thought I'd miss my car, but now the thought of a forty-five-minute commute is distasteful. It's bad for the environment, for starters. But if I'm being honest, I've got too many problems of my own to give a shit about global warming. It's not the drive I dread so much, but the time investment. How am I going to ease my way back into Sam and Lucy's good books when I'm spending an hour and a half stuck in traffic every day?

It's not a definite plan at this stage; more of an overall strategy. Slowly but surely, I will infiltrate my daughter's life again. I'll start picking her up from school a couple of times a week, bringing her back to my apartment for a home-cooked meal. When I know she's home alone, I'll pack up dinner and take it over to her, something she loves, like lasagna or my chicken parmesan. "Leave a little for your mom," I'll say, so that when Lucy finally gets home from work, she can reheat one of my specialties. Eventually, I'll stay a little longer, just to keep Sam company until her mom gets back. Lucy won't have the heart to kick me out when she sees how close Sam and I have become. Sam will get back to her old self and start painting again, and Lucy will be so grateful to me that she'll invite me back home. But how can I execute my strategy when I'm stuck out in Coquitlam, land of strip malls, dodgy pubs, and fast-food outlets?

I'll get another job, one that's in the city. It shouldn't be too hard: I've got the education, the experience, and the contacts—unless Annika has spread word through the industry that I'm a cross-dresser with crabs and a penchant for golden showers.

Almost unconsciously, I walk into the beer store two blocks before my building. My fridge is empty, and if ever I needed an after-work beer, it's today. Sure, it's only one-thirty, but I need to de-stress. I grab a case of Heineken. Given the fact that I could soon be unemployed, I should buy something domestic. But this isn't the time to deprive myself. Walking to the cash register, I plunk the case on the counter.

The clerk, a skinny kid of about twenty, keeps his eyes glued to the open newspaper beside my beer case. "That all?" he asks, eyes affixed to the entertainment section.

"Yep." As he punches in my purchase, I glance at the paper to see what had him so transfixed. It's upside down, but there's a large photo of some woman in her bra and some good-looking young guy. She's got a nice rack. Then the words *Cody's Way* pop out at me from the caption. That's Lucy's show! I grab the paper and turn it toward me.

That's when I see that the woman with the nice rack is my wife, who appears about to eat that Cody Summers kid. I'm stunned. A sickening wave of rage and betrayal overtakes me.

"Twenty-two bucks," the kid says.

I hand over the bills. "Can I take this?" I ask hoarsely, indicating the paper.

"I was reading it."

"I'll give you five bucks for it." I toss a fiver on the counter.

"Okay." He shrugs, handing over my change. "There's a newspaper box right outside . . ." But I'm already leaving the store.

Somehow, I make it home before reading the article. I just can't do it in public. My wife is banging some teenage actor. It's sickening! How can she degrade herself like that? How can she degrade me like that? In the privacy of my apartment I devour the contents.

It's a short blurb. The paper doesn't even know who Lucy is, or the scope of her relationship with Wynn Felker (Cody Summers's real name). She's identified only as "a sexy soccer mom" caught outside Felker's waterfront home. The kid is apparently twenty-seven, not seventeen, which at least makes it less illegal for her to be carrying on with him. That doesn't change the fact that it's disgusting. He's still on some teenybopper TV show and millions of little girls are in love with him.

Jesus Christ! I'm immediately running out the door, car keys in hand. Sam can't see this photograph. She's one of the millions of little girls in love with that Cody kid. If she sees her mom sexually attacking him in the newspaper, who knows what she'll do. "Damn you, Lucy," I mutter as the elevator slowly lurches down to the parking garage.

Within moments I'm behind the wheel and racing toward Crofton House. Amidst my anger at Lucy and my fear for my daughter, one thing has become clear. I can't take a job outside the city. My daughter needs me now more than ever.

Lucy

I WAIT IN the hall as Principal Black disrupts tenth-grade history class to extract my daughter. "Your mother is here," the large woman whispers, her tone pitying. I'm thankful for Principal Black's kindness, but there's something inherently judgmental in her rigid posture and cloying smile. If she saw that photo of me and Wynn, she'd probably feel it her duty to call Children's Services and have Sam removed from my care.

My daughter spots me across the hall, her face contorted with worry. She rushes up to me. "What's wrong? What happened? Is it Dad?"

"No honey, it's nothing like that," I assure her. But to maintain the urgency of the situation for Principal Black's benefit, I say, "I just need to talk to you about some . . . urgent . . . family . . . stuff."

When we're outside the building, Sam says, "What's going on? You're freaking me out."

"Don't freak out." I reach for her hand, give it a squeeze. A lump forms in my throat as I experience a flash of déjà vu. Sam is a little girl skipping beside me, holding my hand like I'm her favorite person in the world. Breathing in, I try to staunch the emotion threatening to overtake me. I look at my daughter and realize that, in about half an hour, she's going to hate my guts.

We're almost to the SUV when Trent pulls in. I hear the squeal of tires before I notice the Lexus speeding in to the parking lot.

"Christ," I grumble, "this is a school zone."

"Why is Dad here?" Sam cries as Trent flies out of the car. "Oh god. Did Grandma die?"

"Grandma's fine," I say as Trent jogs up to us.

He touches Sam's shoulder. "How you holding up, kiddo?"

Sam shrieks, "Will someone please tell me what the hell is going on?"

"Let's go home so we can talk." I make a move toward the car, but no one follows me.

"I'm not going anywhere with you until you tell me what's going on!" my daughter cries.

Trent looks at me. "She hasn't seen it yet?"

"Seen what yet?"

I turn to my husband. "Can you let me handle this, please?"

"Handle what?" Sam screams.

"You'd better tell her," Trent insists, "before she finds out on her own."

I don't like his holier-than-thou tone. He probably thinks that my being caught in a compromising position with Wynn Felker somehow erases his dalliance with his porcine coworker.

But now is not the time to take offense. My daughter looks on the verge of a nervous breakdown.

"Well, honey," I say cheerfully, "you know that I work with Wynn Felker."

Her eyes narrow. "Yeah?"

"We've become sort of friends lately, and sometimes, people get the wrong idea when two adults are friends."

"Be straight with her, Lucy," Trent says.

"Will you stay out of this?" I shriek. "You obviously have no idea how to handle new relationships and children."

"New relationships?" Sam says weakly.

"Nice one," Trent grumbles.

I'd like to kick him in the nuts right about now, but obviously that wouldn't help Sam. "No, no," I say, trying to backpedal, "Wynn and I are just friends, but there's a photograph . . . You know how the media always spin things to make a better story."

Sam says, "A photograph of you and Wynn Felker?"

"I'd been to his house to talk about some work stuff," I say lamely. "And when I left, a photographer jumped out of the bushes and took a picture."

"Oh," Sam says, skeptical but accepting. But Trent just can't keep his big fat nose out of it.

"Tell her the truth," he demands.

"I did!" I lie.

"You're in the newspaper with your shirt undone, practically throwing yourself at that Cody kid."

"What?" Sam shrieks.

"You're such an asshole," I hiss at Trent.

"She's going to find out sooner or later."

"Honey," I say, turning to my daughter, "it's not that bad.

I'd spilled some juice on my shirt and so I had it undone to dry out."

"Juice?" Trent snorts.

"Yes." I glare at him. "Juice."

"Stop treating her like a baby," Trent snipes. "She's not going to buy that bullshit story."

Unfortunately, he appears to be right. Sam turns on me. "First you flash your boob at him, and now this?" Her voice is cruel when she says, "You make me sick."

As Sam storms across the parking lot toward Trent's car, he says, "You flashed your boob at him?"

"No!" I snap. "It fell out—not that it's any of your business."

"What exactly is going on with you and this Cody kid?"

"Nothing! And he's not a kid. Why are you even here, anyway?"

Sam is at the Lexus's passenger door. "Dad, unlock your car!"

"Don't," I tell him. "She needs to come home with me so we can talk."

"Sounds like it's a bit late for that."

"Trent . . ." My voice wobbles. "There's nothing going on with me and Wynn. It was a mistake. Please . . . I can't lose her."

He is surprisingly kind. "You won't," he says, giving my shoulder a brief, reassuring squeeze. "Give her a little time to cool off. I'll bring her home later."

Trent

"I WANT TO see it," Sam says, flopping on the couch. Despite the fact that she's only been to my apartment once, she seems remarkably at home. "If you don't show it to me, someone at school will. And that will be even grosser and mess me up more."

She has a point. At least if her initial viewing of the photograph is with me, I can be there to ease the pain. I grab the newspaper off the floor and hand it to her.

Sam stares at the photo, and for a few moments, says nothing. Other than a distasteful curl of her lips, she seems to have no reaction at all. Then finally, she throws the paper to the floor. "It's disgusting!" she shrieks. "It's even more disgusting than you bringing your girlfriend to my art show."

"Uh . . . thanks." I shift uncomfortably. "That was a big mistake and I'm not seeing her anymore."

Sam picks up the paper, looks at it once more, then proceeds to rip it into pieces. "What is wrong with her? Cody's, like, practically my age."

I clear my throat. "But Wynn Felker is actually twenty-seven, so it's not . . . you know, against the law or anything." It feels strange, defending Lucy's liaison with Cody Summers. I'm sickened by the thought of it. And although I have no right, I feel jealous, possessive, and hurt. Seeing her breasts hanging out in the newspaper makes me livid. Those are my breasts! Why did she have to flaunt them in that kid's face like that?

Sam brings me back to the room. "She's sick," my daughter is saying. "She invited him over to our house and she was all like, Meet my poor sad daughter. And then she hits on him!"

"Well . . ." I'm not sure if I should say this in front of Sam, but the pieces are coming together in my mind. "Maybe Cody was really there to see your mom?"

"But he brought me flowers!" Now she stops, acknowledges the possibility. "Eww! Do you think Cody's, like, her boyfriend?"

The words are like a punch in the stomach. "No," I say quickly, "he's not, like, her boyfriend. She said there's nothing going on and I believe her."

"Well, I don't," Sam huffs, going to the fridge. "Can I have a beer?'

"What?" I boom. "No!"

"God, you don't need to spaz. It's just one beer."

"Forget it." I hurry to the kitchen and shut the fridge door.

"That's what's wrong with this society," Sam says, rummaging through the cupboards in search of something to eat, I suppose. "Parents are so uptight about everything. If this were France, you would already have offered me a glass of wine."

"This isn't France," I mutter. "There'll be no underage drinking."

"Okay," she says, removing an Ikea glass and filling it with water. "I'll just deal with my mom banging the guy I'm in love with without alcohol."

"They're not banging!" I yell. "And don't say *banging*, please."

"Sorry!"

"And you're not in love with him. He's a TV character."

She whirls on me. "He came to see me and brought me flowers!" She suddenly remembers the distinct possibility that the visit wasn't hers. "I'm not going back there."

"What?"

Sam charges back to the living room and sits on the sofa. "I'm not going back to Mom's house."

I'm really dying for a beer myself, but it would be like taunting her. Instead, I follow her to the front room. "You have to go back, honey. It's your home."

Shades of the vicious girl I'd seen after the art show emerge. "So you don't want to spend time with me after all. Was that just your way of getting into Mom's good books again?"

I keep my cool. "Of course I want to spend time with you, Sam. But you don't have any clothes here. You've got school in the morning . . ."

"I'm not going to school."

"Yes, you are."

"How can I? Everyone at school will have seen that photo! They'll think my mom is some child-molesting sex maniac!"

She has a point. "You have to go," I say.

"Forget it. And I'm not going home either."

I look at my daughter, her arms crossed fiercely across her chest. Her jaw, so like her mother's, is set with grim determination. Suddenly I realize I'm completely out of my depth. Obviously, Sam can't live with me in this apartment forever. And she can't quit school. But what do I say? How am I supposed to handle this? I need Lucy.

"I'll go to the house and pick you up some clothes and stuff," I offer, already grabbing the car keys. "I'll tell your mom that you're going to be staying with me for a few days."

"A few years!" Sam snipes.

"But you will be going to school tomorrow. Okay?"

To my surprise and relief, she shrugs. "Okay."

"There are some frozen dinners in the freezer," I say, slipping on my jacket. "I'll be back soon."

She reaches for the remote and flicks on the TV.

"And don't touch those beers," I caution. "I know how many are there." But she doesn't reply. She has already immersed herself in some reality show.

Lucy

"FINALLY," I MUTTER as I hear Trent's car pull into the driveway. Sam has every right to be upset, but running off to her dad's place isn't the way to deal with this. I need to make her understand that there's nothing going on between Wynn and me. And even if there were, it's really none of her business. I am a grown woman with emotional and physical needs. And Wynn is not the teenybopper with the overalls and can of yellow paint she thinks he is.

Yanking open the front door, I prepare to greet my angry daughter. "Oh my god," I say as he lopes up to the door. "What are you doing here?"

"I need to talk to you," Wynn says. "Can I come in?"

"No," I snap. "Sam will be home soon and the last thing she needs is to find you here."

Wynn looks over his shoulder. "We should talk in private. I don't think I was followed, but . . ."

I suddenly have a vision of a swarm of paparazzi on motor-bikes racing into my front yard. All I need is for Emily Sullivan next door to be alerted to my recent notoriety. "Come in."

Alone in my foyer, Wynn reaches for me. "I'm so sorry about all this."

I pull away. "Me, too. I should never have agreed to come to your house." What I really mean is, You should have just agreed to sleep with me instead of rejecting me like some ideal-istic moron.

"Don't say that." He moves closer to me. I'm disappointed that my anger has done nothing to diminish my attraction to him. "I'm still glad you came—no matter what this has done to my reputation."

I take a step back. "Your reputation?"

Wynn looks sheepish. "Millions of teenage girls think I'm Cody Summers. It's not good for ratings when they see me with someone who could be . . ." He trails off.

"Go ahead, say it," I snap. "Someone who could be your mother."

"Well . . . not *my* mother, but Cody's mom."

The whole thing suddenly seems overwhelmingly sordid. "You need to go. Sam knows about the photo in the paper and she's justifiably disgusted. Trent should be bringing her back any minute."

"Okay," Wynn says. "But I came here to tell you that I'm going away for a while. The press is camped outside the studio and my house, and my managers said I should get away until this dies down."

"Good idea."

"I was thinking that maybe you'd want to come with me?"

"You've got to be kidding!" I splutter.

"My mom and my brother were supposed to come visit me here. But I've decided to go see them in New Mexico instead. I don't know . . . it might be fun for you to meet them?"

I can think of very few things less fun than meeting Wynn's family. "I can't."

He seems to have read my mind. "We could go somewhere else then . . . somewhere warm. Sam could stay with your ex for a few days. It would give her time to cool off."

Looking at him, I'm surprised by his earnestness. Yes, there is chemistry between us, and yes, our make-out sessions have been very exciting. But that's all we have—chemistry. It doesn't mean we should go on a holiday together!

Wynn takes my pause as consideration and continues. "By the time we get back, the press will have lost interest. Everything will go back to normal."

"No," I say, but my tone is less adamant than I intended.

Suddenly, Wynn grabs me by the belt and pulls me close to him. Our bodies collide and the attraction is undeniable. "Come on, Lucy. My contract's up after next season. When I'm not Cody anymore, no one will care about the age difference."

Maybe he's right? Wynn's next role has got to be more age-appropriate. He could be twenty-nine-year-old Detective Robbie Madison, or thirty-two-year-old cardiothoracic surgeon Dr. Larry Shoenfeld. And there's nothing wrong with dating a thirty-two-year-old cardio-thoracic surgeon, is there?

"They've been talking about doing a spin-off, *Cody's Way at Berkeley*, but I'm not committing."

That's when I hear a car pull into the drive. "Oh my god!" I shriek. "Sam's here! You've got to go!"

Grabbing his wrist, I try to drag him to the back door, but he resists. "We can't hide from her."

"Yes, we can!"

"My car's out front."

"Shit!" I slap his chest. It's ineffectual, but somehow satisfying. I do it three more times for good measure before I spy the coat closet. "Get in there," I say, shoving him toward it.

But Wynn won't be shoved. "We need to talk to her. We can make her understand."

"Understand?" I cry. "Obviously you know nothing about teenagers!" Of course, I could be wrong. Given that Wynn's entire career is built on appealing to the teen demographic, he may have some useful insights. But he doesn't know *my* teenager.

There's a knock at the door.

"Please," I plead, my eyes welling with tears. "It'll be too much, finding you here."

Wynn looks about to comply when we hear a key in the lock. Before we can react, the door swings open and Trent walks into the room.

"Where's Sam?" I blurt, instantaneously discerning that she's not with him.

"At my apartment," he says. "What's *he* doing here?"

"He was just leaving."

But Wynn is proving less compliant than one would expect from someone his age. He steps forward. "I'm a friend of Lucy's. We work together at—"

Trent cuts him off. "I know who you are. You're the reason my daughter is humiliated and threatening to drop out of school."

"Oh god," I say, fighting back the tears. "She wants to drop out of school now?"

Trent moves toward Wynn. "You're supposed to be a teen

heartthrob. What the hell are you doing running around with someone old enough to be your mother?"

I gasp, outraged. What is with all this mother stuff? Technically, I guess I could have given birth to Wynn when I was thirteen, but it's not like I was sexually active then. Before I can speak, Wynn comes to my aid. "Yeah, Lucy's a few years older than me. What's the big deal?"

"What's the big deal?" Trent booms. He looks at me, his face a mask of anger and jealousy. I should be enjoying this, I think, but I'm too worried about Sam.

"This is not Wynn's fault," I snap at my husband. "If anyone's to blame for Sam's problems, it's you."

"At least I had the decency to keep my fling private," he growls.

"Private?" I snort. "Like bringing that cow to the Crofton House art show was keeping it private?"

"This is not a fling," Wynn says, stepping up and putting his arm around me. "Lucy has made a huge difference in my life. We're friends . . . good friends. And I think we could be more."

Under different circumstances, this moment would be extremely romantic. Under these circumstances, it's a little creepy.

"Get your hands off my wife," Trent growls.

"Look pal . . ." Wynn starts, but is unable to finish as Trent's fist has found its way into his face. There's a sickening crunch as my husband's knuckles connect with Wynn's chiseled cheekbone.

"Stop!" I scream, jumping in between them. Then to Trent: "What the hell are you doing?"

"Tell him to butt out!" Trent hollers. "He is not a part of this family!"

"Jesus Christ," Wynn says, rubbing at his cheek. "My face is my livelihood, you psycho."

Trent takes a threatening step toward him and Wynn retreats behind me—not very manly or sexy, but I'm still on his side. "You need to get out of my house," I growl at my husband.

"*Our* house," he says, pushing past us and heading for the staircase.

"Not our house!" I scream after him as he jogs up the stairs. I leave Wynn massaging his bruised face and scurry behind Trent. "You gave up the right to call this your home when you ran off with that fat slut!"

I find him in Samantha's room, extracting handfuls of underwear and socks from her drawer and tossing them onto the bed. "What are you doing?" I demand.

He doesn't stop. "I'm getting Sam some clothes. She's staying with me for a while."

"Oh, no, she's not!" I say, grabbing a handful of underpants and attempting to return them to her dresser.

Trent blocks my way. "She's upset and humiliated. She doesn't want to be around you right now, and frankly, I don't blame her."

In all our years together, Trent has never pissed me off enough to strike him—until this very moment. I wind up and swing. Unfortunately, all those years without practice have made my punch a little easy to predict. Trent grabs my fist before it connects.

"You fucking bastard," I hiss.

"You selfish bitch." We stand for a moment, eyes locked, our breathing labored. And then Trent yanks my wrist, pulling me toward him. Before I can react, he's kissing me, hard, almost painfully. There is nothing tender or loving about it: it's angry, violent, and so goddamn hot! For a moment I consider pushing him into the pile of underwear on Sam's bed and ravaging him, but sanity prevails. I pull away from him.

"Get out," I croak.

Without a word, Trent continues gathering Sam's belongings, almost as though the kiss never happened. I find this confusing, and for some reason, wildly attractive. But I can't forget that Wynn is downstairs, nursing a dented cheekbone. "Tell Sam I'll expect her home tomorrow," I say in a tone not open for argument. Turning on my heel, I hurry downstairs to make Wynn an ice pack.

Trent

I DROVE SAM up to Crofton House in time for the 8:40 A.M. bell. Thank Christ she didn't put up a fight. After all that Wynn Felker shit last night, the last thing I needed was to get into a scrap with her. She pouted the whole way, of course, but that's starting to seem pretty normal. I sat in the car until I saw her go into the school, just in case.

Granville Street is surprisingly clear, so I push the speed limit just a little. I love driving this car, I really do. It's a bit of a release from all my pent-up frustration. Yaletown living has turned me into a total pedestrian. Not that I want to be sitting in my Lexus for an hour each morning while I commute to mini-mall hell. Forget it. And even if I was okay with the drive, there's no way I could do it now that Sam's living with me.

It's a temporary situation, it has to be. But when I told Sam that her mom wanted her home tonight, she laughed as if I'd said I was having a sex-change operation. I can't blame her.

This whole thing with Lucy and that Cody kid is sickening. I'm glad I punched him, frankly. The little pansy deserved it. I just can't believe Lucy would humiliate Sam and me this way. Yeah, Annika was a mistake, but at least she wasn't a *public* mistake. Lucy always seemed the poster child for good judgment. She was always worrying about what the neighbors thought, what other parents thought. That's obviously gone out the window.

My cell phone rings, causing my stomach to drop a little. If it's Crofton House telling me that Sam's done a runner, I will ground that kid for the rest of her life. Digging the phone out of the console, I check the call display. The number is blocked.

"Hello?"

A male voice with a British accent says: "This is Paul Arnett calling from *In Touch* magazine. Would you like to comment on your wife's relationship with Wynn Felker?"

It's April Fools' Day today. This has to be a prank. But no, given my luck recently, I know it's real. "How did you get this number?" I demand, pulling the Lexus to the curb.

"It must be hard for you to watch your wife carrying on with a teen heartthrob. How does your daughter feel about it?"

"Leave my daughter out of this!" I growl, a wave of fury nearly overwhelming me. But I quickly regain control. "No comment," I say, hanging up the phone and turning it off.

I sit in the car for a few minutes trying to calm myself. This can't be fucking happening. If the press has my cell phone number, they probably know where I live. They probably know where Sam goes to school. We'll be swarmed every time we set foot outside. Our pictures will end up in all the trashy magazines: the poor, pitiful husband and daughter of Wynn Felker's new girlfriend. Well, she's not his new girlfriend, goddammit; she's my wife. Yeah, we're going through a rough patch, but that kiss yesterday proves there's still something there. We've got a kid and a home and we've still got the chemistry. Of course, right now I'm totally pissed off at her, but that doesn't mean I'm giving up on our marriage.

Easing the car back onto the road, I try to push the one recurring thought out of my mind. Unfortunately, it resurfaces, as it has about four thousand times in the past eighteen hours. There's no point living with regret, they say. But whoever "they" are, they probably didn't make a decision that turned out to have such horrible, far-reaching consequences. Yeah, I was selfish and horny and irresponsible, but so are millions of other guys out there. Look at Mike! None of the women he slept with turned out to be a complete psycho who went after his job. Hope didn't bang some twelve-year-old pop star and end up in the tabloids. Do I really deserve all this? Jesus Christ!

I park the car in my building's underground lot and walk, in a kind of daze, to the office. The spring sun is making a rare appearance, and on another day I would have appreciated its warmth. But in my current state, it may as well be pouring rain down on me. I'm not completely depressed about what lies ahead. It's not going to be pleasant, but it's no worse than all the other crap I've had to deal with lately. I guess I'm just resigned. My life has turned to complete shit and I may as well accept it.

Conversations cease abruptly as I enter my workplace. Most of my coworkers avert their eyes; only a couple of the guys give me a nod and a "Hey, Trent." It's not like I give a shit. In about twenty minutes, I'll never have to see any of them again. I head straight to Don's office—no point taking my coat off. He's on the phone, but when he notices me lingering outside, he says: "I'm going to have to call you back."

"Hey," I say, walking into his office.

"So . . . ?" Don says, getting right to the point. "Have you thought about my offer?"

I sit in my usual chair. "I can't go to Coquitlam," I tell him. "My daughter's moved in with me and I need to be around for her."

Don doesn't seem surprised . . . or disappointed. "I understand."

For some reason I feel compelled to elaborate. Normally I'd want to keep this kind of thing quiet, but Don has become a sort of de facto sounding board. "I don't know if you saw my wife's picture in the paper."

"No. Why was she in the paper?"

"Apparently, she's having some sort of fling with Wynn Felker." Don looks at me blankly. "Cody Summers," I explain.

"Oh my god!" Don says and his shock is satisfying. "Isn't he like, seventeen years old?"

"His character is. The real guy is twenty-seven or something."

Don is still disturbed. "My niece loves that kid."

"So does my daughter. Well, not so much now."

"That's got to be tough," he says. "And the tabloids got ahold of this?"

"One of them called me on my way into work."

"Jesus Christ." There's a moment of silence, and I can practically read Don's mind: this guy is cursed.

It's time to get back on topic. "So, I'll email you a formal resignation letter, if that's okay. I take it you don't want me to give two weeks' notice?"

He shifts uncomfortably. "I'm sorry it had to go this way, Trent. You were a good employee up until . . ."

"Yeah, I know."

"I'll still give you a good reference," Don says. "And I know McMillan Securities is always looking for good advisers."

"I'll give them a call."

"And who knows . . . maybe you'll end up back here one day . . . when we've had some personnel changes."

It would be great to think that Don will be able to oust that crazy bitch and bring me back on, but I'm a realist. I shrug. "You never know."

Standing up, I extend my hand. "Thanks," I say, "it was great while it lasted."

Don shakes it firmly. "Good luck to you."

Back in my office, I begin to pack up my personal items. There's not much: a couple of outdated photos of Sam, a framed ink drawing of ants that she gave me for Father's Day. The coffee mug is mine but I'll consider it a donation. I'm going to have to return my cell phone, which is a pain. I think I'll just hang on to it for a while and pretend I forgot. Within minutes I'm done: seven years captured in one medium-sized cardboard box, and it's not even full.

"What are you doing?" Her sudden presence in the doorway scares the shit out of me. I look at her standing there in her cute outfit with her cute hair as though everything is just hunky-fucking-dory.

"Packing up and getting out," I growl. "You should be happy now."

"Happy?" she cries. "I don't want you to leave!"

Why am I continually surprised at what a whack job she is? "You said it was you or me," I grumble. "So now it's you."

I grab the box off my desk and try to push past her, but she blocks my way. I'm tempted to plow right through her, but she'd probably charge me with assault. "Excuse me," I say pointedly.

"Trent, don't go," she says, her voice low. "I'm sorry about everything. I was just hurt and upset and I felt used. I don't want you to lose your job over this."

"Too late." I make another attempt to leave, but she throws her body in my path.

"I saw the photo of Lucy in the paper. I know how humiliated and ashamed you must feel. And Sam must be mortified. I want to be there for you, to help you both get through this."

That's it. I'll risk an assault charge to get out of here now. "Let me through," I say, pushing her out of my way. Fortunately, Annika doesn't scream out in false pain. Unfortunately, she trails me down the hall, yapping like a Chihuahua.

"Why won't you let me support you?" she says, scurrying in my wake. I don't respond, just stare straight ahead and try to ignore the eyes watching us in gleeful horror. "I would never humiliate you like that," she continues. "You can't go back to her after what she's done."

I stop, turn to face her. "After what *she's* done?"

Annika seems taken aback. "Yes," she says, somehow missing the irony. Then I remember that she's a psychopath with no self-awareness. What's the point talking to her? I push my way out the door.

"This isn't over!" she screams from the doorway. Thankfully she doesn't follow me into the street. "I'm not giving up on you, Trent!" she cries as I move purposefully away from her. "I still care about you!" There's a moment of silence. I wonder if she's gone inside, but I'm not about to turn around. But then I hear her parting blow.

"You gave me crabs, you bastard!"

Lucy

I'M STILL SEVERAL yards from the set entrance when I spot them. A crowd of people—mostly men, mostly wearing cameras around their necks—is milling about, chatting and looking bored. Three sawhorses have been erected as makeshift gates to keep the photographers out. A heavyset security guard, about sixty-five, stands nearby with a clipboard in his hand. Shit. I guess it was unrealistic to hope that Wynn's being attacked by a forty-year-old single mother wasn't particularly newsworthy.

Pulling the SUV up to the sawhorse barricade, I wait for the security guard to approach. He saunters over, as do the photographers, their necks craning with curiosity. If they knew that I was the cougar herself, I'm sure there would be more aggressive jostling for position. When the guard is at my door, I crack the window open a few inches.

"Name?" he asks gruffly.

I keep my voice low. "Lucy Vaughn."

"Pardon?"

"Lucy Vaughn," I repeat, in a louder whisper.

"Do you have ID?" he asks. Hurriedly, I dig my driver's license out of my wallet and hand it to him. I wait anxiously as he looks at it then looks at me . . . back at it and back at me. Christ! What does he think I'm going to do—blow myself up once I get inside? If he doesn't hurry up, the paparazzi are going to recognize me. Of course, I'm less recognizable with my shirt buttoned up.

"Okay, go on through, Mrs. Vaughn," he says, in a normal volume that, under the circumstances, sounds like yelling into a blow horn.

"It's her!" one of the photographers cries. "It's her!"

As predicted, they swarm the vehicle, shouting questions and popping flashbulbs.

"Are you dating Wynn Felker?" one yells.

"Have you slept with him?"

"Do you still think you deserve to be fucked by the Choice Hottie?"

"What's the state of your marriage to Trent Vaughn? Are you two getting a divorce?"

Flashbulbs blind me as I hurriedly raise my window. As I wait for the guard to remove the sawhorses blocking my path, I put my head down on the steering wheel to shield my face. This is how Britney Spears must feel. I suddenly have a new empathy for the girl. Not that I'm about to shave my head and stop wearing panties, but this kind of attention could drive anyone to alcohol abuse and poor fashion choices. Eventually I'm able to inch the SUV into the parking lot. To my surprise, the photographers respect the less-than-menacing security guard and return to their previous milling about.

Inside the building it's only slightly less chaotic. A gaggle of my coworkers, Camille among them, surround Tanya's desk, talking in excited whispers. For a split second I wonder if they all know about Wynn and me. The abrupt halt to all conversation leaves little doubt.

"Morning," I mumble, feeling excluded and conspicuous. Hurriedly, I head past them toward my office. Camille breaks free from the pack and follows me.

"Thank god you got in okay. It's scary out there."

"Yeah." I drop my purse under my desk and boot up my computer.

"Don't bother," Camille says. "Shooting's on hold."

"What?"

"Kev, Ainsley, Wynn, and his management team are having a meeting right now. We might go to hiatus early."

"Why?" I say automatically, though I know it's a stupid question.

"For one thing, Wynn's been mobbed. The studio had to send personal bodyguards to his house to escort him into work."

"God!"

"And for two, he's got a shiner. His cheek is all blue and swollen."

"But I iced it!" I cry, inadvertently revealing the source of Wynn's injury.

"Trent?" Camille asks and I nod sheepishly. "I knew it!" she cries jubilantly, then regains decorum. "We were just sort of . . . speculating about what happened to Wynn."

"It was awful," I say, keeping my voice low. "Wynn showed up at my house, uninvited. And then Trent came to pick up some clothes for Sam—who hates my guts by the way—and when he saw Wynn there, he punched him in the face."

"Sounds kinda hot."

"It wasn't!" I cry, remembering the kiss with Trent despite myself. "It was terrible."

"Oh, honey," Camille says, giving me a quick hug. When she releases me she says, "I guess you were right."

"About what?" I snivel.

"That it was wrong to get involved with Wynn Felker. Who knew it would be such a huge mess?"

"I knew!" I wail, fully crying now. "It felt wrong and weird and I was only doing it because I was so angry with Trent. But you said I should go out with him. You said I should give him a chance and have sex in his pool!"

Camille is taken aback. "I never said that."

"You did!" I shriek. "And now Sam's so humiliated that she's staying with Trent. And I'm all alone, being stalked like some poor, defenseless deer."

Camille goes to the tissue box on her desk and grabs a large handful. She hands them over and I wipe the tears and snot from my face.

"It's going to be okay," she says softly. "These things always blow over."

I nod in agreement, though I'm not so sure. Yeah, the press will lose interest in Wynn and his cougar, but will Sam ever forgive my betrayal? Will Trent? Do I even want him to? And what about my job? They've fired me once in the past two weeks, and I'm sure this would just reinforce that decision.

I am somewhat composed, though far from attractive, when Ainsley and Kev march into the room. Bruce trails after, shutting the door behind them. He doesn't look sympathetic as he takes in my red bulbous nose and the makeup under my eyes. Well, he doesn't know what it's like. Only I know how it feels to be pursued and judged . . . me and Britney.

"How you holding up?" Kev asks kindly. I shrug, afraid I'll burst into tears should I try to speak. "Good, good," he continues. Obviously, that was typical Hollywood sincerity. He doesn't give two shits about how I'm really holding up.

Ainsley steps forward. "This is quite a mess you've landed us in."

"Me?" I cry, peering into her round face. "What about Wynn?"

"He's in his twenties. He's a TV star," she says, like this gives him carte blanche to fuck up. "I thought *you* would have had more sense."

"I do!" I snap at her. "He pursued me!"

"And then you brought your husband into the picture," Bruce says.

"I didn't *bring* him in. Wynn dropped by my house uninvited, and my husband showed up."

"Be that as it may," Ainsley says, "it's added a new angle to the story. The press is not going to be leaving you and Wynn alone anytime soon."

Bruce says, "They've got photos of his black eye. They'll be chasing your husband next."

"Oh god!" Tears spring to my eyes. Camille, who is still standing quietly in the room, hands me another tissue.

"This is impacting our shooting schedule," Kev says. "Cody Summers can't have an unexplained shiner."

"There are financial repercussions," Ainsley says. "Wynn's managers are considering suing your husband."

"What?" I shriek. "They can't sue Trent! It's not his fault! Yeah, he punched Wynn, but Wynn shouldn't have been at my house in the first place. I asked him to leave and he wouldn't. Wynn deserved a punch in the face, really."

At that precise moment, Wynn just happens to let himself into my office. Perfect. "Can Lucy and I have a moment?" he says, eyes boring into mine.

As usual, everyone scatters obediently at his behest. When we're alone, he steps toward me, providing an excellent view of the reddish-black bruise along the top of his cheekbone. It gives him a sexy, dangerous look. Damn!

"My managers want me to press charges against your husband," he says. "Would that bother you?"

"Yes, it would bother me!" I say. "My daughter has been through enough anguish and heartache without her dad being thrown in jail!"

"He probably wouldn't go to jail."

"Still! Watching her father being arrested isn't exactly going to have a positive impact on her."

Wynn nods, takes a step back. "I didn't really deserve a punch in the face, you know," he says, sounding like a scolded child.

"I know. Sorry."

He sighs heavily. "They told me to stop seeing you. They said that dating a woman your age sends a confusing message to my teenage fans."

"They're right," I confirm. "One of your teenage fans is my daughter, and she's as confused as hell."

Wynn rushes toward me. "I'm not going to let them tell me what to do anymore. It was you who taught me to stand on my own two feet. You showed me that I can make decisions on my own."

"I never showed you that! How did I show you that?"

Wynn continues. "They want to get rid of you. They think the whole thing will die down faster if you're not working here."

While this should invoke a feeling of panic, it doesn't. Yeah, I need to earn money to maintain my household and support my daughter. But there's always Trent's salary to fall back on for a while. And am I really desperate to continue buying props for the mischievous Cody? Could I maybe find something to do that's just a little more fulfilling? "It probably will," I respond calmly.

"It's not fair," Wynn says. "I'm as much to blame for this mess as you are."

More, I think, but don't bother to say.

Wynn steps toward me. "What if I tell them that if you go, I go?"

"What?" I'm stunned that this boy, for lack of a better term, would put his job on the line for me. I never asked for this! All along I've discouraged and rejected him. Okay, I didn't exactly discourage and reject him when I threw myself at him on the sofa, but still! How the hell did this happen? I should never have gotten Botox.

"They wouldn't really fire me," he says. "I mean, how can you have *Cody's Way* without Cody? But it would send a message."

Right.

He grips me by the shoulders. "Why don't we go to the Dominican or somewhere? Everything is so messed up right now, but if we go away for a few weeks . . ."

"A few weeks?" I cry. "I have a daughter."

"Okay, a few days," Wynn acquiesces. "I know things will be better when we get back. I promise."

I look at him and I'm surprisingly tempted. Maybe it *would* be good to get away for a few days? And it might be better for Sam if I left town for a while. She could stay with Trent, free

from media harassment, until her anger dies down. And perhaps, in different surroundings, Wynn would see that we don't
have a future together, that I have nothing to offer but a jaded
view of the world and a pair of saggy B cups.

Oh, who am I kidding? Going away with Wynn would be
like throwing gasoline on a barbeque. The press would get
wind of it and think we'd run away together. Sam and Trent
would believe it and cut themselves off from me completely.
Wynn's career would be ruined and we'd have to move into
his mother's trailer in New Mexico. We'd fight all the time of
course, each blaming the other for all our problems. I'd turn
to booze, Wynn to drugs. It would all end up in a trailer park
murder-suicide.

But I hide my true thoughts and feelings. "I'll think about
it," I say. His face lights up, but I'm not finished. "You have
to promise me that you're not going to press charges against
Trent."

"Okay," he agrees with little enthusiasm.

"And if Ainsley decides to fire me, I don't want you getting
involved."

"I can't just stand by—" Wynn begins, but I cut him off.

"Let's just let the chips fall where they may, okay?"

"It's not right, though," Wynn cries. "You didn't do anything wrong! If I wasn't stuck playing this stupid high school
kid, our relationship wouldn't be an issue."

"Look," I say, changing tack, "this job doesn't mean anything
to me anymore. But you . . . you're a star. And you shouldn't
jeopardize that for anyone."

No actor can resist a stroke to the ego. As predicted, Wynn
gives me a look of intense gratitude and nods his head slowly in
reluctant agreement.

There's a knock at the door. "Come in!" I call, stepping away from Wynn's grip.

Ainsley and Kev hurry back into the room, followed by Bruce and a tentative Camille.

"I'm not pressing charges against Trent Vaughn," Wynn announces.

Ainsley says, "Well, our filming schedule's royally fucked and someone's going to pay."

"Not Trent," Wynn says. "He's having a hard time coming to terms with my relationship with Lucy. It's normal for him to be jealous and to lash out."

I wince at the reference to our relationship and the sound of my husband's name. Camille notices my reaction. She gives me a look that says: "What the hell is going on here?"

"I'm going away for a while," Wynn says, "to let this all die down. And I'm hoping," he moves to my side and puts his arm around me. I stiffen visibly but keep a smile pasted on my face, "that Lucy will join me for a few days."

I speak directly to Camille. "I'm thinking about it, that's all."

Kev says, "You're destroying your career, Wynn, do you know that?"

Wynn shrugs.

Ainsley says, "Let's get Stephen down here to talk some sense into him. Bruce!" she barks. "Call Stephen. If Wynn wants to flush his career, he might want to think about how many people it's affecting."

"He doesn't want to flush his career!" I cry. "Wynn, tell them!"

"Maybe I do," Wynn says. "Maybe I'm sick to death of pretending to be a high school kid. Maybe I want to be treated like a man."

"It's a jumping-off point!" Kev cries.

"You are a man!" Camille adds. "Everyone thinks of you as a man!"

"You might be sick of Cody," Ainsley barks, "but you're under contract for another year."

"Cody Summers is a great character," Kev tries. "He's really allowed you to grow as an actor."

"I want to be taken seriously," Wynn says, storming around the room. "I want to be able to date someone who's older than me without everyone thinking I'm being molested."

Oh god. I suddenly feel the urgent need to leave. I make a break for the door just as it opens. Stephen and a couple of miscellaneous managers and publicists burst into the room.

"Wynn, buddy!" Stephen says, making a beeline for his meal ticket. "What's up, dawg?"

It's an opportunity I can't miss. While everyone is preoccupied with convincing Wynn not to abandon his career, I slip out the door. Virtually unnoticed, I hurry outside to my truck.

Trent

"SO," I ASK her as we drive down Granville Street that afternoon, "how was school today?"

Sam shrugs. Standard.

"No strange guys hanging around?" I ask, staring at the road.

I feel her eyes on me. "What are you talking about? Why would there be guys hanging around? Are you accusing me of something? Why don't you just come right out and say it?"

"I'm not accusing you!" I say with an incredulous laugh. God, the girl can fly off the handle in a millisecond . . . just like her mother. "I was worried that there might be photographers lurking about."

"Why?"

"To get a photo of you. You're the daughter of Wynn Felker's mystery woman, after all."

Sam is silent for a moment, staring straight ahead. And then, "You really think they'd want a photo of me?"

"Probably."

"For like, a magazine or a newspaper or something?"

"Yep." I glance over to see a small smile on her lips. Oh shit. She probably thinks this is going to make her famous. "Listen," I say sternly, "I don't want you being exploited in the media. You are not to get your picture taken or do any interviews. Do you understand me?"

"How do you mean 'exploited'?"

"Used! Humiliated! Embarrassed!"

"But what if I just want to tell my side of the story?"

"No photos. No interviews. Got it?"

"Okay!" She slouches in her seat. "God!"

We drive in silence for a while, but I can almost hear the wheels turning in my daughter's head. Finally, she says, "It would be a good way to get back at Mom, though."

"What?"

"If we did an interview! Maybe we could get Diane Sawyer or someone to do a prime-time special, and we could tell her how betrayed and grossed-out we feel."

I sigh heavily. "You need to give your mom a break."

"Why should I?" she cries.

"Because she's your mom and she loves you."

"Yeah, right!" Sam snaps. "She loves me so much that she, like, gets it on with the only guy I've ever really cared about."

We come to a red light and I stop the car. Looking over at her, I can see she's serious. "The only guy you've ever really cared about?"

"Yeah."

"Honey . . . Cody is just a character; he's just a poster on your wall. Wynn Felker is not a kid."

"So that makes it okay for Mom to just *bone* him in front of a bunch of photographers?"

"No! I didn't say that! I'm upset about it, too." The light turns green and I ease the car forward. "And she wasn't exactly *boning* him."

"Her shirt was undone!"

I sincerely hope that my daughter is naive enough to think that having your shirt undone is tantamount to boning. Somehow, I doubt it. "Look, your mother has made a lot of mistakes lately, but she's still your mom and she loves you."

"Whatevs."

"You know she wants you to go home," I say.

"Forget it!"

"Sam . . . you can't live with me forever."

I can feel Sam's eyes on me and the anger burning in them. "Right, you don't want me around so you can bone your fat girlfriend."

"I don't have a girlfriend!" I boom. "And stop saying *bone*!"

She settles back into her seat, and we drive the rest of the way in silence. When we reach the apartment building, I scan the sidewalk for reporters. Thankfully, there are none. I guess Lucy and her little boy-toy are really the money shot, not me and Sam.

We're silent as we get out of the car and ride up the elevator to the seventh floor. As soon as we've entered the apartment, Sam storms to the couch and flops down. She flicks on the TV.

Christ, I need a beer. I grab a Heineken and drink half of

it before I'm fortified to face what's ahead. Walking back into the living room, I stand in front of my daughter. "We need to talk."

"I'm trying to watch this," she snipes. I look at the TV. It's a rerun of *The Golden Girls*. I turn off the set and take a seat beside her.

"It's not that I don't want you to live with me," I begin. "I do. I love having you here, but the place is too small."

"Let's get a bigger place," she says.

"Well . . ." I don't want to worry her, but decide she's old enough to handle the truth. "I quit my job today."

"What? Why?"

"It was just time to move on," I lie. "I'll find something new, but it could take a week or two. So I can't be shelling out for a new apartment right now."

Sam is silent for a moment, staring at the carpet. "I can't go back to Mom," she says softly.

"I know you're angry with her, but you deserve to have a proper house and a proper bedroom. You can't sleep on a hide-a-bed for the next three years."

Her face suddenly brightens. "Why don't we move back into the house?"

"Our house?"

"Why should Mom live there all by herself? We can go back to the house and she can move in here." Her voice turns angry. "Then she can have Cody over and they can—"

I cut her off. "Don't go there, Sam."

"Sorry. But can we move back in, Dad? Please?"

She looks at me, so hopeful and expectant, and I realize that I haven't seen that spark, that light in her eyes, in ages. Maybe she's right? We bought that house when Sam was born and she should be raised there. It's stupid for Lucy to live there all alone while we're crammed into this little apartment.

And then I think about telling Lucy she needs to move out, evicting my wife from the house she has always loved and cared for and taken such pride in. It will crush her. It will break her heart. But we have to do what's best for Sam.

"I'll talk to her," I say. Sam jumps up and hugs me.

"Thank you! Thank you! Thank you!"

I close my eyes and savor my daughter's closeness. She was so angry and so far away from me, and now she's back. Moving us into the house is the right thing to do. If it's made her this happy, how can it be wrong? Sam releases me and I take another swig of beer. I decide to ignore the sick feeling burning in the pit of my stomach.

Lucy

IT'S BEEN THREE days since the initial photo scandal with Wynn, two days since I was asked "not to come into the office for a while," and three days since I've seen my daughter.

Frankly, the state of my job is the last thing on my mind. My obsession has become reconnecting with my only child. I've tried calling her—every day since she went to stay at Trent's apartment. She's still refusing to see me or even talk to me. Her anger and betrayal is justified, to a degree, but how long can she keep this up? Does she plan to shut me out of her life forever?

The thought sends a wave of desolation through me so intense that tears spring to my eyes. I fall back on Sam's bed and allow myself to cry for a few minutes. But I don't seem to have the energy for a full-blown meltdown. Instead I lie on my side, staring at my daughter's artwork on the walls. She had such talent, such promise. And now, thanks to her parents' selfish and irresponsible behavior, it's been destroyed.

Wynn's pictures are gone, of course. When—if—Sam finally does forgive me and come back home, she's not going to want to see Cody Summers smiling down at her. I ripped them off the wall with great pleasure, crumpling and tearing them into pieces. I know it's not his fault that all this happened, but I can't deny that it felt good to destroy his handsome face.

As I lie there, staring at a Georgia O'Keeffe–ish floral my daughter did in pastels, I suddenly become aware of the silence enveloping me. The house, once my home, my pride, suddenly feels so cavernous and empty. I realize I am completely and utterly alone in the world. Who do I have that cares if I live or die? Not my husband. Not my daughter. I can't even reach out to my friends. I'm sure most of them think I'm some kind of pedophile. Even Camille, the one who's seen me through so much, seems to have cooled toward me.

Of course, Wynn has called a few times from New Mexico. The press was at the airport to see him off, but so far they haven't bothered him at the trailer park. When he's not suggesting a liaison in the Dominican Republic, he's offering to write to Sam "to explain."

"To explain what?" I'd asked him.

"To explain that I'm not Cody Summers. I'm not some silly high school kid whose life is made up of basketball games and school dances. I'm a twenty-seven-year-old man with very real, very adult feelings for a sexy, vital woman."

"Thanks," I said. "That's not going to help."

I take a deep breath and focus on the one bright spot on the horizon. Trent has agreed to meet with me this afternoon. Frankly, I've been surprised at his reluctance to come see me. Every time I've suggested we get together to talk, he's made an excuse: "I don't want to leave Sam alone" or "I need some time to think." I guess his previous attempts at reconciliation meant nothing. I'll admit they were all pretty half-assed. There was that kiss in Sam's bedroom, of course, but it was just a spontaneous response to our heated fight.

The sound of the phone ringing shakes me from my reverie. It's probably just Wynn again, wanting to tell me how sexy and wise I am. Leisurely, I make my way to my bedroom and the bedside telephone.

"Hello?"

"Lucy . . . it's Hope."

For a moment, my heart soars. It's Hope: my friend, my confidante, my source of support for so many years. I feel a huge welling of love and gratitude toward her for reaching out to me. It's big of her to make the first move. She's always had such a good heart.

"Hey," I reply, through the lump of emotion in my throat.

Hope continues. "I know our friendship has basically been destroyed, but there's something I felt you should know."

In that one sentence, I remember her judgment of my marriage, her betrayal of my confidence, and her holier-than-thou attitude. "Okay," I reply coolly.

"Sarah-Louise brought home a copy of *People* magazine last night."

"Great," I say sarcastically. I feel like adding something like "At least that shows she's remotely human," but decide against it.

"Well, I discourage her from reading such trash. It's mind-numbing pap and promotes body-image issues—especially in young girls."

"And I suppose you think I got Sam a subscription for Christmas. If you called to insult my parenting abilities, I'm not in the mood."

"I called because you're in it."

"In what—*People*?"

"Yeah."

"Shit."

"Yeah, shit," Hope says. "There's a photo of you throwing yourself at Wynn Felker."

"It was taken out of context," I snap. "I was talking to him about work stuff and I'd spilled juice on my shirt."

"Far be it from me to judge what you do with your life," Hope snips. "I just thought I'd warn you."

"Well, thanks."

There's a pause. "We were friends for a lot of years, Lucy, and I still care . . . about you and about Sam."

"Sam knows," I say softly. "She's gone to live with Trent."

"Oh no," Hope says, her tone gentle. Her sympathy proves my undoing and more tears pour from my eyes. There's a longer pause as I try to compose myself. My friend fills the silence. "This will all die down eventually."

"Mm hmm," I snivel.

"And Sam must think it's at least a little cool to have her picture in such a big magazine. I know Sarah-Louise was impressed."

"What?" I cry. "Sam's picture is in there?"

"Yeah . . ."

"Oh my god, I've got to go." I should thank Hope for telling me about the photo spread, for still caring enough about me to protect my daughter. But I hang up without a word. I've got to get my hands on that magazine.

There's a corner store two and a half blocks from my house. Throwing on a baseball hat and sunglasses just in case, I take off. I run the entire way, well, almost the entire way. A marked lack of cardio conditioning has me wheezing and panting through a terrible stitch after a block and a half. But within minutes I'm pulling the magazine off the shelf and hurrying home with it.

Alone in my kitchen, I stare at the cover. Thankfully, a beloved movie star pregnant at forty-five is occupying most of the front page. In the top corner is a photo of Wynn sporting his black eye. The caption reads:

WYNN FELKER
Love Triangle!

It's awful and humiliating, but I can't help but be relieved that they haven't spun this into a one-sided assault by a pathetic, middle-aged stalker. Hurriedly, I flip to the story on page eighty-two.

THE TEEN STAR AND THE OLDER WOMAN

Below it is the revealing photo of Wynn and me in front of his house. Fuck. My pulse pounds in my ears as I start to read.

Squeaky clean teen star Wynn Felker is the object of a million young girls' fantasies. But it turns out that the actor, 27, who's played mischievous teen Cody Summers on the WB hit *Cody's Way* for three seasons, is interested in more mature women. The star has become involved with props buyer Lucy Vaughn, 40, much to the chagrin of teen girls everywhere—and her own husband and daughter.

I think I might throw up. Or possibly pass out. Gripping the counter for support, I flip the page. There's the photo of

Sam in one of those little boxes. The subtitle reads: The Daughter. There's another shot of me in my SUV, head down, looking guilty and sheepish, and one of Trent in his Lexus. His scowling face is barely recognizable as he races past the photographer. Oh great! And there's Wynn jumping off the stepladder with his yellow paint can—just in case our relationship didn't look sick enough already.

That's it! I can't look at it for another second. With my arm I violently swipe the magazine off the counter, knocking the sugar bowl off with it. The porcelain bowl cracks as it hits the hardwood, sending sugar all over the floor.

"*Fuuuuuuuuuuck!*" I scream, rage enveloping me. I want to throw the coffeemaker, the toaster, and the dish rack holding my solitary bowl and spoon from last night's dinner of yogurt and granola. But something keeps me from trashing my belongings. Perhaps it's my looming unemployment and potential inability to replace them. Instead, I hurl a couple of bills tucked into their wicker file onto the pile of sugar, which is hardly satisfying.

Taking a deep breath, I know what has to be done. I have to make my daughter and my husband forgive me. When Trent comes this afternoon, I will beg him to let me see Sam. She won't be ready, but I need my daughter. I can't spend another day away from her, alone in this house with her hating me. I can't do it. Trent has got to understand.

But first I've got to clean up this mess. I gingerly step through the sugar and open the broom closet. Approximately four thousand plastic bags pour out on top of me. It's like a sort of punctuation mark on this scene of chaos and disorder. And it is, frankly, more than I can take. I collapse into the pile of plastic and sugar and let the sobs overtake me.

Trent

"I CAN'T GO to school today!" Sam wails. "Everyone will be laughing at me."

"No one will even have seen it," I try.

"Everyone reads *People*!" She shakes the magazine at me. "Jordan is the one who told me my picture was in there!"

"I thought you sort of wanted that," I say with an encouraging smile. "You're famous now."

"It's my yearbook picture from last year!" she sobs. "I still have my braces on! I look like a knob!"

"You look beautiful."

"Easy for you to say. Your picture is all blurry because you're racing by in your cool car."

I lean over and look at the picture again. The car looks gorgeous and I don't look too bad—sort of dangerous and pissed off, understandably.

"I'm embarrassed by this, too," I say, "but there's nothing we can do now. And at least it's just a small picture of you."

"True," she says, staring at the layout. "It looks especially small next to the double-page shot of my mom boning Cody Summers."

"*Boning* is a banned word, remember?"

"Humping him, then."

I point a stern finger at her. "Also banned. Now," I say, getting back on point, "I'll let you stay home today, but you have to go to school on Monday. Understood?"

She gives a resigned shrug. "Whatevs."

I look at my watch. "I've got a job interview in half an hour, and then I'm going to see your mother."

Sam perks up a bit. "And you're going to tell her to get out of the house and let us move back in there, right?"

Even the sound of it makes me feel nauseated. Can I really tell Lucy to get out after all she's been through? I dumped her, humiliated her, and now she's being publicly vilified for those photographs of her and that Cody kid. How much more can she take? But I've got to do what's best for Sam. And I can't forget that if Lucy wasn't fooling around with some teen-heartthrob cheeseball actor, she wouldn't be in this mess at all.

"I'll tell her," I say.

THE JOB INTERVIEW went pretty well. I'd met Noel Trimble before at a golf tournament and he remembered me. The position his firm is offering is too junior, but he said he'd talk to the "powers that be." "We don't like to let an analyst with a proven track record get away," he said, which makes me think that an offer might be forthcoming. Thankfully, I wasn't too distracted by the impending conversation with Lucy to give a good inter-view. Even more thankfully, he didn't say anything like, "I hear you like to wear women's underwear and have crabs."

And now I'm in front of Lucy's house—*our* house. There's a knot in my stomach as I sit in the car, preparing myself for our conversation. It's going to be bad, almost as bad as when I told her I was leaving. But she has only herself to blame. As I stare at the house, I suddenly have this overwhelming feeling of nostal-gia. Less than two months ago, this was a happy home. Okay, *happy* might be a bit of a stretch, but we were peaceful then, and cohesive. And now . . . Christ, who would have thought we'd end up in such a fucking mess?

I can't delay it any longer. Hopping out of the car, I move purposefully toward the door. I'm a man on a mission: to do the right thing for my daughter. The door swings open before I can knock, and Lucy is standing there, eyes red, nose shining. Every instinct in my body wants to wrap her in my arms and comfort her. But I can't. She's humiliated me and she's humiliated our daughter. I can't let her think all is forgiven . . . not yet.

"Have you seen it?" she says, her voice hoarse.

I nod and step into the foyer.

"How's Sam?"

"How do you think?"

"Oh god," she cries, tears streaming down her face. "I'm so sorry about all this."

Despite my intention to make her suffer, I hear myself say-ing, "I know."

She looks up at me, her eyes shining. "You know this has all been blown out of proportion," she says. "Nothing happened between me and Wynn. Well, we kissed but that's it."

The admission should bring me relief, I guess, but instead I feel a surge of jealousy. "You shouldn't have even done that," I growl, moving into the living room. "You know how Sam feels about that kid."

She doesn't try to defend herself as she follows behind me. I can tell she feels completely defeated. The news I'm about to deliver is going to kill her. The thought prompts a sickening twinge in my stomach. As I pass by the kitchen, I notice that the floor is covered in either sugar or salt and about four million plastic bags. The *People* magazine is flung in one corner. I pause. "What happened here?" In response, Lucy cries a bit harder.

I go sit at the dining table and motion for her to join me. "Take a seat," I say, my tone formal. If I treat this as a business situation, I just might be able to get through it. I've had to fire people before, twice actually. It wasn't pleasant or easy, but I did it. But I've never had to kick someone out of their house. Or to tell them that their only child refuses to live with them anymore.

Before I can speak, Lucy says, "I have to see Sam."

"You can't. She's still really pissed."

"I know," she wails. "I understand that. But I have to see her, Trent. She's my baby and the thought that she hates me . . . Oh god!" She clutches at her chest. "I can't breathe."

"Calm down," I say firmly. The last thing I need is for her to hyperventilate or have a panic attack or something. "Take some deep breaths. It's going to be okay."

I wait while she struggles to compose herself. It could be dramatics, but I don't think so. Lucy doesn't play games like that. Missing Sam is truly robbing her of her breath. Eventually, she seems to relax a bit.

"You okay?"

She nods in response, though she's still crying.

"Okay," I continue. "Here's the deal. Sam wants to move back into the house."

Lucy's face lights up like a Christmas tree, sending a pang of guilt through me. The blow will be all the more cruel for the hope I've just inspired. It quickly fades as she notices my expression.

"What are you saying, Trent?"

"The apartment is too small, it's too far from school . . . She deserves to have a proper home, Lucy."

"What are you saying?" she demands again, more forcefully this time. But I don't need to elaborate. She's obviously figured it out as she suddenly cries, "Oh, Jesus," and drops her head into her hands.

"Look," I begin, touching her arm awkwardly, "it's only temporary. Sam will come around and forgive you. She just needs some time. And I know how much you love this house. I don't want you to feel like you've been evicted."

Lucy looks up then, her eyes wide with panic. She opens her mouth to speak but no sound comes. She gasps for breath— rapid, shallow, unfulfilling breaths that do nothing to inflate her lungs. Her hands fly to her chest, her throat. Oh shit, here we go. I knew this would be too much for her.

"It's okay, Lucy," I say soothingly. "It's okay."

Obviously, it's not okay. She tries to stand but staggers back, clutching the table for support. It's a full-blown anxiety attack. She had one once before when Sam was about six. Lucy's parents had just divorced and then Sam broke her wrist on the monkey bars at school. I remember Lucy's panicked call telling me to meet her at the hospital. She was completely losing it, much like now. I'd told her to sit down and breathe into a paper bag.

"Sit down," I command. "I'll get a paper bag."

Rushing to the kitchen, I rummage through the cupboards, trying not to slip on the mess of plastic and salt coating the floor. Eventually I find a paper wine sack and hurry back to my wife. She holds it to her face and breathes deeply. Within a few seconds, she has calmed down.

There is a long, awkward silence, finally broken by Lucy. "You can't kick me out of my home," she says, staring blindly at the table. "I love this house. I've put so much of myself into it."

"I'm just trying to do what's best for Sam."

She looks up. "I want what's best for her, too. I want her to come home and live with me."

"Well, she wants to live with me right now," I retort. "And she wants to live here."

"So what am I supposed to do? Go out and rent a bachelor suite? Move into my car?"

"You could live in my apartment," I suggest.

"What?" She jumps up. "The love nest where you screwed that fat cow? Forget it!"

I stand, too. "That's over with. You need to let it go."

"Then you need to let this thing with me and Wynn go."

"I'm trying to," I roar, "but every time I turn around, there's a photo of you attacking him in a magazine!"

"I wasn't attacking him!" she shrieks.

"Right," I grumble. "You were talking to him and you spilled juice on your shirt."

"Right," she responds, somewhat hesitantly.

There's a long silence as we each collect our thoughts. I don't know where the conversation goes from here. Obviously, Lucy's not going to obediently pack up her life and move to Yaletown. And did I really expect her to? She's got too much fire to go easily. But I can't keep Sam cooped up in that apartment, sleeping on the Karlstad. It was fine for weekend visits, but it's not a proper home for a teenage girl.

"I have an idea," I say. Lucy looks at me, hands on her hips. "Let's sit down and talk about this calmly."

When we're once again seated at the table, I begin. "Sam wants to live in this house and she wants to live with me. You want to live in this house and you want to live with Sam. I want to live in this house and I want to live with both of you."

"What are you suggesting?" Lucy says, eyes narrowed.

"Let me move back in, too."

She snorts. "You're kidding, right?"

"No, I'm not kidding. I don't have to move back into our bed—"

"Damn right!" she interrupts.

"But I could stay in the spare room. That way, Sam will have to come back to live with you. She'll have nowhere else to go."

Lucy looks about to respond, but she stops. After a moment she says, "What if she runs away or something?"

"She wouldn't. She's wanted us back together all along."

"What about what I want? Am I supposed to forget everything you've done and go back to pretending we're the perfect couple? I'm not Hope, you know."

"I know, babe, and I'd never expect you to forget everything that's happened. But face it: we're better together than we are apart. We've both tried it on with other people, and it's been a complete disaster."

She gives an agreeable shrug. I push on.

"Yeah, there's a lot to forgive, but I'm willing to forget all this Wynn Felker crap." I wave my hand toward the magazine on the kitchen floor. "And we could go to counseling, as a family," I suggest. "It's not too late for us, Lucy."

"I don't know."

"We owe it to our daughter to give this a shot."

Lucy sighs. "I need to think . . ."

"I know it's a big step, but it would be the best thing for Sam. And I think, deep down, you know it would be the best thing for us, too."

My wife is silent, chewing on her lip thoughtfully. I stand. "I'll give you some time. I won't say anything to Sam yet, but she's going to ask about moving back home."

"Yeah," she mumbles, obviously lost in her own thoughts.

I head to the front door and Lucy follows me. When we arrive, I turn to face her. "I hope you'll give our family another chance."

Her eyes well with tears, but she stays mute.

"There's just one more thing," I say. "I've left Shandling & Wilcox. I can't work around Annika anymore." It's not a complete lie, and Lucy gives a slight nod of approval. "So, obviously," I continue, "I'd expect you to do the same."

She raises her eyebrows. "You want me to quit my job?"

"Well, yeah," I say. "I mean, it makes sense, doesn't it? Think about it from my perspective . . . from Sam's."

"I will," she says, reaching past me to open the door. "I'll think about it."

Lucy

THE CALL CAME in on Friday evening. "We'd like you to come to the set on Monday," Ainsley's assistant said.

"Sure," I'd replied, my lack of enthusiasm evident. On the other hand, if they fired me, it would at least take one decision off my plate.

"The media has moved on," the woman continued, "so no need to bring security."

Like I was going to.

The rest of the weekend I spent contemplating my future. I was desperate to be with my daughter again, but was I willing to take her father back in order to do it? Obviously, I could never trust him again. But could I forgive him? I wasn't sure. And did he really deserve my forgiveness? Wasn't he sort of blackmailing me into letting him move home, using Sam as a pawn to get what he wanted? Or did he really just want to bring our family back together? Maybe he'd really changed and my resistance was the only thing keeping us from being happy again?

Wynn called on Saturday night. "Hey, babe," he said, as if we were a couple.

"Please don't call me that."

"Sorry, hon. Did Ainsley call you?"

"Her assistant did. Did you beg them to give me my job back?"

"No," he insisted. "But they did call me to talk about you. I think you're going to be very excited."

"I doubt it," I grumbled. "Buying props hasn't excited me for a couple of years now."

"What if they don't want you to buy props?" Wynn said leadingly. "What if they have something else in mind for you?"

Something else? Like what? I could probably work in wardrobe or set decoration, but neither possibility exactly thrilled me.

"I'll let Ainsley tell you," he said. "I'll be coming home in a few days. They've given me the all clear."

"Great."

"So I'll see you when I get back."

"No," I said firmly. "I can't see you. I'm trying to rebuild my relationship with Sam. That's all I have time for."

"Wait until you talk to Ainsley," he said chipperly. "I think we can figure out a way to make this work—for you, for me, and for Sam."

Part of me wanted him to elaborate, but a larger part, the part that hadn't slept more than three hours a night for almost a week and held the future of her entire family in her hands, just wanted to get off the phone. "I've got to go."

"I'll see you soon."

I hung up.

Now it's Monday. I'm seated in the boardroom across from Ainsley and two men I've not seen before. The taller one, in his mid-fifties, is an executive producer called John something. The shorter and younger of the two is a network exec named Nick. The three of them sit across from me, broad smiles stiffening their cheeks.

"Do you want some coffee?" Ainsley asks, smile firmly in place.

"No, thanks."

"Or a latte or something? Craft Services bought a latte machine."

"I'm fine," I reply.

"Okay," Ainsley says, glancing at her cohorts, "let's get right to the point. Do you still like your job as a props buyer?"

I open my mouth to lie and say, "Absolutely! I love it. Please take me back." But the words don't come. I decide to be honest and let fate take its course. "I've lost all inspiration for it," I admit. "It feels completely meaningless and consumerist and . . . bad for the environment. I'm sick of driving all over the place, polluting the air looking for skateboards and plastic frogs and robotic dinosaurs. I'd like to do something more meaningful."

To my surprise, my answer seems to fill Ainsley with glee. She places a meaty hand on John's forearm before she continues. "I agree with you, Lucy. I think you should do something more meaningful."

I start to stand, assuming I have just been let go.

"Please, stay," the Nick guy says. "We'd like to talk to you about another opportunity with our network."

Obediently, I sit. Ainsley speaks. "When we first found out about your relationship with Wynn, we were upset."

"I wouldn't call it a relationship," I start, but Ainsley isn't finished.

"We were worried about what it would do to his reputation as a teen heartthrob."

I nod, feeling a bit queasy.

John, the producer, jumps in. "But Wynn isn't Cody. He's actually twenty-seven years old. He's just been labeled by America as a kid."

"So your relationship with him isn't as creepy as everyone thinks," Nick adds. "In fact, it's completely appropriate."

"Thanks," I mumble.

"Assuming your marriage is over," Ainsley adds. "Is it? Over?"

I'm not sure how to answer. And I'm not sure it's any of her business. I shrug.

"Okay," John says, "we think it's time to show the world the real Cody . . . the real Wynn."

Nick elaborates. "It's time for Cody to hang up his skateboard and come out as Wynn Felker, the adult."

"Great," I say, "what does this have to do with me?"

Their eyes dart back and forth between one another. It seems they can barely contain their excitement. Ainsley is the first to speak. "What we're proposing is a reality show."

"*Dating Cody*," Nick announces, running his hand through the air to indicate each word of the title.

John says, "It will be a look into Wynn's life as a man and his relationship with an older woman."

"Not that you're that much older," Nick adds quickly. "The public just thinks you are because they consider him a teen."

"But this will show that he's not a teen." Ainsley smiles. "It will be his debut as a grown-up in a grown-up relationship."

I stare at them, speechless.

"What do you think?" Ainsley prompts.

I open my mouth a couple of times, fishlike, before any words come. "I have a daughter," is all I can say.

"Your daughter will love it!" Nick cries. "She'll be a pivotal part of the show."

"But not in an exploitative sort of way," John adds.

"Right," Nick says. "It will make her a star. Just look at those girls from *Laguna Beach* and *The Hills*. They're full-fledged celebrities now."

Ainsley says, "With the bank accounts to match."

"She could segue this into an entertainment career," Nick continues. "Or she could use the money to pay for college."

"You'll be compensated very well," John advises.

"*Very* well," Ainsley says, for emphasis.

There's a beat as they all stare at me. Finally, I say, "And Wynn wants to do this?"

"Yes!"

"He loves the idea!"

"He said it was the perfect way to get Samantha on board with your relationship," Ainsley crows. "And of course, to re-launch his career as a more mature actor."

"I . . . I don't know."

"Trust me," Nick says, "your daughter will love you for this."

"She's the reality TV generation," Ainsley contributes.

"They all want their fifteen minutes." This from John.

I nod vaguely. As disturbing as the thought is, I know they're right. Sam would love this.

"So . . . ?" Ainsley gives me an encouraging smile.

"What do you think?" Nick asks.

I can't think. My mind is racing with abstract thoughts and images: Sam waving to the paparazzi, a little dog tucked under her arm; Wynn and me, holding hands while a seething Trent looks on; a camera crew in my kitchen, still strewn with plastic bags and spilled sugar . . .

I clear my throat before finally speaking. "I'll need some time to process this. And I'll need to talk to my family."

Trent

MY CELL PHONE rings moments after I've dropped Sam off at Crofton. She'd tried to weasel her way out of going, but we had a deal. I let her hide out on Friday, but today she's got to face the music. Surprisingly, she was fairly compliant. As I reach for the phone, I have a feeling it's good news. I'm right.

"We'd like to make you an offer of employment," Noel Trimble says. "We'll courier it over to you this afternoon."

"Great!"

"I'm sure you've got other interviews and may be entertaining other offers, but we'd like to get your answer as soon as possible."

"Absolutely." I do have one interview this afternoon, but I'm not in a position to turn down a solid offer. The sooner I get this job situation sorted out, the sooner I can focus on moving back home.

I'm on a high for the next few hours. Everything is finally

coming together—or back together, I should say. My career, my family, my sanity . . . I consider going to the gym downstairs, but decide against it. I don't want to get all sweaty and have to shower again. Instead, I throw some stuff into boxes. Since my luck has definitely turned, I should be hearing from Lucy anytime now.

My interview at 1:00 goes well and they schedule me in for a second. When I get back to the apartment, Trimble's offer arrives. It's a couple grand more than I made at Shandling & Wilcox, so I decide to accept. I don't have time to mess around with second and third interviews. I've got to get on with it.

At 3:30, I pick up Sam.

"We're celebrating tonight," I announce, pulling out of the parking lot.

"Mom's letting us have the house?" she cries, her pretty face coming alive.

Way to knock the wind out of my sails, Sam. "I got a new job," I say, looking over to watch her face fall. "But I have a feeling we'll be hearing from your mother very soon."

"We'd better," she grumbles, my job news completely forgotten. "I don't know why you didn't just tell her to get out."

"Your mom's been through a lot."

"So have we!"

It's strange how Sam seems to have completely forgotten that I left her mom in the first place, that the only reason Lucy took up with Wynn Felker was that she was so hurt and angry about me and Annika. Ever since those photos were published, it's as though it's been poor, betrayed Sam and me against cruel, heartless Lucy. I'm thankful for this, I guess. I just wish Lucy had such a short memory.

I pull the car onto Granville Street and increase our speed.

I take a deep breath then say, "I think it's time to forgive your mom."

Sam gives a derisive snort.

"Seriously," I continue, "she misses you so much. She hasn't seen you in a week and it's killing her."

"Well, maybe she should have thought about that before she embarrassed me in front of the whole entire world."

"She screwed up, I know. But it's time to start healing this family. I think we should go to counseling."

"Counseling?" she shrieks. "You want me to tell some stranger how humiliated I am that my mom is b—" She stops herself from saying the word. "Messing around with Cody Summers?"

"That's over with," I tell her. "She was feeling lonely and rejected by me and she reached out, I guess."

"Couldn't she have 'reached out' to someone her own age?" Sam cries. "Someone that my friends and I didn't have a crush on?"

"Obviously, it was a bad choice." I think about Annika, the epitome of bad choices. "Sometimes you're lonely and you need someone to be with, and then someone's just there, you know, and they may not be the right person, but you're attracted to them, for whatever reason, and they're attracted to you—"

"Dad! Gross!"

"Sorry. I'm just saying that grown-ups do stupid things sometimes, just like kids."

"Yeah, I noticed."

We drive in silence for a while as I build the courage to make my next suggestion. "Why don't we invite your mom to join us tonight? We could go for pizza or something?"

I expect Sam to blow her stack, but she doesn't. She says

nothing for several blocks, obviously considering the idea. Finally she says, "I don't know if I'm ready."

"I understand. But we'd be together. We could forget about all the crap that's happened lately and just hang out."

"So, we wouldn't talk about Cody or that fat girl you were dating?"

This obsession with Annika's weight really pisses me off. I mean, the chick's a complete psycho, but she's not fat . . . more like curvaceous. Lucy really needs to watch it or Sam's going to end up with an eating disorder. But I guess now's not the time to explain the distinction between voluptuous and obese. "Right," I say. "Those topics would be completely off limits."

My daughter is quiet for another long moment before she grumbles, "I guess we could invite her."

I feel a swell of relief—or maybe it's more like hope? This is a huge step toward getting our family back together. Yeah, it's just pizza, but Lucy's got to appreciate what I'm doing for her here. I reach over and squeeze Sam's knee.

"Thanks," I say. "You're really going to make your mom happy here."

She stares out the passenger window. "Whatevs."

Lucy

I DRIVE HOME from the studio in a daze. There is no way I can process what has just happened and keep the car on the road. It was too insane, too surreal! I've never been one of those people who coveted fame. In fact, I've always sneered at the pomp and pretense. And now I'm being offered a chance to step into the limelight, to become "a celebrity"—albeit along the lines of Bret Michaels and Heidi Montag.

The house is silent and empty as I let myself in, but I'm starting to get used to that. That's not to say I don't long for my daughter's presence, I do. But now it's more of a dull ache instead of a crippling stab of loneliness. I have to believe that her absence is only temporary. Automatically, I make my way to the kitchen. The mess of sugar and plastic bags remains, like some sort of tribute to my emotional breakdown. I didn't have the fortitude to attack the mess this weekend. But for some reason, I now feel capable.

I begin by picking up the large plastic Toys "R" Us bag and stuffing it with smaller ones. There must be some place I can recycle these, though I have no idea where. As I stuff, I realize that the bags aren't just a product of my career as a props buyer; they're practically a metaphor of it: useless, empty, and wasteful. All that plastic will end up languishing in some landfill, leaching chemicals into the soil and clogging waterways long after we're gone. When I've retrieved the sacks from the floor, I attempt to cram the enormous package into the cupboard, but it no longer fits. I'll have to find another way to get rid of them. I can't keep cramming them away until the cupboard bursts and I'm asphyxiated by a landslide of shopping bags.

Removing the broom, I start to sweep up the spilled sugar, lost in my thoughts. Based on the average life expectancy of the North American female, I am exactly halfway to the grave. For the first half of my existence I'd done everything right: worked hard (too hard, probably, but I was committed); married well; bought a beautiful home; and doted on my child. And look what it's got me. Nothing! Everything I wanted, or thought I wanted, is in jeopardy of vanishing.

I bend down and sweep the sugar into the dustpan. It takes some effort—the tiny granules seem determined to flee the bristles—but I work diligently. As I do, my mind picks up speed. I reflect on the day's offer: my own reality TV show. Never in a million years could I have predicted this opportunity. It's so weird, so bizarre! It's also a chance to win back my daughter, make a lot of money, and build a new relationship with a sexy young guy. But do I want the dubious fame? The notoriety? And do I want to raise my daughter in a fishbowl?

Dumping the contents of the dustpan into the trash, I move to the counter. Leaning my elbows on the granite surface, I breathe slowly and deeply to calm my racing mind. A warm white light is filtering through the window; not sunshine exactly, but a welcome brightness in the otherwise gloomy day. I close my eyes for a moment. Behind my eyelids the light seeps in and I experience an unusual moment of clarity. It's not an epiphany, exactly—that's too strong a word. Perhaps *revelation* would be more appropriate. I suddenly realize that I have roughly forty more years on this planet, and how I spend them is entirely up to me.

I can choose to be the star of *Dating Cody*, or I can choose not. I can choose to start a new relationship with Wynn, or I can try to salvage what I had with Trent. Hell, I can choose to be completely on my own if I want. It's an incredibly powerful feeling, the knowledge that my future is back in my own hands. Sure, I'm faced with a plethora of options, but how I proceed is my decision alone.

I stand upright, my body reacting to this jolt of awareness. I'm going to do what's right for me and fuck the rest of them! It might be selfish, but it's a good kind of selfish. It's suddenly so crystal clear. No longer will I exist in this state of anger and jealousy and self-pity! I'm moving forward! I know what I want for the next half of my life—and perhaps more importantly, what I don't want.

At that moment, the phone rings. I lean across the counter and answer it.

"It's me," Trent says. "I thought you'd still be at work?"

"I came home early."

"Okay . . . well, good. Sam and I are celebrating tonight. I got a new job."

"Congratulations."

"Thanks." There's a pause, probably intended for me to ask

about the details of his new position. But the truth is, I don't care. I guess this is a side effect of my newfound selfishness. Finally, Trent continues. "Yeah, so we're going out for pizza and I suggested that maybe you could join us. It took some persuading, but Sam finally agreed that you can come."

"Thanks," I say.

"It wasn't easy. She's still upset with you, but I think she's starting to come around."

"Good. But I can't go out for pizza tonight."

I hear an incredulous snort. "What?"

"I've got a lot of thinking to do."

"So you're going to blow off dinner with your kid? You haven't seen her in a week!"

"I know exactly how long it's been," I reply. "But tonight, I need to figure some stuff out."

"Jesus Christ," Trent mutters. "You're a piece of work."

I know what he was expecting. He was expecting me to thank him effusively for his peace-talk efforts and express eternal gratitude for including me in the invitation. Two days ago, I would have; two hours ago, I would have. But now, I know I need to spend the night alone. By tomorrow, everything will have changed.

"Could you two come to dinner tomorrow? I'll cook."

"I don't know," Trent grumbles. "Once I tell Sam that you're blowing her off, she probably won't want to come."

"Don't tell her that," I say calmly, "because that's not what I'm doing. I'm asking you to give me one night to myself, and tomorrow we'll have a family dinner to discuss our future."

There is a brief pause before Trent says, "Does that mean you've made a decision?"

I hesitate for just a second. "Yeah, I just need to think through a few details."

"Okay then," Trent says cheerfully. "Do you want me to bring anything?"

For some reason, this simple act of courtesy fills me with emotion. "Sure," I croak through the lump in my throat, "bring a salad."

Trent

IT TAKES ALL my willpower not to tell Sam how momentous this impending dinner is. I'm excited about it, for obvious reasons, but I play it cool. There's enough pressure on her as it is, seeing her mom for the first time after all the shit that's gone on. She doesn't need to know that we're all going to be moving back in together.

Sam's quiet on the drive to the house, fiddling with the Saran Wrap on the spinach salad I made. I glance over at her and see the concern etched on her face. Poor kid. She's been through so much in the past couple of months. I'm glad that her life is finally going to get back to normal. One day, we'll look back on this crazy fucked-up blip in our lives and laugh.

I pull the car into the driveway and turn to my daughter. "You okay?"

She looks at me and shrugs. "I guess."

"She's your mom and she loves you," I say, "more than anything in the world." Sam nods and looks as though she might cry. "Give me that salad," I say to ease the tension. "I wonder what's for dinner?"

Following Sam up the walk, I hang back as she rings the bell. They're going to need a moment, no doubt. I can tell by my daughter's demeanor that, despite her rage, she's missed her mom. Within seconds, the door swings open and Lucy is there. Her eyes fall on Sam and instantly fill with tears.

"Hi, honey," she manages.

"Hi, Mom." Sam's voice wobbles. Lucy reaches a tentative hand out to our daughter and touches her arm. It's all Sam needs to fall apart.

"Oh, Sam," Lucy says, drawing our sobbing daughter into her embrace. "I'm so sorry."

"I-I was so embarrassed," Sam wails. "How could you do that t-to me?"

Lucy hugs her, stroking her hair. "I know. I'm so sorry. I never meant for any of that to happen."

"I-I know."

"And you will *never* be humiliated like that again."

"You promise?"

"I promise."

I stand holding my salad, witnessing their touching exchange. It's a relief to have the two women I love back on speaking terms. Sure, Sam said she wanted to live with me full-time, but it's obvious by her current reaction that she's lost without Lucy. I can be a great dad to her, but she's a girl and she needs a female role model in her life. She needs her mom.

The salad is starting to get heavy and the females show no signs of ceasing their love-in. I clear my throat. Lucy looks up, acknowledging me. "Let's go inside," she says.

We head to the kitchen and I place the salad on the counter. "Smells good," I say.

"Enchiladas," Lucy says, giving Sam's hand a squeeze. "Not very original, but I know you guys love them."

"Great." I clap my hands together. "I've really missed your enchiladas." It comes out as a double entendre, but thankfully, neither of them notices.

"Do you want a beer?" Lucy offers, going to the fridge. "Sam, I've got San Pellegrino?"

When we've got our drinks, Lucy suggests we sit in the living room. Sam reclines in a corner of the sectional, looking instantly at home. I perch in the center seat. It's going to take me a little longer to feel completely comfortable back here.

"So," Lucy says, taking the spot between us, "it's really great to have you both home."

Sam and I nod. Sam looks like she might cry again.

"I've got some news," Lucy continues, giving Sam's knee a squeeze. "I've left my job."

"Really?" Sam asks. "Why?"

I give Lucy a knowing look, but her eyes are affixed on Sam.

"I decided that it's not what I want to do with my life anymore. I want to do something more meaningful than go shopping for some TV character."

"*And*, I told you to stay away from that Cody kid." I don't say it though. We don't need to bring that whole mess up right now. Things are going so well.

Sam says, "So what are you going to do?"

"Well . . ." Lucy replies, her face lighting up. "I want to start my own business."

I take a swig of beer. "Really?"

She looks at me. "Really."

"Doing what?" I didn't mean it to sound challenging, but it sort of does. Lucy doesn't rise to it, though.

Instead, she looks at Sam. "Reusable shopping bags."

"Oh."

"But not just ordinary black or beige ones," Lucy continues. "These will be beautiful: an environmental fashion statement."

Is there a market for that? I guess Lucy would know more than I would. She's spent the last eight years of her life shopping. Sam seems to think so because she says, "Cool."

Lucy angles her body toward Sam, excluding me from the conversation entirely. "I want to hire you."

"Me?" Sam asks. "To do what?"

"I want you to be my designer," Lucy says. "It was the art on your bedroom wall that inspired me. I want some of those big floral prints you do. And I was thinking about something cleaner too, maybe like, your insects?"

"Totally," Sam says excitedly. "I think bugs are a really edgy design element."

"I love it!"

"Great," I say, pushing my way back into the conversation. "Have you got the start-up money?"

Lucy turns to me. "I've got some of it, and I'll get a small-business loan."

"You'll qualify?"

"I've already started working on my business plan," she says with a touch of defensiveness in her voice.

I don't want to piss her off—not right before we announce our reunion to Sam. "I'm proud of you," I say, giving her a warm smile. Then I look to Sam. "Your mom's got some more news, too."

"Actually," Lucy says, glancing at her watch, "I think those enchiladas need to come out." She addresses our daughter. "Could you take them out for me? Just cover them and let them sit for a bit. There's a piece of foil on the counter."

Sam hops up. "Should I set the table?"

"That'd be great."

We watch her bounce to the kitchen, happier than I've seen her in a long time. The girl is really forgiving. I guess a short memory is a blessing. I turn to Lucy. "She's really excited."

"Me, too."

"Should we tell her at dinner then—that we'll be moving back in?"

Lucy bites her lip and slowly shakes her head. "No."

I feel a surge of anger—or maybe it's fear. "When then?"

"I can't," Lucy says calmly. "I've given it a lot of thought, and I can't live with you, Trent. Not now, anyway."

"Fine," I snap, standing up. "We won't stay. We'll let you get packing."

"Please," she says, reaching for my hand. "Don't storm off. Let's talk about this."

I don't get why she's so freakishly calm. Lucy's always been the one with the temper. "There's nothing to talk about." I pull my hand away and glance over my shoulder. Sam is digging in the cutlery drawer, oblivious to our conversation. "You don't want to put our family back together, Lucy, so you can move out of the house."

"I'm not moving out," she says firmly. "I'll need the space for my business."

"You're kidding me?"

"No."

"You're putting this . . . shopping bag thing ahead of us? When did you become so goddamn selfish?"

"Yesterday, actually."

"I'm out of here." I start to walk off but she grabs my arm.

"Just hear me out, okay?"

Reluctantly, I allow her to drag me back to the sofa. "We *are* a family, Trent, whether we live in the same house or not."

I grunt. I'm not going to sit here and listen to a bunch of Oprah Winfrey bullshit. But she just keeps on talking.

"We've hurt each other so much these past few months. It's going to take a long time for the pain to go away." She touches my hand in a motherly way. "But we also had a lot of good years together, and we can't forget that either."

Christ! I somehow resist the urge to roll my eyes. "Get to the point," I growl.

"I want Sam to feel she has a home with both of us—here with me, and at your apartment with you."

"She wants to live with me," I growl, though after the tearful reunion at the front door, I'm not so sure anymore.

"I think we can both agree that it's best for Sam to have both parents in her life."

"Yeah," I snap, "but that doesn't automatically mean you get the house."

"You're the one who left," she says, still eerily calm. "I'm staying."

I stand up. "I've got to get out of here."

"Don't go, Trent."

"You've really changed, Lucy, you know that? You're acting like some weird Zen . . . *freak*."

She shrugs. "I'm sorry you feel that way."

"See?" I cry. "I just called you a weird freak and you didn't even react! The old Lucy would have been pissed off. What the hell has happened to you?"

"I don't know. I've just decided I want to live my life differently. I don't want to be angry anymore."

She's definitely been watching too many daytime talk shows.

"Please," she says, "stay for dinner."

"I've lost my appetite." I storm into the kitchen where Sam is folding napkins. "Let's go."

Her cheerful expression fades and I feel like shit. "What? Why?"

"Your mother and I . . ." Fuck. What am I supposed to say? She's finally reunited with her mom, and now I'm dragging her away. Lucy steps forward.

"Your dad needs some time on his own," she says beatifically. "But I'd like you to stay."

Sam looks at me, as if for permission. I can tell she doesn't want to leave, but feels guilty not coming with me. She's such a sweet kid. Yeah, she's acted out a bit lately, but who can blame her? Lucy and I have put her through so much crap. I suddenly feel really emotional. "Stay," I croak. "I'll pick you up later."

"I can bring her back to your place," Lucy offers. "Or she could spend the night here . . . if you want some more time?"

My daughter steps forward, obviously noticing the tears welling up in my eyes. "I want to go back to Dad's place tonight." She places a comforting hand on my shoulder. I press my lips together to keep from bawling. "Is it okay if I eat with Mom, though?"

I nod and kiss the top of her head. Before I fall apart completely, I hurry out of the house.

Lucy

WYNN COMES BACK on Thursday. I'd expected him to stay with his family for the Easter weekend, but he said he had to see me.

"I'm not going to change my mind about *Dating Cody*," I say, leading him into the house.

"What about dating Wynn?" he says, standing a little too close to me.

I step back. "I'm not going to do the show and I'm not going to continue seeing you. If you can't accept that, you can leave."

"Okay," he says, his tone resigned, "I get it."

"Do you want tea?"

"Sure." He follows me into the kitchen and I busy myself filling the kettle. "I'm not here to nag you," he says, taking a seat at the breakfast bar.

"Good."

"But think how good the show would be for your bag business. Everyone would see you and Sam working together to make these beautiful organic bags. They'd sell like hotcakes."

He's right, of course. But I'm not about to sell my privacy or my daughter's right to a normal life just to make my business a success. "I've got a marketing plan," I say.

"You can't buy that kind of exposure," he continues. "I mean, everyone would be using your bags. The environmental impact would be huge!"

"I thought you weren't here to nag me?"

"I'm not nagging."

"Okay, you're just telling me that if I do *Dating Cody*, I'll basically save the planet."

He holds his hands up. "Sorry."

We make small talk about Sam and the weather until the kettle whistles. As I make the tea I decide to ask about his trip, but I keep my tone cool so as not to encourage him with my interest. "How was your visit with your family?"

"Great! I really reconnected with them, you know? I feel bad that I wasted so much time getting wrapped up in the Hollywood bullshit."

I pass him his tea and slide the milk and sugar over to him. "Don't feel bad," I say, leaning on the counter. "You've done the right thing now. I'm sure they're just happy to have you back in their lives."

"They are." He reaches for my hand. "Thanks to you."

Cue a subject change. I pull my hand away. "So . . . what's next for Wynn Felker?"

He shrugs. "I thought I'd be doing *Dating Cody*."

"I think you should finish out your contract and let Cody die a peaceful death."

"It's not going to be easy to shake the image," Wynn

explains. "My agent says I'll have to do something edgy and provocative—definitely something indie."

"Makes sense."

He takes a sip of tea. "So maybe when I've reinvented myself as a gay serial killer you'll date me then?"

I laugh. "As hot as that sounds, I bet you'll fall in love with some gorgeous actress who plays your sister-slash-victim or something."

"Nah."

He will, I can feel it. And in the past few days, I've learned to trust my intuition. Wynn looks at his watch. "Shit. I've got a meeting."

I walk him to the door.

"So," he turns to me, his hand resting on the handle, "could I give you a call sometime—just to check in?"

"It's not really a good idea. Sam's going to be living here, part-time at least. I promised her that this is over. I can't go back on my word."

Wynn takes a deep breath through his nostrils, nods his head slowly. "I understand."

"But I wish you the best of luck. You've got a lot of exciting things ahead of you."

Without a word, Wynn leans in and plants a lingering, wet kiss on my jawline. It's not a simple peck on the cheek; there's a sensual, almost sucking quality to it. My breath catches in my throat, and I feel that same surge of attraction toward him. But in a moment, he's out the door and gone.

I head back to the kitchen and my lukewarm cup of tea. Taking a sip, I allow myself a wistful sigh. It was the right decision, ending things with Wynn. Our brief dalliance had caused way too many problems, and it never would have worked. We're just way too different. Wynn's a TV star; I'm (currently) a house-wife. Wynn was raised in a trailer park by a single mother with a temper; I grew up in the suburbs with Waspish parents whose idea of a tantrum was to close the cutlery door louder than usual. And most importantly, I have a child. Wynn is little more than a child himself. Sure, he's twenty-seven, but it will be years before he understands the incredible love and sacrifice it takes to be a parent. Still, I can't help but wish I'd had sex with him. It probably would have been great.

But I refuse to live with regret. This is a time to look for-ward, to focus on my business, my daughter, and myself. And right now, I need to devote all my energy to getting ReTotes off the ground. That's the name Sam and I came up with: ReTotes. She's already working on a logo.

At least the first step is done: we've named the company and I've secured Sam as my designer. Her cooperation was para-mount to my success. Sure, I could have hired someone else, but if my daughter wasn't invested in this with me, I wouldn't have the same passion for it. Now, I need to move on to the next step.

Wynn's comment about *Dating Cody* being the ultimate marketing tool was bang-on, but it's not like I don't have my own plans. I'll use guerrilla marketing tactics to make these bags the must-have fashion accessory of the season, the enviro "It" bag. And for that, I need Camille.

"I miss you," she cries, when I call her cell phone.

"Me, too. I want to take you for lunch."

"Great! I actually get to eat now that I'm on *Land Divas*."

When *Cody's Way* went to hiatus early, Camille had no trouble landing a job on a new series. As I knew all too well, ex-perienced props buyers were hard to come by. And fortuitously,

Camille's gig on the prime-time dramedy about four gorgeous real estate tycoons could provide me with the perfect marketing vehicle.

"How about we meet tomorrow?" I ask. "I have a proposal for you."

"Tomorrow's great. What's the proposal?"

"I'll tell you tomorrow."

"Tell me now!" Camille squeals. "You know I can't stand the suspense."

"Okay!" I'm too excited to wait myself. I give her a quick overview of my bag business. "They'll be both beautiful and ecological."

"And I can get the Land Divas to use them on the show!"

"Exactly!"

"Love it! I'll talk to our wardrobe girl, too. And I'll call Miranda, who's doing props for *Tight* now. You can get into the gay market."

"That's perfect! These bags won't be cheap. Initially it'll be a high-end line, and I'll make them more affordable as they get more popular."

"I've got to go," Camille says, and I hear horns honking in the background. "But I'll see you tomorrow."

"Can't wait."

"Lucy," she says before she hangs up, "I'm really proud of you."

"Thanks," I murmur, trying to keep my voice from trembling.

Elated by my conversation, I forge ahead. With my laptop on the kitchen table, I research fabric choices. Obviously, I have to use something sustainable, and both hemp and bamboo present good options. Bamboo seems to offer a beautiful, satiny finish, while hemp is more sturdy and rustic. But I don't know enough about sewing and bag construction to make a decision. I order fabric samples, and then, summoning my courage, I make the call.

My heart beats audibly as I wait for her to answer. "Hello?" Her voice is cheerful and singsongy.

"Hi, Hope. It's Lucy."

"Oh . . . Hi, Lucy." Markedly less cheerful and singsongy.

"How are you?"

"Fine. You?"

"Good." There's no point in this idle chitchat. Besides, my nerves can't take it. "I need your help with a business I'm starting."

"Oh?"

I give her the overview. She is far less excited than Camille was. "What do you need me for?"

"I need your sewing expertise," I explain. "Sure, I could order premade bags and have Sam's prints put on them, but I want to do this right. I want to offer different designs and different sizes. These bags are going to be both utilitarian and gorgeous."

"I don't know . . ." Hope says. "I'm quite busy these days."

I refrain from commenting. I know Hope keeps herself occupied cooking, cleaning, and creating practice spelling tests for her kids, but this would be *hers*. This project would be about using her talents for something more than social studies projects and costumes for the school play. It would give her a purpose! Her own money! But how can I tell her that without insulting the last twenty years of her life? The short answer is: I can't.

"Please," I say, "I need you."

There's a long pause as Hope considers this. "Why don't you come over this afternoon and we can talk more about it?"

"I'd love to."

"But we'd need to set some ground rules."

". . . Okay."

"This would be a business relationship, Lucy. I don't want you judging my life or my marriage."

"I wouldn't," I say. "I was out of line before."

"And I don't want to hear about your personal life."

"Right," I agree. "I won't mention the fact that I'm not seeing Wynn Felker anymore."

"You're not?"

"No. It was a mistake that got blown out of proportion, but it's all over now."

I know what she's going to ask before she says it. "Does this mean that you and Trent . . . ?"

"No. Not now at least. I'm focusing on me and on this business and on Sam. That's enough for me."

There's a moment of silence and I can hear Hope breathing. "You sound different," she says slowly. "You sound . . . content."

"Thanks," I say, a small smile on my lips, "I am."

Trent

I PUT A suit on for my meeting. I've never met with a lawyer before, so I don't exactly know the protocol. But it never hurts to make a good impression. Standing at the bathroom mirror, I knot my tie. A muscle in my jaw is visibly throbbing, and I realize I'm clenching my teeth. With a deep breath, I make a conscious effort to relax.

Making my way back to the living room, I slip into my jacket. Okay . . . there's no need to get uptight about this. It's just an informational meeting to find out what my rights are. Since Lucy's done a three-sixty on me, it makes sense to protect my interests. We had a deal: Sam and I were going to move back in and we were going to try to put our family back together. Suddenly, Sam's living with Lucy four days a week, and working with her every day after school. Lucy's turned all "I Am Woman" on me, and I'm left out in the cold.

My thoughts are interrupted by the sound of the intercom.

As usual, the loud buzz in the silent apartment scares the crap out of me. I should be used to it by now. McMillan Securities has sent a steady stream of HR forms and manuals over in preparation for my starting work next week. I press the button to let the courier in, and hunt for my car keys.

He's at the apartment door in minutes, and I hurry to open it. If I don't leave soon I'm going to be late for my meeting—not super late, but five minutes with a lawyer is probably about forty bucks. Pulling the door open, I'm met with a huge bouquet of flowers.

"Delivery for Mr. Vaughn," the guy says from somewhere behind the arrangement.

"That's me," I say, taking the flowers and shutting the door. Sorry buddy, no tip today. I don't have time to rummage around looking for a couple of bucks. Placing the flowers on the table, I tear open the envelope. The card features two champagne glasses clinking together. I open it.

Congratulations!

Handwritten beneath it is:

I heard the great news about your job with McMillan Securities. I wish you all the best in your future endeavors.

Yours,
Annika

It sends a chill through me. Such innocuous words, but the message is clearly ominous. So she knows about my new job. The question is: what's she going to do about it? She's probably on the phone with Noel Trimble right now, telling him I'm a porn addict or something. Maybe she's already gone into the office to alert the female staff to the chronic masturbator joining the firm. I suppose there's a slim chance that she's actually sincere, but I doubt it. Taking the card and the bouquet, I stuff them in the trash.

As I pull the car out of the underground garage, I think about the delivery. It's not the first message I've had from Annika since I stormed out of Shandling & Wilcox. There have been phone calls, a couple of emails, all cordial if not downright apologetic. They've all gone unreturned and ignored. She's got to get the message sometime, doesn't she? If Lucy had let me move home, it would have sent Annika a clear signal: unavailable. But no— the fact that I'm still living on my own gives her some sort of misguided hope.

Half an hour later I'm sitting in a spacious office with expansive views of Chinatown and Mount Baker in the distance. Across a massive oak desk cluttered with files sits Richard Currie. He's about my age, pale, pasty, and thankfully, to the point.

"If the issue is getting back into the house," he says, "I'd advise you to sue for full custody of your daughter. When she's living with you full-time, you'll have a much stronger case to have your wife removed from the family home."

It sounds so harsh when he puts it like that. I clear my throat. "Would I really have a chance at full custody? I mean, Lucy's a great mom."

Richard looks at his notepad. "You said your wife had an inappropriate relationship with a teenager?"

"No," I retort, "he was an actor who *played* a teenager, not an actual teenager."

"But the affair brought negative publicity into your daughter's life, right?"

I nod.

"You could definitely use that against her," he says.

"So I'd basically have to destroy Lucy's reputation to get custody of Sam."

Richard leans back in his chair. "It's not easy to get kids away from their mothers. You said yourself that she's a good mom."

"She is."

"So you'd have to play hardball if you want her evicted from the house."

The words make me uncomfortable and I shift in my seat. "Lucy and I have agreed that it's best if our daughter spends time with both of us. I don't think it would be good for Sam to cut her mom out of her life."

The lawyer leans forward. "You don't have much of a chance then, I'm afraid."

I lean forward, too. "My wife led me to believe that I could move back home to work on our marriage. Out of the blue, she had some kind of midlife crisis and changed her mind. Now she wants to be by herself to start some reusable bag business. Is she allowed to do that—to change her mind on a whim? To opt out of our relationship with no repercussions?"

He glances at his notes again. "You left the marriage in the first place, right?"

"So?"

"Look," Richard says, "if you want to get back together with your wife, suing her for custody of your daughter and having her removed from her home probably aren't the best moves."

I shrug. He has a point.

"I think you need to take some time to identify your objectives."

I'm paying this guy four hundred and fifty bucks an hour to tell me to figure out what I want? I already know what I want. I want Lucy to let me come home. I want her to love me again. I want that comfortable, complacent marriage that I thought was so boring and stultifying. But how do I make it happen, after everything that's gone on between us?

I sigh heavily and run my hands down the front of my pants. "You're right," I say, "I don't want to kick Lucy out of the house and take Sam away from her."

"Then there's not much I can do for you."

A quick glance at my watch tells me I've been here for exactly thirteen minutes. No doubt I'm being charged for the full hour. I clear my throat. "On an unrelated matter . . . How would I go about getting a restraining order against someone?"

Lucy

IT TOOK THREE months to get ReTotes produced and merchandised. But now, only four months later, our company has turned a profit. When I say *our* company, I mean mine and Hope's. Once she was done sewing the prototypes and overseeing their production, I handed her a check. But she wasn't ready to step out of the picture.

"I want to invest in the company," she said. "I want to be a partner."

I was happy to take her on. Originally, I'd envisioned a larger role in the business for Samantha, but she's still just a kid. She was happy to do designs for me, but she wants to spend time with her friends and she recently joined the drama club. Besides, Hope's technical expertise is a huge asset. With her taking care of fabric selection, design, and production, I've been free to focus on marketing. I've thrown myself into promoting our bags, using every film industry contact I have. And tonight's event is a testament to my success.

It's a fundraising gala at the Hotel Vancouver to support an environmental charity. It's very posh and swanky and not something I would normally be invited to. But the evening will include a fashion show of environmental clothing. And ReTotes, coordinated with the outfits, will be featured prominently. It's going to be such great exposure. Elvis Costello will be playing and the press is sure to be there. And while the bags have caught on with the local entertainment industry, I'm excited to bring my product to this wealthy new market.

I toss a lipstick and my credit card into my little black pocketbook as I wait for Sam. The invitations are on the counter, and I finger the silky embossed lettering. The expensive print job is evidence of the evening's high-end flavor. That, and the fact that the event is being hosted by Goldie Hawn. Apparently she lived here for a while and still has ties to the community. And Camille said that the fashion show will even feature two of the Land Divas as models. Obviously, it was their involvement that created the opportunity to showcase ReTotes.

Reflecting on this lucky break, I realize that my years as a props buyer weren't a complete waste. Without my connections to the entertainment business, there's no way my bags would be selling as well as they are. They've been featured on television shows and have had coverage in numerous magazines. And I've recently had to create a website to handle out-of-town orders.

Of course, I haven't used every contact from my television days. I haven't spoken to Wynn Felker since his jaw-sucking good-bye seven months ago. *Cody's Way* continues to air, but I can't bring myself to watch it. I will admit to having searched Google for his name a few times, though. The last time I checked he'd been attached to a movie project currently in preproduction. He's to play the drug-addicted father of a seven-year-old girl. Obviously, this qualifies as a more mature and challenging acting role, and I'll definitely be in the audience on opening night. Secretly, I'm hoping for some full-frontal nudity—just to see what I missed out on. But it's not like I'd ever consider resuming our relationship. That ship has sailed.

Sam walks into the room then. "How do I look?" She's wearing a dark blue, knee-length cocktail dress with a cream-colored pashmina around her shoulders. There's a single strand of pearls around her neck—mine—and silver, kitten-heel sandals on her feet. My eyes mist up.

"You look beautiful." I sniffle.

"Mom," she admonishes, "don't get all emotional."

I walk toward her and take her hands. "You just look so grown-up. Where did my little girl go?"

"I'm sixteen," she says. "Do you want me wearing polka dots and ruffles?"

I kiss her forehead. "Of course not." Then I step back and do a twirl. "Is this dress okay?"

She takes in my black satin sheath dress. "Very sophisticated."

"Do you really mean old?"

My daughter laughs. "I mean age appropriate."

"I'll take that as a compliment . . . I guess."

"Hey," Sam says, "do you think people will throw like, manure at us or something because we're not wearing hemp?"

"No," I assure her. "This is the type of crowd that prefers to throw money."

Retrieving my purse and car keys, we move toward the front door. "Did you call Dad?" Sam asks, casually.

I pause. "No. Why? Was I supposed to?"

She rolls her eyes. "I told you on Wednesday that he wanted you to call him."

"Well, I'll see him tonight," I say, continuing to the door and opening it. "You invited him, didn't you?"

"Yeah," Sam says, following me outside. "But he wasn't sure he could come."

Locking the door behind me, I follow my daughter down the steps. "Does he have other plans tonight?"

"You know how he is," she says, walking gingerly in her heels to the car.

I give a derisive snort as I get into the driver's seat. I do know how Trent is. Since our split last winter, he's vacillated between attentiveness and neediness. He'd been angry at first when I refused to let him move back into the house. But after a few weeks his rage seemed to dissipate and he launched a campaign to get back into my good books. Behind his back I called it Operation Lasagna.

Practically every time Sam came home from his apartment she was carrying a casserole or a pot roast. There was always a note taped to the lid, something like:

Lucy,

Reheat this lasagna in the oven at 350. Hope it will keep my girls warm on this chilly night.

Trent

I appreciated the food. With my business gaining speed, I was only slightly better in the kitchen than I'd been when I worked on *Cody's Way*. But the notes always felt a little manipulative to me. It was true—sometimes the nights were cold and lonely. But I was also enjoying the extra space in the bed, and being lulled to sleep by the rain instead of being kept awake by Trent's incessant snoring. And I liked putting a chick flick on in my room and inviting Sam to watch and fall asleep with me. Of course I missed my husband sometimes. I missed his presence, his companionship, and his cooking. That didn't mean I was ready for him to move back home.

When his crusade didn't produce the results he'd hoped for, the casseroles had stopped coming. In the last couple of months Trent seems to have adopted the role of poor, ostracized martyr. Sam and I continually try to include him in family get-togethers. We've invited him to movies, twice, and over for Thanksgiving dinner, but he always refuses. "I don't want to intrude," he says, or "I don't want to make you uncomfortable, Lucy."

"You don't make me uncomfortable," I am forced to reassure him. "You're still a part of this family."

"So, you won't be inviting a date or anything?"

"What? No!" Eventually, Sam is forced to step in and convince him that his presence is truly desired and we're not just including him out of pity. When he does arrive, I always get the feeling he's doing me some sort of favor.

I'm not sure what prompted this childish behavior. When I served him with the separation agreement, I explained that it was designed to protect both of our interests, and that it didn't necessarily mean divorce was imminent. He'd seemed to accept that, at the time. But shortly afterward he got all weird and hypersensitive. It's as though he can't accept us being together in anything other than the traditional sense. I guess it's hard for him to understand that I have different needs now. I don't want to go back to that stagnant, conventional marriage. I can't! Maybe having sex with him was a bad idea?

I hadn't meant to give him false hope. And it was only a few times. But I'm a red-blooded woman in the prime of her life. I have *needs*. And I still find Trent very attractive. The first time it had been great—comfortable yet still new, somehow. And there's something reassuring about making love to a man who's spent eighteen years studying your body. There was no need to worry about a couple of gray pubic hairs. (I'd spent twenty minutes with the tweezers before I'd attempted to seduce Wynn.) And I knew Trent wouldn't be disappointed when the push-up bra came off and he was faced with the reality of my breasts. That night, I realized that sex with Wynn Felker, as thrilling as it may have been, wouldn't have been nearly as satisfying. Trent knew my body and I knew his. The sex was intimate, effortless, and wonderful.

The second time we made love was great, too. But the third time Trent got all emotional when it was over. He said he couldn't keep doing this if he didn't know where he stood. I got flustered and tried to explain it to him, but I couldn't find the words. I ended up using a space analogy—we were all planets in the same orbit, and though we were sometimes miles apart and moved at different speeds, we were still held together by a gravitational force. This seemed to upset him more.

I pull the Forerunner up to the hotel entrance and hand the keys to the valet. Why not splash out tonight? This is a really big deal for Sam and me—seeing all our hard work showcased at such an exciting event. If Trent can't be here to support us, then that says a lot about our future. Sam and I made the effort. I secured a third invitation and Sam called to invite him. We continually try to include him in these special events, and he continues to act like he needs more.

But maybe Trent's feelings are justified? Maybe he's too traditional to give me the kind of relationship I'm asking for? I want freedom and space and time for me. He wants a key to the house and our undying devotion. If I can't give him that, maybe I should just let him go?

I push these thoughts from my mind as my daughter and I enter the elegant, carpeted lobby. "This is so cool," Sam says, her voice gleeful but hushed.

"I know," I whisper. Taking her arm, we follow the signs leading us up the stairs to the Pacific Ballroom. A vestibule is set up where our invitations are whisked away and our coats hung up. "Uh . . ." I hesitate before proceeding. "I have my husband's invitation here. I'm not sure if he's coming but . . . Could I leave it with you?"

"I'll take care of it." An efficient blond woman with a reassuring smile snatches the piece of paper from me.

Inside, the opulent ballroom is seething with people. Guests mingle, champagne flutes in hand, as liveried servers sashay expertly between them. In the center of the room I spy the runway set up for the impending fashion show. I feel a flutter of excitement. Sam and I meander our way through the crowd as she whispers a running dialogue in my ear.

"Oh my god! There's that guy from the news! You know, the kind of good-looking guy? . . . And there's Richard Dean Anderson!"

"Who?"

"General Jack O'Neill from *Stargate*."

"Right . . . He'll always be MacGyver to me."

"And there's the Attorney General!"

I look at her, shocked.

"What?" she says, her tone defensive. "I'm not a complete airhead, you know."

Putting my arm around her, I give her a squeeze. "I know."

She points conspicuously this time. "There's Sarah-Louise's mom and dad." We make a beeline for their familiar faces.

I feel a twinge of something uncomfortable as I greet Hope and Mike. It's not jealousy exactly, but seeing them standing there as a couple makes me long for that comfort and security. Sam is a great date. She's an integral part of ReTotes and I wanted to share this evening with her. But a small part of me still wishes I was holding my husband's arm. Of course, I can't forget that both Trent and Mike are less than ideal husbands, but then . . . I guess everyone makes mistakes. Everyone except maybe Hope . . .

"Is Sarah-Louise here?" Sam asks Hope.

"No, honey. She's really wrapped up in this paper she's writing about the evolution of capitalism."

"I guess you'll just have to hang out with us old fogies," Mike says to Sam. "Can I buy you a drink?"

"Pop only," I say as they prepare to head to the bar.

Mike rolls his eyes. "Like I was going to get her a dirty martini." Sam snaps her fingers with faux chagrin.

"I saw Camille here," Hope informs me. My two friends are on much better terms now that Hope is working with me. "She was popping backstage to check on the fashion show. Her friend is the producer."

"Maybe I should go back there?" I say. "Just to make sure they've got all the bags coordinated with the outfits."

"They've got people for that," Hope replies. "We're here to enjoy the show. They've even got front-row seats saved for us."

"That's great. Sam is so excited."

"Will Trent be coming?" As always, there's something a little hopeful mixed with something a little disapproving in her voice. Hope seems to think that the only thing keeping my family from a joyous reunion is me. Well, I guess she's right in a way. But I'm not inviting Trent back just for the sake of appearances. I stopped caring about that kind of thing around the time I was featured under the "Cougar Attack!" headline.

I shrug. "We invited him. And I know it would mean a lot to Sam if he showed up."

"What about you?" Hope says, fixing me with an intense stare.

For some reason, I hear myself stammering. "W-well, obviously it would be nice to know that he supports my business, but I don't expect . . . I mean, he's had a hard time respecting my boundaries and maybe he's uncomfortable, you know, being here with me."

"He shouldn't be."

"Yeah, I know, but he's been acting weird lately. I think he's pulling away."

"And do you want that?"

I know she means well, but now is not the time for a mini therapy session. Besides, I don't really know how I'd respond. No, I don't want him to pull away. But I'm beginning to understand that what I'm offering him might not be enough to keep him hanging around. Instead, I say, "Hey look! There's Miranda, a props buyer I used to work with." Rather desperately, I wave Miranda over.

Hope and I chat with Miranda and a few other film industry acquaintances. When Hope is engaged in another conversation, Miranda says quietly, "So . . . we've got this new lighting director who just moved up from L.A. I thought you two might hit it off?"

"Thanks for thinking of me but . . . I'm not interested."

"Are you sure?" Miranda says. "He's cute."

Just then Camille rushes up to us, looking ravishing in winter white. She kisses my cheek.

"I was just backstage and the bags look fucking awesome," she assures me.

"Well, that's the look we were going for," I say, "fucking awesome."

Camille leans closer to me. "Have you seen Wynn Felker here?"

My stomach lurches. Oh god. It's possible that Sam's feelings of anger toward her former crush have mellowed over time. It's just as possible that they haven't. The subject never comes up, so I have no way of knowing.

"Why? Is he here?"

"I don't know," Camille says. "I just thought he might be. Richard Dean Anderson is here."

Miranda places a calming hand on my forearm. "He's not here," she assures me. "One of my friends is a D.O.P. on *Cody's Way*. They're in Miami shooting his spring break getaway."

I breathe a sigh of relief, just as Mike and Sam return. My daughter has a cranberry soda that I unobtrusively sniff for alcohol.

Camille looks at her watch. "We should sit. The show will be starting in about ten minutes."

Our group moves slowly toward the runway and the assembled chairs. The first two rows have folded paper cards on them: Reserved. I find five seats in the front row inscribed with "ReTotes." Hope and Mike take the first two, leaving the other three vacant. Sam and I sit down, the empty chair conspicuous between us.

I lean over to my daughter. "I can't wait to see your designs on the catwalk."

She nods and looks distractedly over her shoulder. I know she's searching for her dad.

"Honey," I begin carefully. I don't want to upset her right now. I don't want this evening to be tinged with more adult drama. But I feel the need to explain Trent's absence. Sam should know that this isn't about her. "I think it's hard for your dad to be around me right now. Our relationship has gotten kind of complicated lately, so . . . if he doesn't show up tonight, I'm afraid it's because of me."

Sam takes a sip of her drink. "Whatevs," she mutters.

We sit silently, waiting for the show to begin. A curtain moves on the stage and I think I catch a glimpse of Goldie Hawn. I lean over to tell Sam. Of course, to her, Goldie Hawn is nothing but Kate Hudson's mother, but she does love spotting celebrities.

As I turn toward my daughter, I catch a glimpse of him out of the corner of my eye. Trent is lingering at the back of the crowd, looking handsome in his dark suit and tie. He has a glass in his hand—rye and Coke, probably. He likes a stiff drink when he's feeling out of place. As Trent scans the crowd, I hold my hand in the air, waving to capture his attention. When he sees me, I beckon him over.

"Hey, Dad," Sam says, jumping up to kiss Trent's cheek. "I'm so glad you came."

"Are you kidding?" Trent says. "I wouldn't miss this for the world."

"Hey," I say, looking up at him from my seat.

"Hey." It's a little awkward, a little cool.

I lift the reserved card off the seat beside me. "Sit down." I pat the chair. "I saved you a seat."

Trent sits, and almost without thinking, gives my knee a squeeze. "You look beautiful," he murmurs, before turning away to talk to Sam. It's an intimate gesture, and his words send a little thrill through me. I look over at him, but he's listening attentively as Sam chatters in his ear.

I reach over and give his knee a deliberate squeeze. He turns to me, a bemused smile on his lips. Our eyes meet and we share a lingering look. "Thanks," I say softly, "for being here."

He gives my hand a pat. The intimacy is gone, and his touch is nothing more than friendly and supportive. "Thanks for including me."

Goldie Hawn walks out on stage and I join the applause of the crowd. In a matter of moments, my bags will be carried down this glamorous runway. My daughter's designs will be showcased for all these people to see. The business that I started, all on my own, is an unqualified success. And Trent is here, sitting between Sam and me, and supporting us. I pause my clapping for just a moment to wipe a small tear from the corner of my eye.

Acknowledgments

Thank you to Ina Brooks for giving me an in-depth look into the life of a props buyer, and for taking me to the set of *The L Word*, where I got to see Jennifer Beals! And thank you to the team at Penguin for all their guidance and support.